OUT OF PATIENTS

Out of Patients

A Novel

SANDRA CAVALLO MILLER

UNIVERSITY OF NEVADA PRESS | *Reno & Las Vegas*

University of Nevada Press I Reno, Nevada 89557 USA
www.unpress.nevada.edu
Copyright © 2022 by Sandra Cavallo Miller
All rights reserved

Manufactured in the United States of America

FIRST PRINTING

Cover design by Trudi Gershinov/TG Design

LIBRARY OF CONGRESS CATALOGING-IN-PUBLICATION DATA
Names: Miller, Sandra Cavallo, author.
Title: Out of patients : a novel / Sandra Cavallo Miller.
Description: Reno ; Las Vegas : University of Nevada Press, [2022] I
Summary: "After practicing medicine for more than thirty years, Dr. Norah
    Waters struggles with career burnout as she hunts for the lost fulfillment in
    her work. Supported by her steadfast dog, a misfit veterinarian, and a pensive
    radiologist, she wrestles her way through a surprising assortment of obstacles,
    sometimes amusing and sometimes dreadful, to make a final decision about her
    future."—Provided by publisher
Identifiers: LCCN 2022003337 I ISBN 9781647790592 (paperback) I
    ISBN 9781647790608 (ebook)
Subjects: LCGFT: Novels.
Classification: LCC PS3613.I55293 O98 2022 I DDC 813/.6—dc23/eng/20220419
LC record available at https://lccn.loc.gov/2022003337

The paper used in this book meets the requirements of American National Standard
for Information Sciences—Permanence of Paper for Printed Library Materials, ANSI/
NISO Z39.48-1992 (R2002).

*To all the determined and
often weary practicing physicians
who carry on and strive
to get it right.*

1

They say a career in medicine is among the most fulfilling pursuits a person can undertake. That as a physician you will enjoy a lifetime of rewards and respect, that the sacrifices are worth it.

They're wrong.

Take this past afternoon. Things weren't going great, and I felt a headache coming on, that familiar nag. Getting enough sleep usually kept those headaches at bay, but sleep had become elusive.

Even though old Ana Merriweather's appointment said she had a hip problem, within one minute of saying hello she wept softly and crushed my hand in a grip worthy of a stevedore. Some of these elderly ladies with tissue-paper skin and feathery white hair have the steely clamp of a welder's vise when they get upset.

Her problem went deeper than her hip. She wore a shiny silver jogging outfit, displaying a designer logo that someone other than me would have recognized. Her skin bore a trace of citrus fragrance, just a hint, just right for the doctor's office, and gray hair floated in a coif around her head. Her lips looked suspiciously free of wrinkles for eighty. That botoxed mouth barely moved when she spoke, as tears wet her cheeks.

I should explain who I see in my practice.

Until a few years back, I cared for patients in downtown Phoenix with three other family docs and a revolving crew of volunteers. Funded by a grant, serving poor and indigent patients, the clinic squatted on a dusty side street beside a parking lot that had crumbled into gray powder. Just a few blocks away you could see the huge limestone municipal courthouse, where every year or two I waste a day if I'm not clever enough to escape jury duty. Trust me, lawyers do not want a doctor on their jury because we're way too opinionated, even when we don't know what we're talking about. It was worthless for me to spend all day there being ignored by attorneys and judges while I worried about messages piling up from my patients. Messages from people who really needed me, instead of some incarcerated drunk with three DUIs who was trying to stay out of prison when maybe that's exactly where he belonged.

My tolerance had dimmed. I was working on it, trying to be more forgiving like I used to be.

I enjoyed my patients at that downtown clinic. Some of them, anyway—there were plenty of duds, like everywhere. We're talking reality here, not a sappy movie where impossible medical miracles blossom at the last minute. Certain people simply make lousy patients, demanding and rude, regardless of whether they ride the bus to see me or drive a new Tesla. Go ahead, people: get mad at me because you made poor choices and now it takes three drugs to control your blood pressure. Kill the messenger.

But many of my patients were humble. They had difficult problems and needed tests and medications they couldn't begin to afford. Many were undocumented immigrants, trying to make a better life for their kids. You couldn't blame them for that—you would do the same thing.

Then the clinic lost its funding. That building was a wreck, with warped linoleum and leaky shingles that apparently no one could patch. One year I even bought the supplies for repairs, but it was like chasing snakes. The whole roof needed replacing. A rusty stain crept across the ceiling, looking a little too much like dried blood no matter how many times it got painted over. I saw patients glance up with concern, as if we stored our failures in the attic. Summer heat oozed through loose windowpanes, and we couldn't exactly seal them with duct tape. We tried, but it looked bad, brittle and peeling. In summer the exam rooms were too warm and smelled like dust and feet. During cold winter rains the patients shivered in their thin paper gowns while the ceiling stain seeped and expanded, a slow bleed.

Eventually the clinic closed down, and my patients scattered like dry leaves in a hot Arizona wind. I scrambled and joined a group with some docs I could mostly tolerate and a few that I appreciated, a practice straddling the Phoenix-Scottsdale border. . .a mixed population of clients. The affluent patients hardly listened to me, while the less fortunate ones barely got by and they didn't listen, either.

And truthfully, I felt worn out by that ragged old clinic. Try telling a sixty-year-old woman with no health insurance, living in a friend's garage, that the stony lump in her left breast needs special mammograms and a biopsy and surgery because for sure it's cancer.

Then after that difficult discussion I would steer her to a weary social worker with chronic back pains because she had to twist herself into pretzels to find the patient an ounce of emergency medical coverage. If she could. Always some version of that, over and over.

Anyway. Enough about those old stories. Back to Ana Merriweather with the hip problem. She grew up dirt poor and came from Central America as a teenager. I can't remember what country because my middle-aged brain can only hold a limited number of facts. But her family became wealthy over time, and they now live in an upscale golf community north of here, so I shouldn't worry about her or feel sorry for her, not at all. Completely first-world problems.

I liked Ana, though, and her story captured my imagination. Her maiden name was Banderas and she looked gorgeous in the wedding photo she shared. Twenty-two-years old, sultry and exotic. I remember her maiden name because I had a crush on Antonio Banderas and Zorro when I was younger. You could see how Ana, with her wild young presence, snagged that tall rich white guy. . . . I'm sure his gringo family was appalled.

I could use a Zorro in my life again. Those flashing eyes, that mischievous smile. A rippling cape and a gleaming black horse. But I digress, and it never helped to ponder my dreadful love life in the middle of work.

Ana raised her kids with an iron hand and made sure they only spoke English. Now she lived with her lawyer daughter who married a gazillionaire entrepreneur, and old Ana never had to lift a finger anymore. They set her up in an immaculate apartment in their immaculate house, with her very own kitchenette and gym.

She was wretched.

"How do you spend your day?" I asked, starting to grasp the picture. I pulled my hand from her clutch to type a few words in the electronic chart, wiggling my crushed fingers to restore circulation.

"I do nothing," she lamented. "There's a maid to clean the house and a cook to fix the meals. There's a nanny for the kids. I go to the hairdresser and the spa and the dermatologist. I sit there with all the other worthless old women who have too much money." Her words melted into despair. "I do nothing."

We discussed alternatives. Do more around the home, or volunteer

3

outside the house. The hip pain never came up. I offered to call her clueless daughter and make suggestions, but Ana Merriweather shook her head. Her eyes carried that look, that haunted misery, that worried me. I'd seen that stare before, and things didn't turn out well.

"I should be more assertive," she continued. "My daughter's too bossy. Those children need me. . . . They need more hugs. And someone needs to teach them Spanish." Her face lit up and she laughed, a surprising musical peal. "I forbid my own kids to speak Spanish, and now I want to teach my grandchildren. How funny is that?"

I laughed too, because it was pretty ironic. Heritage issues shift constantly near the border, each generation inventing itself, looking forward and back at once. Ana vowed to make new plans at home, to find a meaningful role, and return to see me in a month. Maybe we would get around to the hip problem then. I hugged her, my arms slippery against her slinky outfit, and for a moment we were both in a better mood.

I spent thirty-five minutes with Ana, sorting her out. How well she slept, or didn't sleep. Depression takes a while, and later that night I would spend more time documenting our encounter, because I couldn't sit there staring at the keyboard and typing while she spilled her heart. But it might not take much for Ana to endure a bad day and overdose on the addictive sleeping pills she got from a naturopath. I went ballistic about those pills and she claimed she quit taking them, but I bet they're still around. I've seen too many hip fractures from sedated old ladies who get up in the middle of the night and stumble and fall.

I thought naturopaths were supposed to do natural things, like have her sniff lemongrass. They push pills more than anyone.

I'm allowed fifteen minutes for most patients, and I didn't exactly start seeing her on time, so do the math and you can see how I was getting off track.

Then Bobby Farrell called about his wife, Clara, pleading to bring her in for another "emergency." Running so late, I should have sent them to urgent care. But urgent care gets expensive and they've got lousy insurance, so like a fool I said I'd squeeze her in. The nurse Martina—who isn't really a nurse but a medical assistant—gave me one of those scouring looks, like she had a thousand better ideas than working late, and I sure as hell better not expect any favors from her anytime soon. She's good at her job but isn't exactly charitable with her time.

"No problem, Dr. Waters," she said, her voice sharp, clearly not meaning it.

That's when things really fell apart.

2

I want to blame Nellie, even though that's not fair. I've got no one but myself to thank.

Nellie harped away all month, worried about supplies soon to expire. Nellie is a fierce office manager, with skinny arms like twigs and spiky orange-brown hair that's been tinted and streaked into a frenzy and looks like a firecracker exploded on her head. A day rarely goes by without her reminding us how wasteful we doctors are. Sometimes she's right.

Nellie once told me she has Apache blood, which makes her a warrior. I believe it, and I'd rather not be on her bad side. She might have smiled once a few years ago, but I missed it. A serious, taciturn woman. Relentless. I admired her work ethic even though she wasn't always easy to be around.

"You had me order all that injectable penicillin," she complained, "and it's about to expire. We can't even return it because that cheap discount drug company went out of business. What a terrible investment. This practice cannot afford to lose that kind of money."

No kidding. For no clear reason, my income had dropped lately. The other docs noticed smaller profits too. If anything we were busier, more patients, more procedures, so it made no sense. I'm not saying I couldn't pay my expenses, but it costs a lot to run a medical practice and the gains had gone slimmer. Nellie couldn't explain it, which put her in a foul mood and made everyone edgy, wondering if someone had sticky fingers.

Which brings me back to the penicillin. Only one doctor insisted on stocking the penicillin, and it certainly wasn't me. Say hello to healing-touch woo-woo Dr. Brian Mulch, who spouted all day about supplements and vitamins. . .the kinds that don't really make any difference except in his pocketbook. My first month at this practice, I tried to discuss the lack of scientific evidence for what he pushed, like vitamin C for a virus or vitamin E for heart disease. It felt like we spoke different languages, used alphabets with different letters. I soon gave up and left him to his blather.

Call me Brian, he told his patients, *because I don't believe in titles. We're all equal players in this universe.*

Are we? Put a struggling teenage mom next to a private-school prom queen and look me in the eye when you say we're all given equal chances. Yet for such a nature boy, he has a remarkably quick trigger finger on antibiotics, and apparently believes in the power of the syringe and needle over swallowing a pill.

So I guess I had that expensive unused penicillin in my brain when Bobby Farrell brought Clara in with her sore throat. I had a weak moment and I made a stupid mistake. I'm occasionally human, and I will feel bad about that decision the rest of my life.

Clara's nose dripped like a little red faucet. She didn't need penicillin because she had a virus. A bad cold. Penicillin kills bacteria, I explained patiently, and cannot stop a virus. The virus won't even slow down.

"But my bones are so achy." Moaning, miserable, she lolled her head against her scrawny husband for support. Bobby stroked her stringy hair with his diesel-mechanic hands, a greasy black moon under each broken nail, then glared up at me.

Looking back, I probably would have stood my ground if it weren't for the headache, lodged like a claw in my skull. If a medical student had been present, I would have been a shining role model for deflecting antibiotic demands. It's an important skill that doctors must learn, or we'll all die with sepsis ten years from now when antibiotics no longer work. If that sounds dystopian, it is. Likely? Absolutely. Long story short: don't take antibiotics unless you really need them. And eat less meat, because we cram those poor animals full of chemicals. Remember that the next time you eat a hamburger and ingest a dose of tetracycline.

Enough soapbox. No one listens anyway.

"This looks like a bad virus," I tried again, rubbing my forehead. Through the tinted window, muffled by thick glass, I heard the random notes of wind chimes in the courtyard. I wished I could slip outside, lie down, and turn my throbbing head to the sun, bake out the ache. "That's why you feel terrible, and the best thing you can do is rest and let your body fight it off."

"They would've given her a penicillin shot at that urgent care." Bobby's mouth curled like he just bit a lemon.

"That's risky. You can have a dangerous reaction." I said, finding an ounce or two of determination.

"I'm not allergic, Dr. Waters! For pity sake," Clara wailed. She sat suddenly upright, her eyes snapping.

I admit I cracked. Her throat did look quite red, and I convinced myself there might be a small streak of pus along one tonsil. Her neck lymph nodes felt tender if I pressed hard enough. Never mind that her leaky nose essentially ruled out strep. And I knew she would just scuttle over to urgent care if I refused antibiotics. People do it all the time. That urgent care gives antibiotics for everything.

Got a sprained ankle? Dandruff?

Antibiotics.

"You could take oral penicillin," I ventured, seeking compromise. Cheaper, safer. These days I ordered injectable antibiotics only for gonorrhea.

"But I can hardly swallow," Clara rasped. "I'd never get those big pills down."

"All right then," I conceded. I felt myself sink into a bad place. "The nurse will come with the injection."

"Thank you." Bobby nodded smugly, nudging his wife. Big man with his triumph.

"You have to stay in the waiting room for thirty minutes after, though, to be sure you don't have a reaction," I cautioned, starting for the door.

"I told you," Clara enunciated, as if speaking to a dunce, "I'm not allergic."

"It doesn't matter." Clenching my jaw did not help the headache one bit. "You can have penicillin twenty times, then have a serious problem the twenty-first time."

Clara rolled her eyes but said nothing.

I steeled myself and saw the next two patients. As I sat typing up Clara's visit and berating myself about the penicillin, Betsy from the front desk poked her wan face around the corner. She always wore animal-print scrubs, some kind of feral feline, like leopard or tiger, but she looked more like a kitten. Everything about Betsy was washed out, her thin ponytail nearly platinum. It hung down her back like a ribbon of cream-colored silk.

"They don't need to pay today, do they?" she whispered.

"They who?" I replied loudly. I knew better than to let Betsy under my skin, but she could be annoying as hell when she took up a cause.

"The Farrells." Her eyes glinted and she lowered her voice even more, her lips barely moving. "He doesn't get paid till next week."

Betsy took her collection duties seriously unless she decided the patient looked too poor. I didn't really care, for her motives were generous (generous with my income, anyway) and much of the time she was probably right. I actually appreciate well-placed pious fervor that isn't self-serving, and the Farrells were a good place to put it. I'd give Betsy that. But it was defiant—only Nellie could make exceptions to the rule posted on a prim card out front: *Payment Expected at Time of Services.*

Nellie lectured Betsy about her collections more than once. I happened to know that these patients, the Farrells, owed quite a bit to the practice. Never mind our wretched healthcare system and how so many people endure hefty deductibles before their insurance kicks in. So Betsy's devout flame burned hotly for them. I understood, and I suppressed a wicked urge to have her demand every penny right then. What was wrong with me? But the point in using up that precious penicillin meant getting paid for it.

"Have them talk to Nellie," I said, not looking up.

"She isn't here right now." Her nose pinched tight.

"Where—never mind. See if they can put down at least a little toward their bill."

Betsy nodded curtly and left, a scowl of judgment against my soul. Maybe that's what caused the headache, the devil's pitchfork, poking in my brain.

"Dr. *Waters.*"

Jo's voice, quick and high. Jo is my favorite assistant, the one who always smiles. She wasn't smiling now as she pulled frightened Clara through the waiting room door. Jo's worried eyes flew back and forth from me to Clara, and behind her Bobby bounced up and down, his grimy hands flapping in the air. I grabbed Clara's arm and took her into an exam room, mentally cursing.

You incredible fool, I said to myself. It serves you right.

"Can you breathe okay?" I asked Clara calmly, in spite of my hammering heart. I rapidly checked her pulse and respirations, scanning the lumpy welts on her face and arms. She looked misshapen, warped.

"I don't know," Clara whimpered. "I think so."

"A vial of Benadryl, Jo. Right away. Fifty milligrams." I saw no drooling, no gasping. What a break, just the hives. So far.

"Yes ma'am." Jo turned so fast her words hung in the empty air.

"What's wrong with her face?" Bobby demanded, eyes wild. "It's not that flesh-eating bacteria, is it? Dang! I knew we should've got that penicillin into her sooner."

"Clara. Does your throat feel tight? Like you're choking? Open your mouth." I peered in, but nothing had changed. I had to either ignore Bobby or snap at him, so I ignored him.

"No, it's not tight," she whispered, rubbing at a lump on her arm. Her eyes glittered with fear. "It itches real bad."

"Breathe deep," I instructed, sliding the stethoscope across her chest. The air swished cleanly through her lungs, no wheezes. Such luck. With a severe allergic reaction, the lungs could spasm shut and she could die within minutes.

"Hey! What the hell is going on?" Bobby screeched, grabbing my arm and making me drop the stethoscope.

"She's having an allergic reaction," I explained carefully, picking it up. "To the penicillin."

Bobby's arms dropped to his sides and his chapped lips fell into a small round "O."

Jo came back with the syringe of Benadryl.

"Maybe you'd better lie down," I suggested, helping Clara settle. Within seconds I'd injected the drug, while Bobby collapsed onto a stool beside her, clutching her arm.

"She'll be all right, won't she?" he groaned. "She looks awful."

"We'll just let this medication work and she ought to start improving—"

"We're not going to lose her, are we?" he cried, his dirty nails digging into her arm.

"Ow, Bobby. That hurts." Clara pushed his hand away.

"Of course not," I said. At least, I doubted it. "She should be fine soon."

Bobby rested his forehead in the hollow of her elbow, rolling his head back and forth. His lank hair flopped. "I never should've let you give her that shot."

I said nothing. I sat right there with her and typed in the chart, observing her closely. Within ten minutes Clara groggily pushed herself up, dazed from the Benadryl but better. The lumpy hives subsided. Not completely gone, but nearly. Now incredibly far behind, I saw my last three patients, checking on Clara in between, and by the end she looked normal, sleeping and snoring away. Bobby sat in a chair, draped against her on the exam table, sawing logs along with her. I woke them up and sent them home, supplied with medications and strict precautions.

One weak second, one tired decision, was all it took. A million people get penicillin injections every day and nothing happens, then I order it for the first time in years, and I had potential death on my hands.

How could anyone do this, day after day, with such hazards hanging over them? I wanted to walk out the back door and never come back. Two more weeks until my vacation. . .maybe I could keep from killing someone between now and then. Maybe the summer heat had gotten to me, one hundred ten degrees again. No one functioned well in this weather. Maybe it was that flop of Bobby's hair that ever so slightly reminded me of Austin, the way his straight brown hair flipped down his neck when he rolled over to me in bed. My heart lurched. Or maybe it was the radio sermon, droning through my brain. Holy savior, deliver us from the fiery grip of the devil, his sharp red—

"Jo!" I called.

A chunky young woman, quietly energetic, Jo's bright cheeks and bouncy dark curls always looked like she just stepped in from a hurricane, a little rushed, a little breathless.

"Yes, Dr. Waters?"

"What am I hearing over the speakers?"

Jo paused to listen, gazing up, her lips pursed in a cautious smile. "I believe it's a choir."

"Does it seem like they're singing a hymn?" I really should get hold of myself.

"Why, yes. I believe they are." Jo smiled widely, as if nothing could really be wrong. "It's just an accident, I'm sure. Betsy probably switched that on after the patients left. She loves that station. . . . She usually sings along. I mean, after the patients are gone. I bet she forgot when she went home. I think the channel is called KSIN. Kind of clever, isn't it?"

"Jo. There's no place—" I stopped, made my voice relax and tried very hard to forget KSIN. I suspected Betsy left it on for the benefit of my imperfect soul. Whatever happened to positive messaging? Would Jesus approve of that? "Everyone should just leave the music alone."

I stomped to the radio console and snapped it off. Our patients came from many religious backgrounds. If Betsy were still there, I would have talked with her myself. I pictured her pallid face above her stiff starched tiger scrubs, a suffering missionary, tiny bright crosses glinting in her earlobes. Truly a devoted worker among us savages. I had to remind myself that she worked hard and probably meant well. I was the damaged one.

If Nellie had been there like she ought to be, she could manage these personnel issues. But Nellie probably ran to the bank to deposit my money, what little of it there seemed to be these days. Since all the physicians found this matter concerning, we discussed a possible audit to investigate the cause. But so far no one had the energy to make it happen.

I departed, likely to everyone's relief. September means autumn in most parts of the country but not in Arizona, and I braced for the blast of hot air. The sun trudged toward the horizon, still a fierce fire, cooking the atmosphere into a thick molten gas. Cloudless, the sky trashed to glowing ash, like the aftermath of a devastating burn.

I blotted the sweat from my face and tried to fathom why I let the Farrells badger me into the wrong treatment. My focus had slipped, so far off it felt broken. I turned a corner and the low sunlight flashed in my eyes, an orange searchlight, nearly blinding me.

Summer in the desert. Next stop, hell.

Seven more years to retirement. I could barely imagine doing this seven more days. It used to be that I thought about quitting every month or so. Then every week. Now I thought about it every single day.

I had to get out of there.

3

Those who don't know the joy of returning home to a waiting dog simply haven't lived a full life. I feel sorry for them, for their unenlightened existence.

Emcee knows my moods. Whether she approves of those moods is another story. A lab-retriever mix the color of toast, with soft maple-syrup eyes, I named her after Marie Curie, one of the most brilliant early female scientists. We'll skip the part about how Curie accidentally killed herself with radiation exposure. Inevitably, the dog's name got shortened to MC. Then, because she always tried to broker arguments between Austin and me, whining when we quarreled and nudging us apart, she became Emcee.

The dog still longed for Austin. Austin had been gone three months, but she continued to sniff for him around the bedroom, still checked out the spare room he used as his writing den. Now she spent the day alone instead of lounging at his feet while he wrote, or whatever the hell he did all day.

Emcee always insists on climbing into my lap, all sixty-five pounds of her, when I get home. At least one furry leg slides off me because she doesn't fit, but she won't leave until I've scratched her head and rubbed her belly, her tongue slopping out to anoint my arms and face with warm saliva. It's the best. If anything kept me from falling off the cliff, it was Emcee. I could practically hear her thoughts.

Where have you been all day? she asked, lapping my nose.

"At work, same place as always. Trying to keep people healthy."

Why don't you take care of dogs instead? They're so much nicer. She groaned happily as I stroked her chest, her eyes closed.

"Dogs don't need me as much. People keep doing dumb things."

Like nasty smoking? Like not going out for walks?

"Absolutely."

Stupid self-destructive humans.

"Hey, don't act so superior. Dogs eat disgusting crap off the ground. They run in front of cars, which is obviously suicidal."

Emcee kept her eyes shut and pretended to be asleep.

My cell phone rang, so I shoved her off and found my purse. Austin again—my face crimped. He called the night before but I ignored him. So this time I answered, because I might as well get it over with.

"Norah," he said brightly. "How's my best friend?"

"Emcee is good," I replied, neutral. Sometimes I wondered which one of us he cared for the most. "She misses you."

Austin laughed, that good deep laugh of his. "Yeah, that's what I meant. What else could I possibly mean, right? Okay. When can I come see her?"

"How about this weekend, maybe Sunday? You can take her for a walk." That way I could stay out of it. Maybe I could teach Emcee to open the door and I wouldn't even have to be home, since Austin no longer had a key.

"That would be great, Nor. You'll come with us, won't you?" Too eager. The hope shone transparently between his words, like a thin waif.

"I don't think so. It's not a good idea." We discussed this a thousand times. Except for Emcee, I would have cut him off entirely. But the dog loved him and it felt unnecessarily cruel to separate them completely. Even though Emcee lived with me two years before Austin came along, she felt like our custody dog.

"All right." His voice dropped and I imagined the hurt in his clear brown eyes. His disbelief that I hadn't come back around and let this go, that we stayed apart.

"How was the interview yesterday?" I asked. A few days before, he texted me about a promising job with a small community newspaper. He said I'd be proud of him for applying and getting the interview. But I'd been there too many times.

"I knew you'd ask." He understood that petulance did not appeal to me, but he couldn't help himself.

"Austin. You were the one who told me about it. You were all excited—why wouldn't I ask? What happened?"

A short hard sigh. "The guy was kind of a dick. Expected me to come in every day even though I could work better from home. Wanted me to go to local markets and festivals all over the valley, to interview merchants. It sounded miserable, lots of driving. I told him it didn't seem like a good fit."

The job sounded fine to me, interesting and stimulating, but I should have known better than to ask him about it and cannot believe I went there. Telling myself to stay quiet is something I should practice about every three minutes.

I missed Austin. I could admit that. I missed his enthusiasm over silly things, pushing me to lighten up and be frivolous now and then. How he romped with Emcee. His slow smile, his thoughtful face when I talked, his attention to me in bed. When he grew excited about a new story he wanted to write, he lit up like a hundred candles, and we could talk half the night. I teased him about his chestnut-going-gray beard that kept changing, different patterns every few months: a full beard like a bear, a prissy van Dyke, that ludicrous handlebar moustache. Like he kept trying on personalities.

And there sat the problem. In his fifties, Austin still didn't know who he was, and maybe never would. He seldom held a job for long because no job ever "fit." Suck it up, I say—we all do. We all work when we'd rather not, we're all disappointed with our careers, our jobs that seemed like such shining opportunities a few decades ago. Austin is a good writer, but he gets in his own way. He'll spend an afternoon getting one sentence perfect, then he'll change it the next day, or delete it entirely. He possesses three partly written novels and passed up two good jobs with benefits last year. I suspect there were other offers he hid from me. Jobs where he could write newsletters and advertisements for big corporations, and still have evenings and weekends for his novels. One position he actually started, but then he dropped it after six weeks because the boss acted "weird" about deadlines.

He wanted more time to work on his real writing, he claimed, but then he didn't. Nothing got done. I can't name one project he finished in three years. There was a poem he wrote that I really liked about a storm crossing the desert, but he only submitted it to one journal for publication and after that rejection he quit trying.

Meanwhile, I started feeling like his cash cow. Moo.

I can't remember when I gave him access to my bank account for some expenses, then I sort of forgot and left it that way. I mean, we had lived together a long time. He started buying me expensive things I didn't want, like modern sculptures for the backyard because I once admired a Brancusi. I guess I'm not fond of misshapen metallic horses who look like they're writhing in pain, even though that spindly concoction still stands in my backyard because I don't know what to do with it. Fortuitously, a sagebrush cropped up beneath it and is slowly obliterating the outline, so I hardly notice it now.

Then Austin wanted to get in better shape, so he bought himself a top-notch mountain bike that he used exactly once. Without asking, he "gave" me a pricey vacation package in Santa Barbara, a place I had little interest in going. And so on. Let me repeat that my money paid for all this.

After a while, it started feeling like abuse. Financial abuse.

Over and over, we discussed how he needed to contribute. That's how Emcee got her name, intervening when we bickered. We never shouted or raved because neither of us were prone to drama, but we sniped and whined. Just ugly, and I hated it. I hated myself for not rising above it, but I apparently could not.

Contribute something, anything, I said, work part time at the doughnut shop. I didn't care, because it was the principle. I'm not wired to support a mooch. He promised to get a job, but then he didn't. Although he never said it exactly, I know he thought it was stupid because I made plenty of money. That obviously was not the point. He's a smart man but refused to embrace this.

I drew a line in the sand. He still found no job that fit, so then he had to leave. And now we negotiated over the phone.

"You should come early in the morning to walk Emcee," I said. "Otherwise it's still too hot."

"How about evening?" he asked quickly. "She loves evening walks."

"That won't work for me." I fudged, for I had no plans. I just didn't want him there at night, because that could inadvertently lead to supper or bed. It happened once and I regretted it.

We hung up. Then I called Clara Farrell to make sure her hives hadn't recurred. I woke her up and it took her a few minutes to figure out who I was and report she felt fine.

I'm a walker. I like to get out and move, find my stride, cover ground. Dogs make the best accomplices. Sometimes I think a great deal while I walk, and other times I don't think at all. After talking with Austin and Clara, Emcee and I traveled a long way and I imagined what a great walker I would be after retirement. A sensational walker, all over the country. In my head, I tried composing a resignation letter to my partners, a task always skulking in the dark corners of my brain. Somewhere down there deep, black and cold, where all the hard stuff dwells.

The moonless night surprised me, for I expected a moon. I like to track the moon and its phases. It's not a conscious thing, just one of those daily details I know, like knowing the days of the week. Most physicians are detail people because they have to be, because missing or neglecting even a single small item can turn disastrous. If your doctor isn't a detail person, find a new one. So it threw me off when I realized I didn't know if the moon had gone missing because a new phase, that minimal rim, had already set, or because a fuller moon had yet to rise. It seemed a signal for how far I'd slipped lately.

Emcee and I journeyed a few miles on that walk, but my thinking went in circles, even after I shut it off, and I returned to the same place, ultimately going nowhere.

I wished I could be a different person. Austin had admirable traits, but a little fiscal responsibility would have gone a long way. I wished I could let it go, wished that he didn't make me feel mistreated. Let's just say I was not very happy with who I was those days, but didn't know how to be someone else.

4

My mother frequently called me on the phone.

At eighty-six, she seemed blissfully unaware when I might be working. Let me correct that: she seemed blissfully unconcerned when I might be working.

Don't get me wrong. Engaging and fairly intact for her age, Mom simply lived in her own world. But then, she always did. Her calls came in little flurries, and I rarely returned them until after I got home.

"How come Austin never answers your phone anymore?" she demanded.

"Because Austin's gone," I said patiently for the hundredth time.

"I know, I know. You told me. I just don't like it. . . . I miss him. When are you going to make up and get back together?"

Austin cherished my mother, and frankly I'm surprised he didn't keep calling her himself. They could chat for an hour about her peevish Sun City neighbors and whether Mom should invite the mailman in for coffee.

"He's only seventy-five and he won't retire," she carried on with admiration. "He's quite handsome and fit by Sun City standards. And he's got big quads and biceps from carrying all those packages. I might ask him in. Most of the rundown old geezers around here couldn't deliver mail to more than five houses without needing dialysis."

Austin laughed and egged her on. I overheard their conversations because she nearly shouted, a reedy voice, making Austin hold the phone away from his ear. He balanced a notebook on his knee and jotted down snippets of her words, gathering materials for one of his endlessly languishing novels.

What with Emcee and Mom both adoring and yearning for Austin, my ego suffered when we broke up. Sometimes I think they would have contentedly traded me for him. Maybe they should have. Maybe I should live alone in a closet.

"Does the mailman even like coffee?" Austin goaded her.

"Honey. I don't really mean coffee." She laughed and Austin snorted.

My mother knew all about quads and biceps. A retired anatomy professor, I can probably blame her for how I ended up in medicine. Throughout my childhood, she waxed eloquent on the intricate machinery of the body, told me bedtime stories about red blood cells fighting their way through the chambers of the heart, carrying their little backpacks of oxygen molecules on a wild ride to the far reaches of the limbs, all the way out to the fingers and toes. I still remember the adventures of Reddy and Steady, those plucky little corpuscles. But she spared me no reality—Reddy and Steady perished after four months of journeys, gobbled up by the spleen and replaced by their millions of cousins.

A strange childhood. Definitely a vivid image of the human body.

So now with Austin gone, I entertained her by myself, but I felt like second fiddle.

"Who are you seeing now?" she demanded.

"No one, Mom. I'm taking a break. Reevaluating my life." I kicked my shoes off and sprawled with Emcee on the couch. The dog gave me a narrow strip of cushion and took up the rest for herself, then twisted her neck and grinned at me. Ingrate.

"That's dangerous, reevaluating. Be careful," she warned. "Don't do it. You'll think too much and you'll get stuck, and the next thing you know, you'll be ninety and wonder what happened to all those years. Or you'll do something stupid and regret it forever. What little forever you'll have left."

She blew her nose vigorously, making me wonder if it was her allergies or a few tears, thinking of the past. After my brother, Ben, died, she sat in the kitchen for weeks and stared into space. Or sometimes she doodled endlessly, filling her sketchpad with intricate drawings of lungs. The large spongy lobes, cradled in the ribcage. Wide tracheas, forked carinas, tunneling bronchioles. The little bubbles of alveoli, like cul-de-sacs, the last stop for inhaled air. . .in normal lungs. Ben's lungs had been anything but normal.

Or maybe she thought of my dad, twenty years older, long gone.

Such a drawn-out pause in conversation rarely happened.

"You okay, Mom?"

"Damn allergies. Used to be people came to the desert to escape pollen. Now it's everywhere. That's what happens with too much irrigation, too many canals and dams. They never should have let the city grow this big."

"I might drive out for a visit this weekend," I said, thinking perhaps she felt lonely. An hour's drive for me, Sun City covered many square miles of flat desert northwest of Phoenix, one of the first communities in the country to legally ban children.

"Nah, don't bother. There's a big dance party on Saturday and I'm part of the decorations committee. I think that mailman is going to be there, too. Maybe you could come out the next weekend."

Great. My mom had plans for the geriatric prom while I sat home by myself, studying medicine. Learning exciting topics like treating kidney disease and a new technique for removing infected toenails.

Typical.

5

Every academic season, I took on a fledgling medical student, tucked them under my wing, and started teaching them to fly. I enjoyed these raw souls, keen to see actual patients and taste the thrill of practicing medicine with a real human instead of theoretical cases in textbooks. One afternoon every week, this eager first-year student appeared before me to learn how to talk with patients, examine patients, and create a professional note in the chart. How to organize a dozen symptoms and shuffle them into possible diagnoses, then make a treatment plan. Female students gravitated to my practice because they saw me as some sort of role model, however jaded.

This year, I had two taxing students, both males. The first one came through the normal route, but the second one did not.

George Clark got assigned to me in the usual manner, which means someone picked him from a list and put us together. Probably less scientific than the Hogwarts sorting hat. George had a forgettable name. A forgettable bland round face, soft light brown hair, the kind of young man who in college studied for his classes or played video games far into the night and hadn't spent much time outdoors. Smart, no doubt, or he wouldn't be there, but he had the cautious nocturnal eyes of a high school mathlete and he probably majored in physics. George was nice, shy, and fearful of talking with patients. He didn't know what field of medicine he wanted, but I figured he should probably be a pathologist and spend most of his time with microscopes and tiny transparent slices of human organs.

Then a month into the season I got a call from Dr. Angelo Candore, an assistant dean at the medical school, wondering if I could possibly take on one more student for the year. Because I always did such a good job, blah blah blah—he laid it on thick. Another male, of all things. Jeremy Newell, he said, would be an easy ride, downright brilliant, a quick study. His original clinical preceptor hadn't worked out, a poor match.

I should have asked more questions, but I assumed that if a really sharp student got paired with one of the weaker docs out there, the student might have balked. I knew a few of those docs and they scared me a little. They ordered too many labs and X-rays, a shotgun approach. They used expensive brand-name drugs when a simple generic would do fine and referred almost everyone to specialists for the simplest problems. At least part of their current knowledge came from the lips of slick pharmaceutical reps who spouted blatant advertising veiled as research. At a medical conference those docs were more likely to be found on the golf course rather than in the lecture hall. Their charts were often a mess, and they should hardly be seeing patients, let alone teaching students. Some were old, but some were not.

To be clear, I'm not perfect, not even close. Look at my penicillin debacle. But I study nearly every day and take a little pride in my work, no matter how limited modern medicine can be. When I don't know something, I look it up. A really important skill for family physicians is knowing how to find good answers. I call patients to check on them when I'm worried. You have to make the effort, be responsible. Otherwise go work for an insurance company.

If Candore knew how I really felt about medicine, he never would have asked. I'm not sure why I didn't refuse, either. Maybe I was afraid to hear it out loud, from my own mouth. *I shouldn't take on another student because I might quit before the year is over, Dr. Candore. I'm too tired to read like I should and I can't keep up with the endless charting.* It would have been entertaining, to see his reaction.

So now I taught Jeremy Newell on one afternoon and George Clark on another, and it was frankly too much. It slowed down my flow and I scheduled a couple fewer patients those afternoons so I could supervise the students properly. George needed a lot of work on interview skills, and I discovered quickly that Jeremy needed even more work on being a human. Yes, he was smart in some ways, but he was also an arrogant jerk.

I didn't mind coaching George because he tried. He wanted to improve, and my heart went out to his sad, hopeful expression when he came up short. What he really needed to do was talk to random people every day, to practice being friendly and curious, make small talk. I told him that, and he looked at me like I just asked him to run naked down the street. My guess is that in college he had a small group of geeky guy friends who studied together, and maybe once a month a geeky female joined them for fifteen minutes. That's possibly the extent of his communications with the opposite gender.

When I asked him about the sexual history on a female patient, the one he just talked with who needed contraception, he flushed dull red and stammered that she just wanted to renew her prescription for the pill, so wasn't that enough to know?

"That's the most important," I agreed. "The last thing anyone needs is an unwanted pregnancy. But this is your opportunity to provide some other very important information. Any idea what that would be?"

George turned redder and mumbled a few words into his laptop.

"What's that?" I asked.

His voice raised a fraction and he looked at my shoulder, somewhere south of my face. "You mean sff szz?"

"George. Speak up." This truly pained me.

"Safe sex?" he blurted, suddenly too loud.

Behind him, Jo startled and looked at me. Jo liked the med students and offered them little treats like chocolates, and she enjoyed teaching them how to give vaccines and attach the EKG machine. She sort of adopted them like little pets, a comparison I kept to myself. I could tell she liked George and worried about him.

"Yes!" I crowed. "Safe sex, absolutely. Good job."

After that accomplishment, I joined George with the patient and demonstrated a conversation about partners, condoms, and STD testing. Small steps. George would always be timid, sweet and awkward. I wanted to give him enough skills to get through med school without feeling bad, without being picked on by the occasional obnoxious attending or chief resident. There were always a few who thrived on putting others down; medicine remained sadly populated with a handful of them. Weak egos, mean spirits. After George survived training, he could pursue pathology or research or some equally studious, reclusive work where he would flourish.

Later that day I suggested he practice on me, to pretend I was a new patient and take a sexual history. "The more times you do it, the more natural it becomes. It feels clumsy now, but you'll get better, trust me."

George coughed and seemed to choke on something, but the patients were gone, and I had plenty of time to let him recover.

"I don't know, Dr. Waters," he said miserably. "I hate role playing."

"So do I," I confided, "but it actually helps. Come on, only a few sentences. Don't worry, I'll just make up a history, nothing personal. And look me in the eye." I put on a blank pleasant expression and a cheery high voice because I'm not good at acting like a patient. I hadn't seen my own doctor in quite a while.

"Is there anything else you need to know about me, Dr. Clark?" I asked, all chipper.

"Um." George consulted his hands, his bitten fingernails. His eyes reluctantly climbed to my face, briefly connected and skipped away, as he muttered, "Are you currently sexually active?"

"Why, yes I am," I affirmed brightly.

"Is that with men, or women, or both?" he managed, a throttled sound. Another fleeting eye contact. I had to be quick to catch it.

"Oh, goodness. Just with men."

George sighed from the tips of his toes. "Do you use protection?"

"Why, not very often. Do you think I should?"

He sighed again and shot me a tortured glare. "Can we stop now? I know what to say."

"Of course," I agreed, back to my normal voice. "Good job, George. It will get easier, I promise."

Still, I preferred George and his struggles over Jeremy Newell, with his smug know-it-all smirk. Jeremy has close-cropped curly blond hair and oddly asymmetrical lips, like each half of his face has its own emotions. He took a flawless sexual history when appropriate. Except he explained it back to me like a weather report, dry and a little snide, as if amused at the patient's answers. It felt odd and disquieting.

"This is a forty-year-old white heterosexual male, who's here because he's anxious about everything. I think we can safely label him as one of the 'worried well.'" Jeremy spoke formally and sounded bored. Although he looked at me levelly, his right upper lip lifted as he said *worried well*, a tiny sneer. "He's afraid he might have a sexual disease."

"Does he follow risky behaviors?"

"No. He always uses a condom." Now his mouth remained still but one eyebrow rose. I'm not certain how a person can make an eyebrow appear sarcastic, but Jeremy managed.

"Did you ask him why he was worried?"

A short puff of air emitted from the corner of his mouth. "No, Dr. Waters. He worries about everything, like I said, and he's not very bright."

And I had to work with this student for almost a year? We went to see the patient. I greeted him warmly and asked about his job at an electronics store, and within two minutes he admitted to an unanticipated and unprotected homosexual encounter. Hence his worry. I talked to Jeremy about using open-ended questions and how to keep the patient from shutting down. The left half of his face looked bored and the right half grimaced.

During Jeremy's first month, a door stood slightly open and I saw Jo demonstrate for him how to perform spirometry on a patient with emphysema. Jo's enthusiasm helped, as she vigorously coached the patient to take a huge deep breath and blow out hard, measuring their lung capacity. Right in the middle, Jeremy answered a call, pulling his phone from his pocket and walking out of the room without an apology, speaking loudly to someone about a test. Startled, Jo lost her momentum and had to start over. Never mind that I always told medical students to keep their phones off when with patients.

"What are your future plans?" I asked Jeremy later. My fingers crossed that he didn't say family medicine, so he wouldn't want a letter of recommendation from me.

"Neurosurgery," he said shortly, his cold eye scanning me like I was a poor specimen of some inferior species.

"Well, good for you. It's a long road, but we'll always need neurosurgeons."

I left it at that. Maybe Jeremy would get better as we came to know each other. Maybe he would relax. Maybe not. But I had better things to worry about than haughty med students who looked down at family medicine. We're used to that. We're used to most specialists looking down on us; they don't begin to understand what we do. Instead, I planned to go home and worry about myself. My lagging income. My distress over Austin. My pathetic personal life. The upcoming first meeting of the admissions committee for the medical school, which I let myself be talked into again.

I was likely not the best person to be choosing next year's medical students.

Then I discovered something new to fret about. Climbing into my car, I saw a white unlined index card slipped under my windshield wiper. Annoyed, assuming it to be an advertisement, I groaned and got back out, pulling it off and burning my fingers on the metal blade. A thick black border ran around the card, like a Victorian funeral announcement. A broad cursive script: *You Suck*

6

I looked up from my office desk and there stood my practice partner Emily Thatcher, her dark red hair waving and crackling, flying around her shoulders like a magnetic field. She had been bugging me to go out with her for weeks, and even I could become a little bit contaminated with her positive energy now and then. No one could not like Emily.

"Come on, Norah," Emily pled, eyes sparking. "I need a night out, and I'd rather not go alone. I've got a babysitter and everything. Well, not a babysitter—they're too old for babysitters. Their dad is coming over."

"Emily. You must have younger and better friends than me. What good would I be at a pickup bar?" I eyed her skeptically, digesting the dynamic of her ex-husband staying with the girls while she went out looking for men. But then, I'm older and not always as modern as I'd like to think. Not that Emily was a youngster, but her vitality at forty-some years old seemed pretty impressive. I probably had that in my forties, but it's too long ago to remember.

Emily shook her head. "I don't go to pickup bars. I go to nice places and enjoy a drink. Maybe I meet someone, maybe I don't. The whole point is to get out and have some fun, have some laughs. Let go of your stress."

I stared at her over my eyeglasses. "Do I look like someone who has random fun at bars?"

"You could be. Come on, don't be such a grump. It'll be good for you. Besides, you always make me laugh."

I suspected she didn't really need my company. She worried about me; she practically said so. What did that mean, that it would be "good for me"? Perhaps she thought I was depressed. Good call, Emily.

"I sort of embrace my grumpiness," I pointed out. "It's who I am."

Emily laughed. "Oh, Norah. That's bullshit and you know it. I need to go home and put on my evening face, then I'll come pick you up. Is eight-thirty okay?"

"Eight-thirty? Isn't that kind of late?" I might be in pajamas by then, reading, or watching some worthless movie on television. Cuddled up with Emcee, maybe a glass of wine.

"No, silly. If anything, it's early. I've got to run and spend some time with the girls first. See you then." She slipped out the door, gone before I could decline.

So that's how it happened that I turned up with Emily at an expensive resort, drinking a too-sweet cocktail and watching people hook up. Entertaining, at least. Emily looked quite pretty, smoky eyes and tight black capris, a shimmery green tank top that glowed against her red hair. Divorced for several years, her children now teenagers with lives of their own, Emily had started looking around. I liked her daughters, spunky and always overloaded with school plays and soccer teams, funny and a little crass.

I tried not to think about that chance I had, ten years ago. I could have adopted that baby. The young pregnant woman was desperate to find someone trustworthy. It could have worked, but I lost my nerve and now I'll never know. Having a ten-year-old daughter might be nice.

I told my brain to shut up. Water under the bridge. I would likely have been a terrible mom, too wrapped up in my work, too many late nights catching up, too preoccupied with patients. Not everyone has to be a parent, and some shouldn't.

Contrast Emily's chic appearance with mine, me in my best jeans and a simple white blouse. My favorite silver earrings dangled along my neck, and my hair was clean and fluffy. I wear it in layers now, loose and wavy around my face, and the gray mixes in nicely with all the shades of dark and light brown, a little gold here and there. I don't really look almost sixty. I had put on lip gloss and plucked those damn little hairs at the edge of my chin. I'd stared at the wrinkles in my neck. Welcome to ageing. Emily said I looked great, although she had to say that since she made me accompany her.

But so what? I didn't look to replace Austin any time soon. Maybe never. Some of us do better solo.

Perhaps this could be my moment, here with Emily. How would she react if I leaned over, put my lips near her ear and said quietly *Hey, I'm quitting at the end of the year?* Then I couldn't back out—I'd have to follow through. I tried to imagine how restful retirement would be, getting a good night's sleep without worrying about which patient I'd messed up. Just do it now, I thought, say it before you chicken out.

I had always wanted to be a doctor, cannot remember a time when I didn't. That sounds corny, but it's true. There weren't any light bulb moments, no brilliant revelations. I played doctor when I was three years old, bandaging our dog's paw, helping my Grammy exercise her new hip. Bringing my older brother Ben his medicine when he coughed. I even had a small pediatric stethoscope to listen to his bony chest, all the burbles and wheezes inside his lungs. Why my mother endorsed that I can't imagine, but it worked for me. I loved it.

Ben suffered—and I mean *suffered*—from severe cystic fibrosis. He had the same mixed brown hair as mine, bright with flaxen lights, like a field of wheat above his thin face. People with difficult cystic fibrosis tend to be small and often don't grow like they should. Thick mucus clogs their lungs, so obviously they don't breathe well. But no matter how bad he felt, how hard he worked for his oxygen, he always made time for me.

"My lungs are pretty tight today," Ben would tell me. His chest whistling, eyes large, cheeks gaunt. He didn't like to cut his streaky hair so it often hung in his face. . . . I think it gave him a place to hide from the world. "Fix me up, Sis."

I filled his nebulizer and adjusted the mouthpiece, rewarded with a smile. Then he coughed, dense gurgling bubbles, lips tinted blue. He gripped my hand while I waited for him to get his breath back, ready with the mist.

By the time I turned seven I could manage his breathing machine, measuring just the right amount of meds. I penciled the schedule of his treatments in a daisy-decorated notebook. I learned to interpret his peak air flow meter, that plastic tube with a red slider which measured how deep he could puff. It felt like a secret code to his lungs, and I had all the parameters memorized. Ben said no one could calculate his nebulizer needs better than me.

On good days, he read to me with marvelous drama: *Treasure Island, Watership Down*, everything by Roald Dahl. On his bad days, I read to him with attempted drama: *Lord of the Flies, Huckleberry Finn, To Kill a Mockingbird*. My father, who lived with us intermittently, sometimes protested that the books were too old for me, some too violent. My mother shrugged and said children will police what they can handle. I think most of us know better than that.

When Ben was twenty-two and I turned eighteen, a college freshman, I went as an aide with a medical mission to Guatemala for a month. While I was gone, having a great time and fortifying my dreams of physicianhood, Ben came down with pneumonia and died.

"Hey," Emily said, her elbow in my side. She bent toward me, away from the friendly looking guy beside her in shirtsleeves and a tie and nodded across the room. A dim comfortable space, glints of light off bottles and glasses. Voices murmuring like a background sea, a faint spool of piano music. "That man is watching you."

I hadn't noticed because I rarely notice things like that, and because I was busy staring into my drink, thinking about Ben. He surfaced at the strangest times, even after forty years.

This man appeared about sixty, dark gray hair. Thick in his middle but craggy features, decent looking. He caught my glance and smiled, so I had to look away slowly, like I was just scanning the room and accidentally crossed his face. I thought I'd escaped but then he stood up, holding his drink, and started over.

"Nice evening," he remarked. Confident, he leaned on a chair and studied me openly.

"Is it? I think it's still over one hundred outside." I suppose it wouldn't kill me to be sociable, but I hardly know how to flirt and pretty much disdain it. Someone once accused me of unflirting.

"Hm." He pulled back, as if recalculating. I wondered how soon he would leave. He did smell pretty good, a woodsy aftershave. He went on. "I guess I thought you wanted company. The way you were looking at your drink, kind of lonely."

Good lord. Lonely. How trite can you get? A faint Texas twang, so probably a visitor. Many businesses hold conferences in Scottsdale hotels every summer because half the rooms are empty and the rates are so low. Bargain basement prices to come roast yourself to death.

"No, I was thinking of my dead brother," I said.

He squinted. "Well, that's a new one. I guess I can't top that."

I nearly smiled. Okay, now I almost liked him. "You're welcome to sit if you have nothing better to do. But I'm just here to ride shotgun for my friend." I canted my head toward Emily, who now shared sips of a cocktail with the other guy.

He pulled the chair around, ordered another drink and gestured at the room. "You can help me scout out the crowd. Who do you think would like me?"

I took my time. I slanted a little away from him and perused the scattered people, the single women. Some slick and overdressed, dripping with gold jewelry, some barely covered by beachwear, freckled and sunburned, as if they just came from the pool. Probably they did.

"That depends," I commented, still scanning. "Are you looking for true love, or just lust?"

He laughed and turned back to me, moved his face in front of mine so I'd have to look at him. "Are you sure you're not interested?"

"Not happening," I assured him. Not mean, just matter of fact. He sighed loudly but gave up, respecting my words.

We sat there talking off and on for another thirty minutes until I got bored with him. Nice enough, not stupid, but I wasn't hunting and he was no Zorro. I grew quieter and soon he left for a better prospect on the other side of the bar.

Animated and laughing, Emily chatted with the shirt-sleeve guy. Sometimes you can look at a man and tell he's probably decent, a sort of honesty in his eyes, and he had that vibe. Emily slipped me an amused glance now and then, enjoying herself. It made me feel good because she deserved it. She worked hard and loved her girls and it gratified me that she wanted to be my friend. And her husband had been a two-timing ass.

But Emily wasn't going anywhere soon, so I said goodbye and summoned an Uber. I had missed my moment to announce I was quitting, and I could see the chance wouldn't be back, not that night.

When I reached home Emcee frisked around me, thrilled, eyes sparkling. *Where have you been? I haven't seen you in days!*

"I was just here a few hours ago. Remember your supper?"

No. I don't think you fed me. I'm really hungry. She circled, prancing, her food dance.

I gave her a dog biscuit and I tried to read a medical journal, but it was an article about heart disease that seemed both too complicated and too boring at once. So we spent the rest of the evening falling asleep to a stupid movie. You would think Hollywood could create an original plotline every now and then. And why could I fall asleep on a couch watching television, but not in my bed?

I'm sure Emily thought I had a good time, and she could keep that delusion because it would make her feel better, feel like she's saving me.

But my self-assessment held true. I was grumpy, and I functioned better solo. Maybe not the best life, but apparently mine.

I kept trying to figure this out. I truly did.

7

The office financial meeting at lunch did not go well. Although patient volumes remained steady, all the physicians experienced a drop in income. We came together to brainstorm.

Office manager Nellie glared like a cornered bobcat and insisted every single penny went where it belonged, that each payment got logged properly and deposited. Just to be certain, she ran to the bank every day now, so no checks or cash or insurance payments sat unattended overnight. Each bill had a corresponding deposit or "past due" entered in the ledgers. The books, she declared, looked impeccable. Insurance companies were not denying or reducing payments any more than usual. I mean, that was an endless battle because insurers always pulled that sort of delaying crap. And Nellie diligently upgraded our billing codes, if appropriate, whenever she could.

Her orange-and-brown streaked hair burst from her head like an explosion and quivered when she spoke.

Betsy, the pasty receptionist, sat quietly and nibbled her baloney sandwich, a paper napkin tucked in to protect her starched leopard scrubs, the fabric stiff as cardboard with hardly a wrinkle. And I wondered how anyone can eat baloney, that mash of pig snouts and ears and genitals. You can feel gritty little bits of bone. I know she's poor, but isn't peanut butter just as cheap? At least it isn't pulverized pig parts, shoveled up off the slaughterhouse floor and poured into a blender.

Being a detail person is not a calming trait. I probably read too many labels.

Betsy did not seem like a bad person; she just vexed me because I let her. Self-righteousness puts me off. Add it to my list of failings. She drove an ancient Ford Pinto, a sunbeaten brown, prone to languish in our parking lot for days at a time when it refused to start. When that happened, her husband dropped her off and picked her up until the car could be coaxed to cooperate, but no one ever met him or even saw him. A phantom spouse. Maybe his car looked even worse, maybe they were embarrassed. Watching her peck at her sandwich, her eyes down, it occurred to me that he might be difficult, and I made a mental note to talk with her.

We had five physicians in this practice, including me. There was Emily Thatcher, my bar-scene friend. Brian Mulch, the nature boy so fond of penicillin and every vitamin ever discovered. Wanda Cunningham, maybe the sweetest thirty-year-old on the planet and naïve as a hatchling hummingbird; she's tiny, about four-foot-eleven, and always reacted with astonishment when someone did something foolish. Which meant she was astounded every few minutes. And finally our senior partner Zane Grayson, early seventies, whose parents clearly had a sense of humor. Zane started the practice by himself years ago, back when you nailed up a shingle and people came in. No contracts with insurance companies, no signing up with state health plans, no computers—just shelves full of paper folders. By now he probably should have retired, but he practiced better medicine than most docs half his age and his patients adored him.

All of us worked with medical students except Brian Mulch, a blessing for those students who might have been stuck with his reckless approach to supplements. Mulch never met an herb he didn't love and managed to tout obscure purposes for them all.

"So what do we think is going on? Where's our dough?" Zane groused. He has a wide chest and thin legs, a prominent belly. Typical older male habitus. A gruff voice. But his eyes gleamed playfully. "I mean, it's not a fortune, but something's off. Norah? Are you skimming from the top so you can fund a new homeless clinic downtown?"

"Very funny," I said. "I wish I was. Except I think my income is down more than anyone's. Right, Nellie?" Nellie's face went a little purple but she gave a jerky nod and I went on. I guess I wanted to stir things up, and I abandoned vague diplomacy in favor of vague confrontation. "This feels like one of those murder-mystery parties. Like, it must be someone in this room who knows, right?"

All eyes opened wide at that. Nellie and Betsy and the four medical assistants, including Jo, looked sideways at one another. A mixed bunch, they were solid workers who knew their jobs and cared about our patients. Sometimes they called in sick more often than seemed reasonable, but I tried not to judge. Okay, I didn't try very hard. Except for Jo, relentlessly upbeat, who never called in sick that I could recall. And calling in sick didn't mean they were embezzling.

"It could be one of the doctors, too," Nellie pointed out, staring at me.

I nodded. Fair was fair. "It certainly could."

"Now, Norah. This probably isn't intentional, you know? Couldn't there be some hidden error, some kind of system problem?" Wanda Cunningham, a motherly physician and ever the peacemaker, chirped in her high birdlike voice. Her small sharp nose and her dark curls gathered up in a topknot made me think of a little crested woodpecker. "Maybe we should hire an outside person, a professional auditor. You know, so we won't be suspicious of each other. That's just a horrible feeling. I love each one of you and there's probably something we haven't figured out. I can't imagine anything dishonest."

Brian Mulch rolled his eyes and said nothing, looking at his phone, not paying much attention. The MAs, the medical assistants, looked back and forth and Betsy nibbled away.

I felt less charitable than Wanda. Obviously, I knew it wasn't me, but it could be anyone. Maybe Nellie—maybe she had a reason to look so grim all the time. Or maybe Betsy's poverty drove her to it, though it seemed unlikely that her moral self would condone theft. I mean, she listened to a radio station called KSIN. No one knew what her invisible husband did. Perhaps credit card debt? Once I noticed she carried an expensive handbag, something my mom tuned me into because she always railed about her concept of frivolous things. But we all have something—I enjoy pricey walking shoes when cheaper sneakers would probably work just as well. The bag was likely a knockoff, anyway. Maybe I should secretly look for the label, but that felt theatrical. I could hardly imagine getting down on my knees and crawling under Betsy's desk to check the seams and tags while she went to the restroom.

Who else? Emily raised two teenagers mostly on her own, not cheap. I wouldn't put anything past Brian Mulch. Zane neared retirement and physicians notoriously planned poorly for that. Wanda, easily distracted, could be wreaking havoc and misdirecting money without realizing it.

And who knew about the MAs? I would never doubt Jo, the most straightforward person in the world. They sat together, a little clump in blue scrubs, as if banded together in denial. They all had personal problems: Nadine with an alcoholic partner who climbed on and fell off the wagon frequently, Priya prone to morning tardiness though always willing to stay late, Martina who sometimes waxed dramatic over the barest insult, real or imagined. But everyone has problems, and I suspected it wouldn't be terribly difficult for a clever person to swindle our system. Medical practices are notoriously easy targets.

Jo caught my eye and made a tiny grimace as she glanced around the room. I could tell she didn't like this and wanted to leave. Not too long ago, I asked how her life was going.

"Oh, Dr. Waters." She blushed, a little flummoxed. "My life's not much."

That took me aback. "Of course it is. Everyone's life is important. Your goals, your hopes. You know."

"I'm pretty simple. I like living with my mom. We go shopping on the weekends, maybe see a movie. Maybe we'll take a vacation next year—that might be nice." She brightened, as if glad to come up with that.

"But how about friends? Any special people, any loves in your future?" Probably I acted too persistent, but I couldn't really believe her. I valued Jo and wanted to connect better.

"Oh, Dr. Waters," she repeated. Her sunny face clouded. "I was married once, when I was too young. A bad decision. I don't think I have the nerve for that again. Or the energy."

That made me sad, but why should it? Why should I impose my arduous overdrive, my endless quests, on a quietly contented person?

"Well, I think I envy you," I said. She smiled unconvincingly and seemed relieved I stopped trying.

Pay attention, I told myself. Zane was talking.

"A professional auditor costs a fortune. I hired one once, a while back, and I regretted it," he complained. That was probably twenty years ago and it probably cost a few hundred dollars back then, but no one said anything. He pulled a foil square of antacids from his pocket, pushed out a tablet and slipped it in his mouth. "And they always find other things to charge you for. Before you know it, they'll want to overhaul our whole system. I say we sit back and see what happens over the next few months. Maybe it'll straighten itself out."

Nobody argued overtly with him, but no one really agreed. We talked a long time. We got nowhere, everyone defensive and cross. Nellie promised to investigate the expense of hiring a consultant.

I actually didn't care that much, because no matter how we sliced it, I disliked private medicine. I realized I'd made a mistake, joining this kind of practice after that downtown clinic folded, but right now I lacked the gumption to start again somewhere else. While not a financially attractive option, quitting altogether seemed a better idea. Maybe I could go work in a research lab, wear a hazmat suit and seal myself off from everyone else. Off from the world.

I worried how appealing that felt.

I saw now that I was happier drawing a salary, focusing on my patients and not wasting energy by figuring out how to bill the maximum, not ordering a test because it brought in more money. I'm not wired that way; in my old clinic, we cut costs wherever we could and sometimes where we couldn't. But now I could charge a fair amount for an office urinalysis or an EKG, whether the patient really required it or not, so you can see the temptation. No one needs that clouding their judgment, and I'd rather not have money in my head when making decisions.

As we broke up the meeting, Zane's face puckered and he punched another antacid tablet from the foil and popped it in his mouth.

"What's going on?" I asked. He looked tired.

"Damn heartburn," he growled. "I shouldn't drink so much coffee."

"Maybe you should see your doctor," I suggested, poking his arm.

He laughed and squeezed my shoulder. "I would, Norah, if I knew any good ones."

"No, really." I shook my head, concerned. He'd been using those antacids for months.

"Hey." He pulled up a white card from his pocket, handed it to me. "Is everyone else getting these weird things on their cars?"

Another black-bordered card, thick handwriting: *You Old Quack*.

"What the hell," I said, flipping it over, looking for more, something revealing. But of course there was nothing. The same handwriting. I was struck by the Os, double-looped, one small loop inside the larger one. "Yes. I got one a few days ago. It informed me that I suck."

"Well, it's not completely false," Zane said thoughtfully, taking the card back. "I might be sort of an old quack. Oops. Sorry Norah— I didn't mean to imply that you might actually suck."

"This is ridiculous. Who would do this? It's so. . .immature. Besides, you and I rarely see the same patients." Zane's senior patients sought him like a cult, seemed leery of the other doctors. It felt unlikely that the same person would be unhappy with both of us.

Aggravated, I stalked through the halls and asked all the physicians, then returned to Zane.

"Just you and me," I reported. While it seemed stupid and childish, it made me uneasy. No one wants to be called names by an unknown culprit for unknown reasons.

Zane shook his head and pushed out another antacid, slid it into his mouth.

"Zane," I insisted. "I mean it. Go see your doc."

"Oh, Norah. Calm down. I'm fine. You don't get to be my age without a few aches and pains. Some days more than others." He sent me a reproachful look and thumped my back to reassure me. Then he retreated to his office.

Making people feel better wherever I turn, that's my specialty.

8

The next day I needed to finish my morning patients right on time. The first admissions committee session began that afternoon, and I hated being late.

I blame Jeremy Newell, my newest medical student. For unclear reasons, he changed his half-day to that morning. I should have told him no, but because I entertained so many negative notions about him, I conceded. A mistake, since I must work extra efficiently to arrive in downtown Phoenix by noon.

What was it with medical students this year? Could I not get assigned a normal one? Instead I had the yin and yang of learners. The dark and light, fire and water. Jeremy and George. I told myself to just roll with it, teach them enough to get by and not stress over them. No, apparently my ego needed to analyze and try to fix them. Make a difference in their lives. Maybe I worried that my failure with Grace, a previous student, might repeat itself. I may have mentioned how doctors often obsess about doing things right.

Anyway, I thought Jeremy might enjoy a patient who required a neurosurgery referral. Right up his alley. He could perform a thorough neurological exam and demonstrate his amazing skills. At least three times, he'd boasted about working with a neurosurgeon last year, a friend of the family who let him "do just about everything." I let that hyperbole go and tried not to picture Jeremy accidentally slicing through someone's spinal cord. Jeremy alleged his neuro knowledge to be far superior to his modest first year of training.

My patient Hilda Reed came in to review her diabetes. She also had a very small and very stable tumor in her head, a benign meningioma, due for follow-up with her neurosurgeon. Seeing the neurosurgeon and hearing his reassurance always calmed her, for she would likely never need surgery. Hilda was talkative and mildly anxious but amiable, and I figured Jeremy would be fine with her. I didn't expect him to know much about head tumors no matter who he worked with last year.

Jeremy surprised me when he exited the exam room rather soon, visibly excited.

"I think she should go to the emergency room, stat," he asserted urgently. "Her headache is an eight out of ten since this morning, and when I did her neuro exam, her feet are numb and her reflexes are weak. I'm worried her meningioma is suddenly expanding."

"Interesting," I said, not convinced.

Lodged against the frontal lobe of her brain for years, Hilda's tumor was a blip. For it to start enlarging at this point seemed quite unlikely. Improbable things do happen in medicine, but it didn't make sense.

"Let's take this apart," I suggested as Jeremy bounced a little in place, impatient. "Did you read the chart and notice where the tumor is?"

"Right frontal lobe," he snapped.

"Excellent. I'm sure you haven't studied this yet, but do you happen to know the symptoms caused by a frontal lobe problem?" I gave him a moment to shine if he could.

His features sagged, as if sensing a trap, though his upper lip leered. His expressions were downright disorienting.

"Headache," he said. I swear he rolled his eyes a tiny bit.

"Partly true. Any tumor can cause headache, although frontal tumors usually don't. But they might create personality changes. It's unbelievable now, but doctors used to perform frontal lobotomies for mental illness, back till the middle of the twentieth century. Their patients became dull and emotionally blunted. Became depressed. It's fascinating, and frontal lobe tumors can cause the same symptoms."

"She's pretty dull."

That was just plain mean, and Hilda did not deserve that. I had tried to guide him softly, but his attitude did not bring out my best side. A side which has grown smaller with age.

"All right then," I said formally. I kept my voice neutral, or tried to. "By what nerve pathway does a frontal lobe tumor cause her feet to be numb?"

Both sides of his face pulled together for the first time and looked pretty hateful.

"I'm not sure," he finally admitted. Surly, like it killed him to say so. "But her headache is eight out of ten, so we can't ignore that."

"Let's go see her." I'd observed Hilda walk in thirty minutes earlier, waving to me and chatting with Jo. If her pain was an eight, then I was a giraffe.

I worry most about doctors and students who can't admit when they don't know. Nobody knows everything, and medicine can change so rapidly that it's impossible to stay on the cutting edge of each new discovery every single minute. It's all right not to know—you just have to know how to find the answer.

Needless to say, this took a while. I reframed the pain scale for Hilda, describing what the pain scale means, that a ten feels like you're actively on fire.

"Oh no, then, not an eight," she proclaimed, eyes wide, chins trembling. She looked as if she might cry, a puddle of fear. And no wonder—I discovered that Jeremy, in all his first-year wisdom, already told her she needed brain surgery. First year? Make that his third month.

"Then I guess my pain is about a four," Hilda went on, a meek glance at Jeremy. "Maybe because I didn't get my coffee this morning, and sometimes I get a caffeine headache if I don't. Do you think I can stop for coffee on my way to the hospital?"

Jeremy made a noise deep in his throat, like a rhinoceros with indigestion.

This is common, for a patient's story to change. It's frustrating, but understandable. They suddenly remember something else. They may be nervous or confused. Sometimes the doctor interrupts them and they lose their train of thought—physicians are notorious for interrupting. Jeremy didn't grasp that if her pain didn't match her appearance, he should dig deeper. Anyone with eyes could see that Hilda didn't have high-level pain. . .she just didn't understand the pain scale. I don't blame Jeremy for that. He's new. But I do blame him for telling her the wrong thing and terrifying her, before he ran it by me.

I took my time explaining and Hilda finally relaxed. I didn't fault Jeremy publicly in front of her, while wanting to wring his neck. Outside the room, I showed him her last diabetic exam four months ago, and every four months before that, all documenting her diabetic neuropathy and numb feet. That her problem list included

Chronic mild neuropathy, bilateral lower extremities. Her feet had been numb for years.

On Jeremy's first day with me, I made a big deal about how he must thoroughly review a chart before approaching the patient.

I left in a mad rush because of the admissions committee, and had no time to rectify with Jeremy. He sat there finishing the note, slamming the keys as he typed, and when I apologized about leaving before him and took off nearly running, he did not look up.

This could not go on all year. We needed a frank discussion. Somehow I must find a way to get this hostile young man to meet me halfway. . .there must be a way to unlock him. Even a third of the way would be progress. I did not look forward to that talk.

Nobody listens. Sometimes I feel like a tiny squeaky voice in a wind tunnel, about to be blown away.

9

I hated being late to a committee meeting.

By the time I parked and walked across campus, the sidewalks blistering in the midday sun and radiating heat like plutonium, my bedraggled sweaty entrance felt highly disruptive. Those sidewalks may be lined with tall palm trees, graceful and stately, but they cast minimal shade on anyone walking by. I stalked into the building thinking of all the work I'd left behind, despairing about when I would get to it, despondent about Jeremy and dreading our inevitable talk.

Never mind that I found another note on my windshield: *Have a bad day.*

What was this, some sick game of gotcha? I tossed the card behind the seat and refused to think about it. For now. Maybe I could squeeze in some chart notes during the midafternoon break, if no one minded me being antisocial. They probably already thought of me like that anyway.

For some diabolical reason, the door to the meeting room opened right behind the podium, so everyone saw me creep in. I tried to duck aside, but I'm not invisible. I slouched over to my group, mouthing "sorry, sorry" all the way. The committee chair, an uptight forty-ish woman with short sable hair and spiked purple heels, aimed her laser pointer at the ceiling and paused her presentation. She smiled tightly and waited till I sat down. Women can be less tolerant than men, and that's a fact. It's a fact that I just made up, but it felt real enough right then. Being faux-annoyed at her helped distract me from my anger at Jeremy and my disquiet about the index cards, so I guess I settled into that even though it didn't work. The chairwoman was actually a perfectly reasonable person and I knew that. I kept thinking how to coexist with Jeremy, or at least to tolerate him, and fast. I could not spend the next nine months in a lather.

Anyway, being on this committee was a volunteer position. Next time I came in tardy, they could dock my pay.

The admissions committee consumed an inordinate amount of my time, over thirty hours a month, reviewing bulky files and meeting to make hard decisions. Annually, our medical school got over five thousand applicants vying for one hundred spots. Considerable weeding occurred before I saw a file, someone else plucking out and discarding those with lower college grades and weaker scores on the Medical College Admissions Test, commonly known as the MCAT. The magic combination of a perfect grade-point and a strong MCAT should guarantee a student's placement.

But it didn't. Some students got everything right and still did not make it because too many others were equally prepared. Maybe they floundered during their interview or wrote an odd personal essay. One year an applicant entered a poem instead of the required essay. Maybe he attempted to stand apart as creative, but it was not even a poem he wrote. Just something trite about resilience that could have been in a greeting card. Please.

Or maybe an applicant got lukewarm letters from college professors, or even chilly letters. I've seen comments like "she will likely develop more maturity over time." Good grief. At least pretend to have a pleasant personality. Fake it. Faking it is part of being a physician anyway: pretending patience when you want to scream, pretending poise when you want to cry, pretending gravity when you want to laugh.

Some applicants tried three years before letting go of the dream. Some spent a fortune and wound up at a Caribbean med school, only to get wiped off the island by a hurricane.

For what it's worth, here's my advice. Study really hard, no matter how smart you were in high school. I'm not saying the highest-scoring eggheads make the best physicians, because they often don't. But they frequently get in. It's just how the world works.

Be curious and kind. Do chores for your professors until they adore you. Their letters of recommendation will glow with genuine enthusiasm, and we can tell.

Be humble when interviewed. If you're a nervous introvert, practice a million times on your friends and your dog. A cat might do, and for sure a cat will be more critical. The extroverts often interview better because extroverts just do. Fortunately, many premed students are quiet nerds like you.

Anyway, there I was: late, overheated, and in a crappy mood because of Jeremy. My group waited, so I scrambled to set up my laptop, log in, get my head straight. They didn't really care because they've all been there, but I still felt bad for holding them up.

My team this year appeared fairly good. We had a bleeding-heart internist who saw positivity regardless of red flags. She helped balance my cynicism. There was a psychiatrist whose cool eyes seemed to analyze each one of us for mental disorders, but his concise comments carried depth. The newest member, a soft-spoken radiologist, looked glad to be out during daylight. His serene face somehow appeared amused without smiling. An older moody ENT surgeon was the only thorn, a man with whom I almost never agreed. And finally, our one nondoctor member to keep us grounded, a nurse from the county hospital.

We quickly accepted the first three students on the list. It's a yes/no/maybe system: fifteen applicants to rate, and each one got accepted, rejected, or placed on hold. The "maybe" rankings would shuffle up and down for the next five months.

The surgeon, Carter Billings, jumped right in. "I'd like to advocate for the student from Idaho. Not everyone has to be from around here."

I must have grimaced.

"What, Norah? Do you think all our students should be Arizonans? We need some geographic diversity, not just a bunch of desert rats who still live at home with their mommies. She's sharp as a knife—look at her scores. And she's an accomplished rock climber. That takes some gumption."

"Yes, I'm sure it does," I agreed. "But I worry about her letters and interviews."

The psychiatrist nodded, studying his computer.

"They're not that bad." Carter waved his hand, unconcerned.

"They're not that good," I replied. "A lab professor said her best trait was 'efficiency' and nothing else. Her research mentor said she 'wrote good reports,' but nothing else. These letters are only half a page long."

Most letters exuded praise and filled an entire page, sometimes two. But such minimal letters as these? They were trying to tell us something.

"College professors," Carter snorted. "What do they know?"

I carried on gamely. "And her interview scores are pretty low.

One person found her prickly. Another said she acted bored. Even I could pretend better than that."

"You can't always go by an interview," Carter complained. "Some people get nervous."

"You're right. But she didn't seem nervous. I mean, everyone's nervous to some degree, because that's normal. Besides, she missed the whole point of the video game, even when the proctor reminded her."

One piece of the interview involved this game where applicants navigated a video maze, then reflected on the experience. They were coached beforehand that the outcome didn't matter, that they didn't need a high score—it was all about the process. Applicants discussed their frustration and anxiety, talked about determination and how they learned. How to adjust and move on. This Idaho applicant didn't get it. Obsessive, she kept trying to beat the maze, asked twice for more time. When the proctor pushed her to reflect, she claimed she was used to winning and didn't appreciate an exercise designed to thwart her.

"My point is," I concluded, "I worry about her ability to be collaborative. That she'll be difficult. Defensive."

"I know that type." The county nurse sighed.

"She does have a nice personal statement," the internist said.

The psychiatrist raised his eyebrows and looked back and forth between Carter and me, like watching a tennis match. I noticed the radiologist studying me a little more closely than normal. Here we go, I thought, me putting my foot in it.

"No. I disagree." Carter crossed his arms. "This is a great student. She's smart and well-rounded. She's a rock climber and has lots of hobbies. She hunts and she's a great shot—she's won competitions. She's focused and hard-working and I think she's exactly who we want. She's my kind of girl." He raised his hands, apologetic. "Sorry, ladies. I should have said woman. I'm just the wrong generation."

He was younger than me.

The group went silent. The psychiatrist leaned forward, rapt, as if witnessing a fresh diagnosis. Unexpectedly, the radiologist broke the moment.

"I have to concur with Norah," he said.

I turned my head to read his tag again, since I'd already forgotten his name. Middle age is hell on my quick recall. Peter Calloway. In his fifties, unruffled. Thick ginger hair and scattered freckles, with a hint of frost at his temples. He glanced at me and the merest smile touched his lips.

"I'm not saying she's a bad applicant," he went on. "I just think we should be cautious. It's no fun working with an overconfident student. Sometimes they're hard to teach."

I might warn him to avoid Jeremy Newell. And it annoyed the hell out of me that Jeremy surfaced again in my thoughts. It was bad enough having him in the office; I didn't need him constantly inside my brain as well.

Ultimately, the process was democratic. We voted, and she got put on hold for later consideration. The rest of the meeting went smoothly: more acceptances, some rejections, and the rest of the applicants a "maybe" with Idaho. Carter recovered quickly, like it was nothing, not personal.

As we packed up our laptops, Calloway the radiologist spoke up again. "Hey. Anyone want to catch an early supper? There's a new Thai restaurant down the street that's getting great reviews."

I looked up and found him inspecting me. Really.

"So sorry, I can't tonight," I managed to say. "Maybe next time?"

"Sure." He still stared at me, unsettling.

No one else took him up on it, either, so I felt a little bad. But not so bad that I changed my tune, which would have seemed weird.

I don't know why I declined, either, since I had absolutely no plans and I was hungry. I knew I should expand my social connections, too, although I suspected nonmedical people would be healthier. Medicine had consumed my life for way too long.

I think I panicked. Maybe it was Austin—a few months on my own wasn't very long after three years. Maybe I wasn't ready to meet new men, potentially start something. And even before I say this next sentence, I'm aware it isn't fair, because I know tons of great physician men, smart and intuitive, generous and wise. But between Jeremy Newell and Carter Billings, I'd drunk my fill of medical males that day.

10

A medical practice is a little village. The docs and staff inhabit the place while patients come and go like visitors. Sometimes they're happy shoppers, sometimes unwilling tourists. Sometimes we lighten their loads and other times we don't have what they need. Or what they think they need. That's the tricky part.

The medical students are like apprentices. They don't get paid, but neither do I for supervising them. I consider it a mission of mine to help students and I enjoy it, usually a rewarding arrangement both ways. People like Jeremy, toxic and self-centered, were not new to me because there are plenty around in all walks of life. But I'd never had to mentor such a grating soul.

When medicine throws you a problem, the last thing you should do is run away. Instead, you run toward it to solve it. I knew I must work more with Jeremy, find something decent within him. Help him tap into that.

Usually I saved twenty minutes after each student's session to discuss their progress, so I vowed to make that really count with Jeremy.

"Why did you choose neurosurgery?" I asked one day in our little chat. We had just discussed his last patient, with whom he'd done a marginal job. He failed to address the woman's heavy alcohol intake even when she admitted right out loud that it might be a problem. He moved on without comment, leaving me to explore that with her. So afterward we reviewed what to say, how to react, how to support her, while Jeremy pretended to listen and studied the window. So I took it a step further and pointed out how a drinking history would be critical for his future work: he could hardly risk an alcohol withdrawal syndrome after surgery. If a patient stopped alcohol use too suddenly it could cause seizures, and the patient could even die.

At the "why neurosurgery" question, Jeremy gave me a look, like he couldn't believe he had to talk about such a stupid thing.

"It's the top," he said shortly, checking his watch. "The top of the totem pole. I like setting my sights really high."

"In what way do you see it as the top?" I persisted doggedly, resolved to wiggle underneath his prickly surface. I swear he sighed.

"It takes the most training. The most dedication. You have to be just about perfect." He returned his cold eye to me. "That's the kind of challenge I want. I want to—" his voice caught then recovered— "to show that I can do it."

I heard the break but nodded. "Well, that's inspiring. It takes lots of courage to tackle that career. Is your family excited?"

He bristled. "You mean, like, my parents? My brother?"

"Sure. Unless you have your own family? Spouse? Kids?" He shook his head once, dismissive, like I must be the thickest person he knew. I plowed on. "I just imagine some people will try to talk you out of it. Because of the hard work, the long hours."

His gaze tightened. "Of course they're excited. Why wouldn't they be? My older brother just started a neurosurgery residency at Mass Gen, and everyone is incredibly proud. He's like—brilliant."

"Impressive. You come from quite a family." I truly wanted to make Jeremy feel good about this, talking to me about his dreams. Surely we could find some link, some bond.

"Yeah." His face darkened. "They'll see."

I wanted to say *they'll see what?* but knew better than to probe just then. I felt pleased that by digging a little harder I had unearthed a kernel. Maybe a little one, maybe large, too soon to tell.

For the record, I happen to know a few excellent neurosurgeons. Both have a keen desire to know their patients well, and they would never ever miss or ignore a drinking problem.

Emcee and I were almost ready to run away. One more day. Arizona has ample places where you can hide or disappear. . .it's a fairly empty place.

The Mogollon Rim called to me. The broad Colorado Plateau ends there, those uplifted lands of northern Arizona thick with pine forests, prone to wildfires. To the south, the lower section of Arizona abruptly falls away and drops thousands of feet. Then the desert takes hold and runs off into Mexico. But up on the Mogollon Rim, scattered campgrounds abound, and some have large enough spaces to afford privacy.

I'll give Austin credit. He hooked me on camping, even though he owned no equipment except a ratty pup tent. I bought the new roomy tent and stove and sleeping pads and portable lights and all the dozens of items needed for comfortable camping. I'm too old for roughing it completely, or maybe I simply don't want to. I appreciate a toilet and clean water from a tap.

What I really treasure is lying back and surveying the sky. Day or night. No distracting television or radio, no news. No messages, no patients or clinic problems, no running to the store or tackling the to-do list. No medical students, no inhibited George or contemptuous Jeremy. No going over the financial ledgers again and again, trying to find my disrupted income. I seriously needed to consider buying a new car, but now I felt cautious.

Sunlight trickles through pine needles, clouds raft the blue. After Phoenix night skies, too light-stunned to ever be truly dark, the starry radiance is magical. Rain works fine too, pattering on the tent, or even a heavy drumming downpour. Sturdy and tight, the tent can take it. You resign yourself to some mud. It dries. I could hardly wait.

But first things first. I had to finish all the tasks on my last day and squirm away from my partners.

Wanda Cunningham came first. I sat in my office minding my own business, chewing my lunch and wrapping up a thousand loose ends. Hummingbird Wanda came whirring in and perched on the edge of the other chair, her quick bird eyes searching me up and down.

"What's up, Wanda?" I asked. Seeing her over lunch was rare, for she often ran behind and worked through without stopping. She of course made certain her MA took a break. Wanda is a hard worker, a truly kind soul, and a decent doc. We just didn't talk that much, didn't have much in common. She's got four kids and goes to mass every Sunday or more, and I honestly couldn't imagine how she kept it all together.

"You're going camping for your vacation?" Wanda cocked her head. "How nice and relaxing."

"Yes, I can't wait." I glanced at my work but she didn't take the hint.

"Are you going with your boyfriend?"

"Wanda. We broke up months ago. . . . I thought you knew." She did know, I'm quite certain, but I let it be. "No, I'm going alone. Well, with my dog. Better than a boyfriend."

"Oh dear. Is that a good idea, Norah?" Her startled look, where she can't believe you said something so foolish. Her topknot of dark curls shivered. "Is that safe?"

"Probably safer than driving to work every day." I smiled because she meant well. I think.

Wanda peered at me closely, then bobbed her head away, then back again. "Are you okay, sweetie?"

"Well, I'm really busy today. You know, getting everything tucked away before—"

"No, I mean. . .you just seem a bit down lately."

I wanted to tell her to stick to her own knitting, but I could never be short with Wanda. It would be too much like kicking a puppy.

"Not at all," I assured her. "I think I'm just going through an adjustment."

"Oh. I guess that's to be expected." Relief flooded her face, then she quickly sobered again. "But if anything changes, if you're having trouble, you'll let me know, won't you?"

"Of course." I produced my most credible smile.

Wanda was remarkably easy to reassure. She went off, happy with her effort to keep me sane. But the parade had just started. Not five minutes later, Emily stood in my doorway, her dark red hair wild with static.

"So. Camping by yourself. What's that about?"

I could count on Emily to be more direct, but I did not welcome her attention. If this didn't stop I'd be there till midnight, still working.

"Some of us like solitude. It's sort of a personal meditation retreat." Which was a lie, because I'm a complete disaster at meditation. But it sounded noble.

"Here's an idea." A determined expression. "My girls have never been camping, and I'd love to take them. Can you imagine what a riot that would be? Only we wouldn't be able to go for a few weeks because of their soccer. I know this seems pushy, but would you be interested in postponing your trip until then, and we could all go together?"

I gave her a jaundiced look and said nothing. This felt like something she just concocted.

"Really, Norah. You have to admit it—that could be so much fun. My girls are too urbanized. It would do them good to get away, get out in the woods. We would laugh so much!"

It actually did sound appealing. But the logistics were impossible. My patients had been cancelled and my gear nearly packed, the campground reserved. Besides, I doubted Emily could pull it off. Her girls were too busy.

"That sounds wonderful," I replied. "But it's too late. All the plans are made. Let's do it, though. Maybe next spring?"

Emily sat down, put her hand on my arm. "All right. I like that you're looking ahead."

"What? Am I missing something? Do I look like I'm about to die?" Me getting cranky.

Emily shrugged and patted my arm. "Breakups can be hard."

"Good lord. Are you serious? Breakups can be liberating too. Does everyone think I'm suicidal or something?" This had to stop. I sat back and pulled my arm away. I didn't need petting.

"No, of course not." Emily's features scrunched. "If you say you're okay, then you're okay. I'm sorry if I'm being heavy-handed. I just worry about you lately. You seem kind of blue."

"I'm okay," I confirmed, still crabby. "Put your mind at ease and let me finish my work."

Emily smiled, not convincingly, and left me alone.

The afternoon patients were lining up, and it was no walk in the park. Manny McIlroy wanted to talk about his recent prostate cancer, in remission though too soon to say cured. Only now he suffered urinary incontinence and impotence from the surgery. Only "impotence" is a word no longer used, and we now call it erectile dysfunction, a more clinical term that leaves power off the table.

I can probably credit Mom for my comfort in talking with people about their genitals. Only an anatomy professor would be determined to educate her children about that in such detail. Once when Ben was about eleven years old and I was seven, she made a model penis out of a long balloon, the kind that you twist into animals. She even kinked on two testicles. Then she filled the balloon with water to demonstrate the hydraulics of an erection. She taught the proper words, the corpus cavernosum and corpus spongiosum, and used a ballpoint pen to draw in the urethral meatus. Only she got carried away with the fluids and the balloon burst, much to Ben's delight. Already pink with embarrassment, the rupture sent him into fits of laughter, which got me giggling helplessly, and neither of us could stop until it prompted an asthma attack and Ben turned a little blue. I ran for his nebulizer, still sniggering.

"What did the urologist say?" I asked Manny, not sure why he'd come to me when he already saw a specialist.

Manny looked both sad and angry, his ruddy face flushed. "He makes jokes about it. Funny guy. He laughs and says 'urine trouble'. . .you know, like 'you're in trouble'? Get it? Then about my pecker he says 'things could be looking up.' Sometimes I want to punch him."

We discussed medications and injections and devices for erectile dysfunction. Manny perked up a bit, realizing he had options. I imagined the surgeon intended to get around to it, but I felt bad for Manny and spent extra time.

Then Manny chuckled, a twinkle in his bright blue eyes, and he lapsed into a Scottish brogue. "Well, m'darling. If I cannae make the thing stand up tall anymore, there's a great deal o' bonny women who'll be resting easier."

You can't predict where the bright spots in a day will bloom. Manny was a full-blown rose.

A long afternoon, but mostly rewarding. Nothing easy, nothing cut and dried. Everyone needed to talk. Mostly good patients, all with real problems. No one surly or defiant, no one acting like I owed them good health because they demanded it, no matter how unwilling they might be to earn it. Every now and then those petulant people stayed home and I felt in my element, listening, sorting, treating.

Come on, Norah, I told myself, settling in with my charts after everyone had gone. Focus, and maybe I could be out soon. The building clicked and ticked with winding-down noises, the windows cooling as the sun retreated, the wood contracting. Peaceful sounds. Cool air streamed through the vents onto my head, stirring my hair, a comfortable artificial breeze. I couldn't wait to feel real wind through the pines, inhale forest musk. I tapped through another note and picked the next one off my queue.

Electronic medical records, EMR, contribute hugely to physician burnout. No more illegible hand-written notes, no loose pages, no lost files. But, incredibly time-consuming, wrestling with illogical, poorly constructed algorithms and mandatory checklists. Most physicians spend hours every day just charting their encounters, in addition to the time spent actually seeing patients.

Wanda told me how she finished later at home so she could have dinner with the family. Then she tapped away into the night, after the kids went to bed. Once she awoke with her head on the desk and her hand on the keyboard, a long line of question marks streaming across the page. We laughed at the metaphor, though it wasn't really funny.

Not to mention prevention, trying to ask about diet and exercise and cancer screening and pregnancy planning and contraception and depression and drug use and cholesterol. Tobacco and alcohol and seatbelts and firearms. All the required inventories. If I performed all the recommended preventive services for each patient, it would take an extra seven hours a day. This is true. . .someone studied it. Once upon a time we became physicians, but now we also must perform as secretaries and transcriptionists and file clerks and coding authorities and billing experts and regulations enforcers.

Maybe this was the crux of my anguish. Stuck in an endless grind that no one could possibly accomplish. No matter how hard I worked, how much I tried to do everything right, I could not. No one could.

I jumped when Zane Grayson suddenly appeared at my door. I thought I had the place to myself.

"Zane," I exclaimed, hand on my heart. "You scared me to death. Don't sneak up on people."

He regarded me sourly, sucking on something, probably another antacid. A shock of white hair sprayed from the back of his head and his tiny reading glasses glinted; he looked like a crazed old professor, but the kind everybody loved.

"Are you all right, or what?" he growled.

"Of course I'm all right. Or I would be, if people would leave me alone and quit asking me if I'm all right." Was I truly radiating a suicidal vibe, or were my colleagues going nuts?

"What's this crap about you camping alone?"

"It's not crap. It's a damn retreat that I invented for myself. I'll come back renewed and refreshed. A new woman, all full of sunshine and rainbows. I'll probably be riding a unicorn."

Zane laughed. "Then I'd really worry about you. You'd have lost all your best qualities."

"Did someone put you up to this? Who's talking about me?"

"Eh. Everyone loves to gossip."

Zane gazed about, my stacks of work, the mess of journals. Sticky notes, reminders. Lists on my board. My favorite framed photo of a monster thunderhead, heaped with menace. A photo of Emcee, sitting behind the wheel of my car with one paw up, like she's about to drive off. Austin's photo—gone. Just an empty space on my wall. An empty space inside of me.

"Everyone can mind their own effing business," I said.

Zane rubbed his large nose, tinted with rosacea and broken veins. "Do me a favor. Just tell me where you're camping, in case we need to find you."

I sighed and wrote down the campground name and location on a paper, handed it to him without comment. The thickly wooded campsite had no cell service, one of the reasons why I chose it. But I didn't tell him that. Instead I asked if he'd gotten any more missives on his windshield.

"As a matter of fact, yes." He pulled a card from his pocket, passed it over. "I'm starting to take it personally."

You Should Retire, Old Man.

He scowled. "It's rather insulting."

"What the hell, Zane. Should we be worried?"

"I'd worry, except that the message is fairly accurate."

A strange anxiety filled me. "Whoever is doing this knows us. Knows which cars we drive."

"Eh. It's so passive." He waved his hand. "It's like a troll, just not online."

"If you say so. But I think I'm glad I'm leaving for a week." Women worry more about such things than men, and they should because they're more vulnerable. I just couldn't fathom how nervous I should be, and for once Zane wasn't helpful.

"Well, have a good time. I'm sure you will. And Norah—take care of yourself, okay?" He paused. "I'd probably retire if you weren't here to keep things real."

That got to me. I stood up and gave him a little hug, which seemed to please and embarrass him.

Driving home, I realized all my partners seemed worried about me except Brian Mulch. Which either made him perceptive or uncaring. Maybe a little bit of both.

Every evening after work, I always hoped for an entertaining sunset to escort me on the drive home. The desert is rightly renowned for that, that revolving blaze of color that starts subtly in the east, tinted with pastels, then combusts violently across the sky in burning red and orange. The fever subsides into tender pinks and grays, soft as cotton, drawing up a blanket for the night.

That night I got nothing but a hot bare cloudless sky that converted with zero fanfare from burning cobalt to baking black coal. Harsh, uninviting. Sometimes Phoenix makes it easy to leave.

12

Instinctively, Mom knew I might be shifting. That maybe I stood on some sort of brink.

She started calling that same day before my vacation, as my partners questioned my mental health. Three messages. Mostly about her curmudgeon neighbor Johnny Quart, who hammered on her door that morning, incensed because the rose-hued gravel of her front yard dared to intermingle with the small ivory stones of his "lawn." I once met Johnny Quart, a tiny, stooped man with hardly any teeth, skin like beef jerky, and a startling wavy black toupee who stalked the perimeter of his property many times a day, alert for transgressions.

"You do know, Mom," I reminded her again, "that unless you need something urgent, I won't call you back while I'm at work."

"I should hope not. I hope you've got better things to do than talk to me about my petty squabbles. Even I wish I had better things to do."

"All right. I just wanted to make sure you understood. What's with Johnny Quart?" I called her back after ten o'clock that night. Heaven knows when she slept, for she always seemed to be up.

"I fixed the problem," she chortled. "I picked out every little piece of my pretty rose gravel while he watched. With my tweezers—I took a long time on purpose. I told him my fingers were too arthritic to pick up the gravel, although of course that's not true. My finger joints are hardly knobby at all. Then I made a cute little border out of lasagna noodles to keep the stone species from co-mingling. He's such a racist. I thought it looked pretty like it was, the way the two colors of rock blended together. Mixed races usually do come out better, don't they?"

"Mom."

"What? Was that offensive? I don't see how—it's a compliment."

"Mom." I learned in childhood to sidestep such comments. "Lasagna noodles?"

"It looks really good. That little ruffle on the edge of the noodle is quite decorative. And anyway, I think old Johnny might have rickets. You should see how bowed his legs are getting. You could throw a cantaloupe between his thighs."

She gabbled on while I packed and tried not to imagine the noodles when it rained. It might be awhile, but it would rain again eventually. My packing didn't take long because I already laid most items out. It's not like I needed to dress up for camping, and I preferred simple meals. Plus wine and chocolate for evenings, naturally. I stuffed my warm quilted jacket in the duffel, then pulled it out. The temperature in Phoenix hovered at ninety-three degrees, making it impossible to imagine wearing the thing. Then I looked up the forecast for the campground and shoved the jacket back in, all while listening to her carry on. I put the phone on speaker so her shrill voice filled my house.

"How did the dance go?" I asked, ready to move on from Johnny Quart.

Mom exhaled heavily. "I may have to give up on that mailman. All those old biddies crowded around him and I couldn't get close enough to say 'hello, sailor.' The next time when I think I need a change in my life, remind me not to move to some stupid retirement community where the female ratio is ten to one. It seemed like a good idea five years ago, but I was deceived by their glossy advertising. Never believe a brochure, because they're always full of lies. The mailman never even saw my sexy hair."

She did have unusual hair. Many women her age clipped their locks short for easy care, but not Mom. White as snow, blinding in the sun, her hair flowed long and thick, almost down to her waist. I tried not to picture her naked. . .she probably looked like a withered Lady Godiva.

"Mom. The female to male ratio cannot possibly be ten to one. You just made that up. Besides, I thought you liked all the activities and social events around there. You said it was great to see so many seniors having fun."

"Norah. I'm pretty sure I never said that."

"Well, my memory isn't what it used to be." Of course she said it.

"Hah! If you want to be depressed, let me tell you a few stories about my memory. It'll make your blood run cold."

"Okay, maybe next time. I don't really want to be depressed. And

I need to get some sleep. Maybe you should stick with your first idea, asking that mailman in for coffee."

"Norah." Her tone changed, now serious. Probing. "What's going on with you—why are you so unhappy? Is it Austin?"

Talking about myself with her usually backfired, for Mom rarely put another person first for very long. She tried her best, but her nurturing moments came hit or miss. She succeeded better with Ben; when he died, she stayed present with him, almost all of the time. Since I wasn't there, I didn't witness it, but I pieced it together from what she said. And even though I know it wasn't my fault I took that medical trip, that he would have died whether I'd been there or not, part of me will never be right.

Ben's death broke her for a few years. Like all of us.

"I never said that I'm unhappy," I said.

"Oh, right."

I could imagine her face. Sometimes she crossed her eyes.

Unlike my medical partners, Mom never questioned my solitary vacation. The original Liberated Woman, she partied in the mud at Woodstock and got arrested for protesting Vietnam outside the White House. For years, she pointed to a blemish on her wrist which she claimed to be a scar from handcuffs and police brutality. Maybe it was, but eventually the mark got overtaken by a brown age spot and she quit mentioning it. Earlier, at twenty-one, she hitchhiked across the country alone. She never married my father and often made ribald comments about a man's only real purpose. About a decade ago, well into her seventies, she attended Burning Man and loved it. Apparently her spontaneous discussions with people about human anatomy—and I mean all parts of it—became quite popular. I couldn't imagine how she hadn't contracted AIDS or syphilis, but she lived a charmed life.

She went on. "I know you're not happy. You're the child of my loins and I'm channeling you tonight. Who are you seeing now?"

"Still no one." My words bitten short. I guess she wasn't channeling me very well or she would have conjured that. "Right now, that's what makes me happy."

"It's your work that's upsetting you, isn't it?"

"Of course it's my work. I never have enough time with my patients and they never listen anyway. The insurance companies try not to pay and my income is dropping. And I don't like people anymore. I'm thinking of quitting."

Whoa. I thought those points all the time, but I almost never said them out loud.

"You have to do more with your life, sweetheart. Get out and mingle with men besides doctors. Aren't doctors kind of boring? Start some hobbies—you've never had real hobbies. Why is that? I know, I know, you'll say that reading and walking and movies are your hobbies, but are they? Do things like that even count? Ben loved chess, and your dad would have golfed every day if he could. Maybe you should play golf. . .that's a good way to meet men. Or you could become one of those Big Sister things. Wouldn't helping a child from the barrio be a good idea? Or—"

"Wait a minute. Go slower. Let me get a big piece of paper so I can write all this down."

I'd heard this rant, or some version of it, about five thousand times. And it annoyed me because I didn't know if my pursuits were hobbies or not. Why did she get to decide if they were? They can be actual careers, and even walking is a sport. And no, I had no "usual" hobbies because nothing like that ever stuck. Did that make me pathetic, or original? My volunteer work involved medical students and the admissions committee. Already this year I'd been offered and turned down other volunteer positions at the rape crisis center, the suicide hotline, a homeless shelter, and a drug rehab unit. All medical, all interesting, all desperately in need of help. So far I'd said *no, maybe next year.*

"You don't have to be so sarcastic." Mom acted wounded. "I'm just trying to help."

I took hold of myself.

"I know, Mom. I'm sorry. I just need a break, that's all." She was eighty-six, for crying out loud. I could hardly expect her to change. "I'll call you when I get back."

13

Living in Phoenix ruins your body's thermostat.

Before long, ninety degrees Fahrenheit feels "cool-ish" and one hundred degrees isn't half bad. Fifty becomes downright frigid, gloves and knit caps. And even though I knew this, knew I should pack warmer clothes than I thought I'd need, I almost didn't take my wool socks and heavy jacket.

A week in a tent with a big dog might not sound ideal but was exactly what I wanted. I staked my tent under a massive ponderosa pine and relaxed for the first time in months.

The diurnal rhythm of sun and stars, the whispers of trees.

No people. Perfect.

My campground neighbors, a bent elderly couple in a small RV, kept to themselves. They were so quiet, in fact, that I wondered if they might be mute. Her permed white hair frothed around her head and his bald dome shone like copper. Every now and then I heard a tinker or scrape from their camp, but that was it. If they spoke to one another, they used stealth-level whispers I couldn't detect. It almost made me curious, made me want to say hello and see what happened. Then I remembered why I was there and left them alone.

The other side of my campsite dropped into a wild ravine choked with rocks and dry weeds. Again, perfect. I'd chosen the spot carefully.

I'm not a journaler. I never felt compelled to jot down my thoughts or document my anguish day by day. Until recently, that seemed to me self-indulgent, like an adolescent penning her immature soul.

Dear Diary: Jeremy is mean and stupid. All my practice
partners ganged up on me because they think I'm suicidal.
They're so lame. Luv ya, N

Instead, I like to walk and figure things out. Get in touch with myself, whoever that is.

Let me put the record straight: I was never suicidal, just unhappy. Disheartened, deeply disappointed. At both of us. Yes, I weathered a spell after Austin left when I wanted to sleep all the time. To not deal with that heartache. A spell when I thought maybe it wouldn't be so terrible if I didn't wake up the next morning. That's supposed to be a suicide-thought equivalent, whatever. I would never do that to Emcee. Yes, a few times I wore scrubs to work instead of my usual clothes, because I hadn't done the laundry, or because the clean laundry sat in the dryer too long and I couldn't summon the energy to turn on the iron and press out the wrinkles. So what.

Up on the rim, dawn took forever, as if reluctant to end such a good run of darkness. Stars dimmed gradually, until I realized they were gone and the sky had gone fleecy gray. The east brightened and clouds tinged peach, coy with pleasure at the new day.

The fact is, human life is outrageously brief. Eighty good years for most, if they're lucky. We've been around in some form for a few hundred thousand years, give or take, and no one knows or cares about 99.99 percent of us. My little speck will be no different. Modern history only goes back four or five thousand years, less than a grain of sand, a blink. . .pick your metaphor for the void. So why would I shorten what little chance I have to find myself? Which is simply a human conceit, as if there's anything to be found. We mostly make it up as we go.

Emcee and I took long walks, spent hours exploring the forest, nearly got lost. This might sound careless, but the trees looked a lot alike. Brown leaves dropped thickly, for autumn had arrived up there in the woods even if not in Phoenix. Those crisp leaves crackled underfoot, a crunchy caramel-colored shell for the earthen floor. I thought about just not returning. Disappearing, driving north. Getting some menial job, living in a shack. Maybe that's how we found ourselves, paring down to our core, seeing what's left. The other docs would miss me for a while, but not long. They all had busy lives that didn't involve me. The world turns.

But disenchantment with medicine wasn't just me. Physicians all over the country fought burnout in record numbers, and everyone and their brother had a personal scheme to fix them. Like yoga, for crying out loud. Almighty yoga crops up everywhere. Sorry for the sacrilege, but it never appealed to me. Just don't ever say that to someone who believes in its mystical secrets.

"You should come to yoga with me," Wanda peeped last month. "It's soooo relaxing. And self-affirming."

"Not a yoga person," I said, some chill in my words. Even thinking of it made me edgy.

"That's because you haven't given it a chance!" Her eyes shone.

"Wanda." My tolerant voice. "I have tried yoga more than once, and I didn't like it. Not everyone has to enjoy the same activities. I'm sure there's things I do that you would dislike." Such as posting sarcastic reviews of crappy movies.

I didn't look good in tights. Bulges appeared in my early fifties and they wouldn't leave. Me trying to mimic a rubber-jointed woman who belonged in the circus as a contortionist did not feel affirming. And I already knew how to breathe, thank you.

People—including other doctors—unthinkingly turned burnout into a physician's own fault, for not relaxing seriously enough. For not yoga-ing (or meditating or running or mindfulnessing) intensely enough to become sound. As if the problem was them. Me.

What would fix me would be better healthcare systems, not spending hours grappling with a convoluted computer program. Where I got more than ten minutes with an addict. Consistent medical billing and affordable insulin. Free insulin. Where medical students didn't lose their glittering idealism in a few short years, while a handful of ego-besotted attending physicians badgered them into despondency. Until some students lost themselves under the crushing demise of their dream. The statistics on physician suicide are dreadful—every day, at least one physician or medical student is lost forever. What an unforgiveable waste.

These now-deceased physicians had interacted daily with other doctors. Doctors who one would think might notice, might wonder about them, ask how they're doing. But they often did not because everyone had their head down, laboring away, long hours. Everyone had to get through the long day. So I'll give my partners credit there, for showing they cared about me. For asking me if I was all right.

The sunsets crept in, ushering night along, relief from the sun's piercing eye. I sat on boulders along the rim and surveyed miles of trees and stone below. Emcee leaned against me, warm and shaggy and real, and we watched shadow muffle the world as it does day after endless days, year after endless years. Millennia, eons, epochs.

Everyone swoons over being mindful within a moment, appreciating a flower or a fragrance, but no one seems mindful of the universe. No one gets warm and comfy about the abyss.

It's still hard to think about Grace, my med student almost two years ago. Patients liked her—she knew when to take someone's hand. She understood silence. If people-skills and listening skills don't come naturally to a person, teaching them is an uphill trek, often partial at best. That's why I worried about George Clark. I suspected Jeremy Newell might be unsalvageable, but of course I would try. Somewhere far inside his warped façade lurked a person in pain, if I could dredge that deep.

But Grace. . .she laughed easily at first, despite her fragility. She studied intensely, almost frantically, looking up diagnoses and treatments. Perfectionism shows differently in different people. If I brought it up, she denied any problems, no worries.

"I'm good, Dr. Waters. I love coming here." Yet she seemed desperate, facing the tasks before her, and through the year she quit laughing. Her face sunken, a little haunted. She moved on to the next level, done with my tutelage, and we fell out of touch.

Then late the next spring, a year after I last saw her and the month I cut Austin off, I discovered that Grace had dropped out of med school, depressed and barely functioning. I still had her phone number so I called her, but she barely spoke. Vacant, dull. I wondered if she was on medication. After that, she quit returning my calls. No one seems to know what happened to her.

First Austin, then that.

I felt terrible that I hadn't grasped the extent of Grace's distress. That maybe I could have helped her more. Giving up on medicine can shatter a student's soul. The arduous path to becoming a physician has crushed many sensitive selves.

I only confided in Zane.

"You can't always fix the world," he told me kindly. "You hadn't seen her in a year—you don't know what happened. What makes you think you could have predicted this? You're not a wizard."

A long time ago, I almost thought physicians and wizards were the same, except physicians had the advantage of science. But science is a tool that's tricky to wield, and some days now I'd prefer to be a wizard. People would rather believe a wizard than a scientist anyway, something I will never understand. Or they'll believe some worthless internet hack burning up cyberspace with paranoia and mock miracles. If a cure seems too good to be true, you can damn well bet it's false.

And the fact is, I did see it coming, sort of. I saw Grace change, less mirth, less joy.

Every night in the woods, I poured myself a cup of wine and opened my notebook. I clutched a pen and experimented, tried writing my resignation letters, tried to explain myself. I wrote many first lines.

Dear Zane: If it weren't for you, I never would have stayed here so long. . .

No. Too maudlin.

Dear Emily: Remember how you knew when a divorce was your only option? Well, I'm divorcing medicine. . .

No. A weak attempt at humor, and too insensitive to Emily.

Dear Wanda: You've taught me a great deal about tolerance and kindness, but I. . .

No. That wasn't true. I felt increasingly intolerant and unkind.

Dear Brian: I'm writing to you last because I'll miss you the least. . .

No. Too mean. But honest.

I would give my practice the rest of this year and see. I would do my best to prepare George and Jeremy to be good physicians. To try to make up for Grace.

Trees give me comfort. Ponderosa pines thrive in northern Arizona. . .splendid trees, tall and wide, protected by dense bark that resists wildfires like armor. I sat under my campground ponderosa and watched chips of sunlight dance around me. Touching that bark felt like holding a hand, that textured skin. When I scratched deep into the grooves, a sweet scent escaped, like vanilla. I thought a great deal about thick skin and endurance.

I ignored the reality of bark beetles, small insects that can bring down a forest. Because who is to say that a beetle's right to survive is inferior to a plant's? Well, most of us would say that, but we could be wrong.

I thought about my personal bark beetles.

No one uses the word *psithurism* anymore, the sound of wind through trees. At night the breeze climbed and the pines spoke for hours, their long low moans. Pleasure. Lament. Emcee snuggled alongside me, her toasted warm-dog smell, her cold nose against me.

We should live here, she said.

I have a job, I remarked.

Humans, she sighed.

14

Packing up and driving back to Phoenix wore me out. I dawdled leaving the rim, reluctant to face a miserably hot Sunday afternoon in the city, especially since no one appeared at my campsite to claim it. Eventually I gathered my grimy gear and hit the winding highway, dropping through pinyon and juniper, down to the desert floor. The heat, that familiar ogre, rose up and crouched over us. Suddenly saguaro cactus appeared, stabbing stickery fingers at the searing blue.

Whenever I drove into my garage and opened the car door, Emcee always leapt out and galloped to the back yard. She ran around catching up on smells, checking out what lizards or roadrunners might have tracked across her realm.

This time she didn't.

"Come on," I called, clapping my hands. "Let's go. Lots to do."

Instead, Emcee stood weakly on the seat and trembled, her hind legs bent. Her eyes deep. She took one step forward and her back end collapsed, plopping her down.

A sensation like a bowling ball crashed inside me.

What could have happened? Emcee was too young for a stroke, had incurred no spinal or back trauma. I stroked her head and she weakly licked me, but she didn't move. Feeling desperate, I threw my arms around her and clumsily lifted her from the car, placed her on the garage floor. She tried a shaky step and her hips buckled again. She sat there, panting and staring dully, and sent me a miserable look.

Help me, she pleaded.

Twenty minutes away, the emergency veterinary clinic glowed in the dusk, the parking lot crowded. Emcee couldn't really walk, so I clutched her again, struggled and stumbled to the door. A whine escaped her when I lurched. Someone inside must have seen me because all at once an overweight young man in red scrubs appeared, his arms and neck thick with rolls of fat. He hoisted her easily from my tenuous grip and carried her into an exam room, bypassing the dozen staring patrons with dogs and cats lining the waiting room. Thank goodness for that, because I was about to lose it.

The portly young aide—he looked about eighteen years old—gently settled Emcee on the table and inclined his head toward the door.

"Uh. You might want to go close up your car and lock it. You know?"

"Of course," I fumbled, not realizing I'd left the car open. "Will she—"

"I'll stay with her. Go ahead." A calm presence beyond his years, he ran his plump hand down her back and she visibly exhaled.

I rushed out and returned. My hands shook slightly, my voice unsteady. Hold it together, I commanded myself. Truthfully, I wasn't sure I could handle this. Diagnoses flew through my head. A tumor. Meningitis. A spinal growth. It occurred so quickly, without warning. A ruptured disc? But she didn't seem to be in pain.

"You need some water?" he offered me kindly.

"No. I mean, yes." Disorganized, I remembered I hadn't drunk enough fluids during the hot afternoon drive.

He handed me a water bottle and petted Emcee's head before he left. "Hang in there. Dr. Parker will see you soon."

Soon is an imprecise concept. I sat with Emcee a long time, caressed her soft ears, rubbed her chest where she loved it. She watched me sadly, as if she understood the magnitude of the situation. I talked quietly, which seemed to help, and she quit shivering. Frayed, I fought back tears. Whatever caused this would not be good news.

The door flung open and a man stood there, stern, observing us. It felt strange, not exactly a friendly vibe. He looked middle-aged, weathered and hardened, as if he'd seen too much. A line of concentration formed across his straight black brows, his dark eyes roaming over Emcee.

"Dr. Parker. Owen," he announced, but he didn't look at me because he concentrated on the dog.

Emcee strained to stand at seeing this stranger, but she gave up, defeated, which made my throat catch. His dark hair fell forward and he swiped it back, a few bars of gray. Overly tanned skin, not aging well.

"When did the paralysis start?" he asked. "I mean, the weak legs."

I swear it seemed like he was talking to Emcee, the way he looked at her directly, man to dog, so it took me a moment to remember I was meant to answer. My head felt out of place.

"Just late this afternoon. When we got back from camping." I collected myself. "And it's okay if you use big words. I'm a people doctor."

"Really." His eyes connected for the first time. Dark blue, nearly black, shaded in deep sockets. Flicked across me.

At that moment I noticed myself. My grubby T-shirt with a dirt stain on one sleeve, ratty cut-off shorts. I mean, really ratty, threads hanging down, torn pocket. Dried-muddy shoes. Having had no thorough shower in days, I reeked of campfire smoke and old sweat, and my hair hadn't seen a brush since early morning. Self-conscious, I put my hand on Emcee to draw attention back to her.

But he no longer cared about me. His hands now explored her, inch by inch. He didn't conduct the usual physical exam, where the vet checks the eyes and ears and gums. He didn't listen to her heart and lungs, didn't palpate her liver. He didn't check her spine, which I very much expected. Meticulous, his fingers slid under her coat and inch by furry inch he combed her body. Murmured every now and then, *atta girl*. Emcee closed her eyes, trance-like as he traveled her skin.

"Aha. Here it is." His fingers halted along her ribs and he threw his first crooked smile my way. Reaching into a drawer, he pulled out forceps as I craned to see the little lump under his other hand. "Keep her still."

A few seconds later he held up the forceps for my inspection, grasping a fat bloody tick. Revolted, I stared at its smooth distended body, a gray globe with waving threadlike legs.

"Tick paralysis," he proclaimed, triumphant. Openly grinning. He bore a stubbled salted beard, one of those growths that might be stylish, or maybe just signified neglect, like he hadn't bothered to shave that morning. Neglect, I decided—he didn't seem a trendy guy.

"That's good?" I asked weakly. Not sure if I should smile back, not completely certain how favorable this news might be.

"Damn right it's good. Completely reversible if you catch it early. Which I think we've done."

I sat down abruptly, swamped with relief, my knees weak. My

eyes damp. I scrunched them tight to regain control. Then I sensed something and sprang open my eyelids to find him beside me, his face close. He smelled like antiseptic and wet cats.

"You okay?"

"Yes, of course," I stammered, embarrassed. I straightened and tried to cover it with curiosity. "So, it's what? Some sort of infection from the tick?"

"No." He sat down. "A neurotoxin. From tick saliva."

My brain struggled to imagine the tiny amount of this toxin that swam in the tiny amount of saliva that a tick could produce. The incredible potency of that chemical, able to paralyze a big dog with just a few molecules. I mean, it's not like a tick went around drooling copious secretions from its little bitty mouth.

Parker's moment of celebration seemed over, and he retreated back to his somber self.

"The toxin should slowly wear off, but it might take a day or two." He watched Emcee silently again, evaluating. "You can take her home, but you'll need to check on her frequently. She'll need help."

Monday—tomorrow—would be my first day at work in a week. A packed schedule, a million messages. I'd be there many hours, a long day. For a moment I thought I could do it, take Emcee with me. She could lounge in my office while I worked, and I could assess her between patients. But that meant I would need to check on her all night, too, making certain she didn't deteriorate. And she would need assistance going outside, all night and all day long. Overwhelming.

"We can keep her here for a day, monitor her," he offered, seeing my expression.

"That would help," I admitted. "My work is hell these days. Sometimes I hate it."

Looking back, I can't believe I said that. It must have been the stress. But it bounced off him and he smashed it right back.

"Hate? Just be very glad you didn't go into veterinary medicine. Worst profession ever." His mouth grim.

I just nodded. Not the time to compare our bitterness; it wasn't a contest. I didn't like him all that much and had no interest in a discussion. We all have our sad story, our disillusionment. Enough.

As I checked out, standing at the desk, he passed by holding a fluffy guinea pig, or maybe a really strange dog. A worried old man in a beret shuffled after him toward the back rooms.

"Don't worry." Parker nodded my way as he went through the door, suddenly intent on me. His dark eyes flashed, a cryptic smile. "We'll take good care of her. You should come back tomorrow night. . . . I'm on till eleven."

Exhausted, I drove home and emptied the car. I just left it all— the dirty camping gear, my soiled clothing—in a heap on the garage floor, to be dealt with later. I had to unwind and get some sleep.

But I kept seeing that last shadowed gleam of Parker's dark eyes. Something shrewd or furtive. Like a thief, but not a thief. The closest thing to Zorro eyes I'd seen in a long time.

15

True to expectations, Monday deteriorated quickly. Too many of my patients thought I was the only doctor they should see, the only one who could solve their problems. They were generous and didn't complain that I took a vacation—they simply waited for me to return, no matter what their symptoms. Common sense has apparently become a lost art.

A little chest pain? *I'll just wait,* they thought. *What could go wrong?*

Phyllis Marr started her menstrual period the day I escaped into the woods. At fifty years old, her last period came three months ago, so she thought she was done. Only this time the bleeding didn't stop. Instead, it grew heavier. After discovering I wouldn't return until Monday, she made an appointment and endured.

"Not your best decision," I commented, pulling on exam gloves. I'd known Phyllis for a while and we could have that sort of conversation. "That's a lot of blood to lose."

"I know, I know." A sheepish wince. "I do feel a little lightheaded. But I wanted to wait for you."

"What if you couldn't breathe?" I asked. "Would you have still waited?"

"Well, I'm not insane."

Our uterus is a strange organ, wonderful when you want it, impossibly irritating when you don't. No other organ comes with a timer. Although the heart ticks like a clock, the uterus has this thirty-day meter that kicks in pretty reliably for decades. Every month the hormonal alarm clock twangs and the ovary punts out an egg, which tumbles through the tube and into the uterus, ready for sperm. *Pregnancy now?* the system says, all ready to go. If fertilization doesn't happen, there's a menstrual period instead, and next month it happens all over again. *Now?*

Phyllis's uterus got to produce two kids; mine got nothing. So sorry, my uterus, about your worthless existence. You made me pay for it: nausea from birth control pills, messy diaphragms and jellies, weight gain and acne from progesterone injections. After a while, I wised up and just insisted on condoms. Then menopause came along. Emancipating.

But back to Phyllis. The uterus has another timer, for when it's time to quit. The organ stops trying and closes shop. Only it can act ambivalent and doesn't shut the door tight, dribbling blood off and on. A faulty arrangement, but it hardly mattered back in prehistoric times when humans only lived to forty anyway. It's a modern problem, this business of living past reproduction.

That's where Phyllis found herself. Although I knew she needed hormones to control her uterus, I still must examine her to confirm that nothing else confused the picture, like a tumor. Let me state the obvious, that conducting a pelvic exam during heavy bleeding is no picnic. By the time I finished, the room smelled dank and red smears stained the table paper. Bloody latex gloves topped the trash. Yep, medicine is pure glamor.

Somehow Phyllis was hardly anemic, so she left with prescriptions and careful instructions. Her uterus would likely behave under my hormonal guidance. Meanwhile I took a short break and called the veterinary office to check on Emcee.

"She's doing so well!" piped the receptionist. "Do you want to talk with Dr. Parker? I mean, he's not here right now, but he will be later. He can call you."

"No, I'll come tonight and pick her up." The idea of speaking to him on the phone felt odd. His moodiness made me tense and I wanted to see his face. I was out of sorts for many reasons, but usually Emcee and I took a walk early each morning, and without her there I simply didn't go. So I felt sluggish and dull. Apparently I'm part dog myself and I need my walks.

Relieved about Emcee, I got back to work. I probably ate lunch but mostly that hour I telephoned people. I called a woman about an abnormal mammogram—more studies needed, most likely not cancer, but no guarantees. Of course, I said it more sensitively than that. More calls about a dozen other things, some important, some stupid.

Then the afternoon dragged on forever. My assistant Jo hung in there with me, and her hurricane energy and quick cheery smile kept me going through the absurdity. Fortunately she's fairly immune to my sourness and carried on like I was easy to work with, while I despaired over my patients' appeals.

No, you don't need X-rays for your three-day back pain from shoveling gravel since it's already getting better. No, don't spend a hundred dollars on that luxury massager for your sore shoulder because it's obviously a fancy vibrator. Instead you should perform the stretches like I recommended last time, which you haven't done even once. No, the chiropractor's spinal adjustments will not improve your diabetes—your sugar is two hundred seventy. I don't care what he said, you should eat fewer carbs. No, your insurance won't cover his treatments and it shouldn't, because they're worthless for this. No, your insurance will not cover this drug you actually really need for your osteoporosis and don't ask me why because I have no clue.

Modern medicine felt more like a farce every day. So much for my retreat. That wore off fast.

Finally I sat working in my office when Nellie appeared, her face tight as a snare drum, and reluctantly handed me my financial statement for the previous month. I stared at the numbers. After calculating my share of overhead, my personal salary had dropped significantly below the usual. Figure in my week off, and I wouldn't garner much after paying my mortgage and utilities. And during summer, needless to say, air conditioning fees were astronomical. Living in Phoenix, you barely run a furnace all winter long, but the AC is a greedy monster.

"I'm really sorry," Nellie finally said, her voice brittle. "I can't explain it. I can hardly sleep these days."

I ran my hands through my hair. "I don't think anyone is blaming you, Nellie."

"Aren't they? I know I'm the obvious crook here. I mean, my hands are on all the money, right?" Her voice sounded rough with distress and her eyes looked sick. "I need this job, Dr. Waters. It's the only thing that keeps me going. I used to think I was good at it."

"Well. I'm sure you are." I heard myself and realized I probably did not sound convincing. "You've always been on top of things."

"Until now," she moaned. "I saw Dr. Mulch give me such a look yesterday. Like he thought I was the most worthless person here."

"Oh, Nellie. He always looks like that." Brian had a pretty low opinion of our boring and traditional approach to patients. "Have you looked into hiring someone to investigate?"

She nodded brusquely. "Dr. Grayson and I are working on it."

"Good. I'm sure we'll get it straightened out." I left it at that. I couldn't be this distracted while managing patient data. I would make mistakes if I let this consume me right now.

I got back to work, thinking I needed to get Emcee soon. My house felt so empty without her that morning, that lazy swish of her tail when we talked. *Hurry back,* she always said. I imagined her caged, morose, raising those big eyes every time a door opened or someone spoke, looking for me.

It occurred to me that I never told Austin about Emcee. Was he entitled to know? Her recovery seemed imminent, so probably it didn't matter. I picked up my phone, put it back down. I tried to picture both of us at the vet clinic, like the divorced couple whose child is hospitalized. Then I imagined Parker's deep eyes, watching our awkward interactions. Forget that.

Betsy appeared at my door, her white hands fluttering, the tiny grain of diamond on her finger catching the light. I wondered why on earth she was still there. Why hadn't she gone home yet? Maybe being extra diligent about the billing since we had that meeting.

"Oh, Dr. Waters. Oh dear," she stuttered, glancing toward the front office, eyes wild.

I stood in alarm, grabbing my stethoscope and prepared for an emergency. Maybe someone in the waiting room, a sudden attack of chest pain. "What is it?"

"Dr. Grayson. He's been admitted to the hospital." Her wide eyes skittered away from me and searched up and down the hall, as if there must be someone better than me to tell. Unfortunately for her, I was the only one around. "Dr. Mulch just happened to be there and talked with him. He just called me, asked me to cancel all of Dr. Grayson's patients this week."

A dozen scenarios leapt in my brain. Seventy years old and more, overweight, stressed, Zane could have anything. A heart attack, a stroke. Uncontrolled diabetes causing a coma, a pulmonary embolus, who knew? I had no idea what his health problems might be—we didn't talk about such things. I'd been badgering him to visit his physician about his heartburn, so maybe a hemorrhaging ulcer? I had not seen him in the office all day, so perhaps he actually went to his doctor.

Betsy just stood there as if struck dumb, mouth open, hands clasped together near her throat. Her pink-and-tan leopard-spotted scrubs made her seem eight years old. Then tears suddenly welled up, which shocked me. Was he dead?

"Well, what happened?" I cried. I wanted to shake her. "Is he alive?"

Betsy's voice dropped to a whisper as she twisted her fingers and the tears plopped down her face. "Dr. Mulch says it's cancer. He has a tumor in his colon, and they're operating tomorrow morning." She dropped to her knees right there in the doorway, raised her arms, and appealed to the ceiling light, her cheeks glistening. "I'm praying for you, Dr. Grayson! I'm praying for you!"

What a relief, was all I could think, not something immediately life-threatening. I guess I shouldn't be happy at that news, but it could have been so much worse. I'd imagined him dying or dead. I knew Betsy felt close to him, sometimes confided in him—maybe he served as some sort of father figure to her. Or grandfather. But I felt so thrilled he wasn't dead that I forgot to be sensitive.

I clapped my hands at her and said, "Betsy, get a grip. He's not going to die tonight—you can pray later. Get on the phone and start calling his patients who are scheduled for tomorrow."

Her little mouth dropped open again. She swiped the tears with her hand and glanced at the clock behind me. Really. I swear, hot then cold, her emotions were downright befuddling.

"If you can't stay and make the calls," I said, a little harsher than I meant, "just tell me and I'll do it myself. Or I'll call Nellie and ask her."

Betsy clamped her lips, looking a little trapped. "I'm supposed to be home."

She seemed almost desperate. I really should ask her about that, about her husband, but this was hardly the moment.

"Well, can you or not? Just tell me."

Her chin rose with purpose. "I'll do it for Dr. Grayson. No matter what."

"Thank you. And don't worry, you'll get paid overtime," I snapped, grabbing my purse. I couldn't quite read her expression, but Betsy needed money, didn't she? "I'm going to the hospital."

16

No one looks good in a hospital gown, not even glamorous women and handsome men. Something about that loose cotton wrap, with its tent-like drape and unraveling hems, just turns everyone generically sickish.

Zane smiled when I entered the room. His belly rose up like a hill and one skinny hairless old-man leg stuck out from beneath the sheets, which for some reason went to my heart.

"Bad news travels fast, I see," he remarked, a little too jovial, returning my small hug. "How was your camping retreat? Glad to see you made it back."

His wife, Tara, tall and seasoned as a tree, sat alongside the bed, an unreadable expression on her solemn face. She kept her gray hair bobbed short and practical, the sort of cut that went from dripping wet to bone dry in three minutes on a summer day. I knew she spent many hours tending her prize-winning vegetable garden—no small feat in Phoenix—and I'd been lucky enough to consume quite a few of her lush tomatoes and zucchini. Her thin lips now pressed together, wary. A tinge of hope. She glanced at Zane and noticed his bare leg, reached over and twitched the sheet across him with a small roll of her eyes. I smiled at her, a brief shared woman-joke. Men.

"What's going on?" I asked, ignoring his question. His eyes looked wrong, small and helpless, then I realized he wasn't wearing his glasses. But the vulnerability felt real.

Zane pointed at his lower belly, sank his finger in the flesh, acted a little proud.

"Guess who has a tumor."

"Oh for heaven's sake," Tara groaned. She turned toward me, shaking her head. "He had his scope early this morning, Norah. It's a pretty big growth in his colon, but so far they don't see any spread. The scan just got done and doesn't show anything in the lymph nodes."

"Like that's always reliable, those scans," Zane said, derisive. "I could be chock full of little tumor cells, having a party in my lymphatics, and they might not show up on the scan."

"You see what he's like?" Tara picked up his hand, patting it, and

I could see her worry. "I don't know how you put up with him at work. It must be hell."

"Norah knows how to manage me," he said gruffly. "She's smart enough to ignore me."

"Not true!" I protested. "I'm just glad you're so cantankerous. No cancer will dare come back once this is out of you."

Tara stood and smoothed her skirt, then headed for the door, a faux-comical scowl. "I need a break and a cup of coffee. Keep him entertained. He's much more terrified than he acts."

"Damn right I'm terrified. What if I wake up dead after my surgery?" he called after her. She made a curt noise and her footsteps diminished down the hall.

We sat silent a moment. While a cynic like me found Zane's and Tara's gibes inspiring, we all knew the reality. The older you were, the more dangerous anesthesia became. And healing would take a long time, especially with his plump abdominal wall.

"You told me to see my doctor," he finally said, truculent. "See where that got me? This is all your fault."

"Right. I caused the cancer." I regarded him fondly while my spirit sank. He wouldn't return to work for weeks, months. He would endure a temporary colostomy and a second surgery later to put his guts back together again. I inappropriately thought of Humpty Dumpty. He might never return to work...likely would retire, even if everything went well. The practice would not be the same.

Zane's mouth puckered and his half-bald pate shone in the soft light. "Listen, Norah. I've been doing a lot of thinking this weekend. Too much thinking, no doubt. I must have known what was coming. But I've been a stubborn, foolish old man. I've ignored my symptoms and procrastinated. Put off the usual screening tests. Maybe it's a stupid male problem, or maybe a stubborn doctor problem. Or just me personally. Arrogance and denial, thinking it couldn't happen to me."

"No—" I started.

"Just listen." His eyes turned sad, looking down at his belly, then jumped up at me. "You have to take care of yourself. I mean it. Tell me if I'm wrong, because I bet I'm not. Are you up to date on your Pap, your mammograms? Have you had a colonoscopy?"

"Really, Zane. That's a little too personal." Don't turn your spotlight on me, I thought indignantly. Of course, I was overdue for all that.

"Oh please. Like you're offended. I'm talking doc to doc here, but also friend to friend. I mean it, Norah. Promise me you'll do it."

What the hell. This was too annoying—I had no intention of seeing my physician any time soon. But I could hardly tell a man with cancer that I wouldn't do a simple thing he asked.

"Fine," I said shortly. "I promise I will. But only because you have cancer and I can't be rude to you right now. Even though you're pissing me off."

Zane laughed, put his head back and roared. Then Tara stood in the doorway, steaming coffee in hand, staring back and forth at us.

"Do I even want to know what this is about?" she asked.

"No." I know I sounded crabby. Acting grumpy is a good way to hide distress. "Your husband is harassing me."

She stepped over and kissed his cheek. "One of his best skills."

We talked a long time; they obviously welcomed the distraction. I told Zane that Betsy was praying for him.

"I'll guess I'll take all the help I can get," Zane acknowledged.

"No, really," I said. "She's extremely upset. If I didn't know better, I'd say she's pretty fond of you."

"She's a tormented young woman. Her husband. . .well, he's not so good."

"Have you met him?" I turned suddenly curious about the furtive man.

Zane shook his head. "No one has."

Now I felt bad. "I'll try to be nicer."

Zane grinned. "Well. She also can be a pain in the neck."

Eventually they asked again about my vacation, my so-called retreat with Emcee.

"Oh crap," I exclaimed, startling. I had lost track—it was nearly seven o'clock. "I have to go get my dog."

We said our goodbyes, and in retaliation I made Zane promise to live through the surgery. I got out of there fast, because you never want a cancer patient, one about to go under the knife, seeing how upset you look.

17

The Amigo Veterinary Hospital never closed. A normal pet clinic during the day, after dark it turned into an all-night emergency facility. People showed up when their dog just ate four chocolate bars or when their cat tangled with the neighbor's much bigger and meaner feline. Next door, linked through a narrow passageway, stood an adoption shelter where muffled barks crept under a bright blue door. Occasionally a low miserable howl.

This time I sat out in the waiting room with the ordinary traffic, no dramatic rush to the back with my paralyzed dog. An extremely fuzzy, orange-striped cat drooped in the arms of an old woman with ratty gray-blond hair and a large bumpy skin cancer on her cheek. A basal cell cancer, a pearly clump. I debated advising her to take care of it.

There is no protocol for these situations. Apparently no one in this poor woman's acquaintance insisted she see her doctor. Possibly a recluse, maybe no close relatives, no friends. Perhaps she was mentally ill, for she murmured endlessly, barely audible, and her eyes never left the cat. I thought maybe I should stick my neck out and just say something. Maybe I should slip her a little handwritten note. Maybe I should mind my own business.

Someone called her to the back and the opportunity disappeared. Then I felt guilty I hadn't acted. At one point in my life, a long time ago, the world seemed much more black-and-white, much more right-and-wrong, than it does now. I guess when your spirit pales to a washed-out shadow, you grow tentative.

So I sat there waiting my turn, disgruntled and weary. I kept thinking about Zane lying in the hospital with his cancer belly, about Tara with her plucky teasing. I hoped his surgery was scheduled first thing the next morning because a study once showed that morning operations might have better outcomes. Our society created rules for how long a trucker can drive a semi, or how long a pilot can fly a plane, or how long a medical intern or resident can work without rest—but attending physicians and surgeons follow no regulations. A harried surgeon in the operating room maybe slept thirty hours ago, but no rule said they couldn't keep it up until they nodded asleep in an open abdomen.

I finally made it to the exam room. The door opened and Emcee trotted in, wiggling and wagging, and joyfully climbed up into my lap. *Finally,* she said. She wobbled just a little and I grasped her, clumsy. I buried my face in her soft coat, her feathery tail swishing the floor. We had a moment.

Parker stood there, watching us with those dark eyes. His grizzled beard had grown longer and looked worse, too scraggly, and his lab coat could have used a wash.

"Well," he said finally, coming in and closing the door, "you sort of look like hell."

"Excuse me?" Flabbergasted. Automatically, though, I glanced down at myself, my professional work clothes. Patent leather loafers, black slacks, a cleanish blue shirt—I looked fine. I'd quit petting Emcee in my aggravation and she nudged my hand hard. Her hind legs slipped off my lap.

"No offense." He smiled and stepped over, steadied the dog's back end. "She's still slightly weak."

What a peculiar person, insulting one moment and helpful the next. I didn't even bother to glare, just scanned him with a vinegar look.

"Guess you haven't seen yourself lately," I retorted.

He turned and checked his reflection in a small mirror behind the sink. Leaned his head one way, made a face, then turned it the other way. Laughed at himself.

"Ha. You're right. But what I meant was that you seem exhausted. Dark circles under your eyes. And you seem upset." He shrugged, a hint of contrition. "I'm sorry. I should keep my mouth shut. Forget I said anything."

I stared at him without an ounce of forgiveness.

"Anyway. Emcee is doing really well." Formal now, he straightened and scribbled in a file. Hearing her name, Emcee went to him and raised her paw. I swear, I never taught her that and she'd never done it before. He leaned over and grasped the paw just like she was human, shook it like shaking her hand goodbye. It was the strangest damn thing, as if she thanked him. Like they had their own little relationship. Then she twisted her head, took a quick look back at me like saying *he's all right by me.*

That moment knocked something loose inside my head.

"I just got some bad news," I admitted, surprising myself. "I had a lousy day at work because no one ever listens and no one ever believes me. And then I found out my older partner has colon cancer. I just came from the hospital and that's why I'm so late."

"Well. That sucks."

"Yeah." I stood, gathered Emcee's leash, headed for the door. I don't know why I told him that and I didn't want his condolences. Why would he care, anyway? It didn't affect him. "It does suck, and it's endless. But thanks for helping."

"Wait." He put his hand on the doorknob, then thought better and let go so I could escape if I wanted. He crossed his arms instead. "What else do you do? I mean, what do you do besides work?"

What else? He had the brains of a grasshopper, jumping randomly from one topic to the next. Probably did too many drugs when he was younger. He looked the type, a devil-may-care vibe, rebellious in his day.

"I do nothing. I practice medicine. I study medicine. I volunteer in medicine." The acrimony bothered even me. "I walk my dog. That's about it."

I hurried out the door. Unfortunately, he followed me to the lobby, but I pretended not to notice and hunched my shoulder toward him. He stood there while I chatted with the receptionist and tried to pay my bill.

"Wait a sec," she kept saying, peering at the computer. "This isn't adding up. I can't tell if all the charges have been entered."

So I waited, trying to be patient, while Parker just stood there watching. It felt awkward and inappropriate. I ignored him and turned to leave.

"Hey." He flashed a smile. "I asked you about what you do because we really need help next door at the shelter. We need people to walk the dogs. Since you're a walker, I just thought you might be interested, that's all. It's good for stress, clears your head."

"I hardly have time to walk my own dog." I awarded him a tiny caustic smile. But only because Emcee liked him.

"Think about it," he called after me.

As if.

18

Jeremy grew more accustomed to our small dialogues. He looked less persecuted, more relaxed. A little more engaged. Or maybe he simply resigned himself to my whims and just went along.

I worried about his narrow thinking. Jeremy latched onto a diagnosis quickly and he rarely considered other possibilities. Once locked in, he stubbornly defended his judgment. . .as if he'd been around in medicine long enough to have much judgment. He seemed determined to prove me wrong.

When I met with George, we had entirely different interactions. We scrutinized the ins and outs of his patients: the ups and downs of symptoms, the comings and goings of aches and spasms, the patient's fears in the night. Our discussions became rich and revealing. We wandered into the merits of generalized vs. specialized medicine. George's ideas came hesitantly, with many pauses, but thoughtful.

With Jeremy, I had to convince him that I might actually know something.

One day Jeremy's patient, a cheerful sixty-year-old woman with glowing lime green nail polish on her lengthy fingernails and long black hair with green streaks, had recently developed constipation. Jeremy had no subtlety when it came to disapproval; I saw him squint at her green highlights with censure. Picking my battles with him hurt my brain.

"How do you feel about that case?" I asked him later at our little meeting.

"I think I was right in the first place, that it's ordinary constipation. She needs more fiber in her diet, and she needs to hydrate better." His expression almost triumphant.

"A good working diagnosis." I nodded. "But she did say that her diet hasn't changed, and she's only been constipated for a month." I paused and got nothing. "So what do you think about the Benadryl she's taking?"

He waved me off. He'd missed the Benadryl on her initial history because he didn't ask if she took any over-the-counter meds. "Unlikely. She doesn't take it every day. Just every two or three days."

I don't like being waved off. And he only knew about the Benadryl because I inquired.

"Do you know the half-life of that med?"

"I think it's. . ." Now he looked angry. "No, I don't know. Not exactly. Probably two or three hours, since you can take it four times a day."

"Jeremy." I leaned forward, earnest, seeking a crack in his shield. It had to be there somewhere; none of us have impenetrable walls. "It's okay—I don't expect you to know that. You'll never know everything. Doctors look up stuff all the time." He pulled back, like I'd gotten too close, his mouth still tight, so I tried to be even softer. "Benadryl can last up to twelve hours in some people, and may take all day to completely clear their bodies. A potent antihistamine like that can dry up a person's allergies, but it also dries up their colon. Which causes constipation."

"But you can take it every six hours," he countered, digging in.

"True. Yet many people experience a more prolonged effect, including sedation. Sometimes all day. It's always important to ask about over-the-counter drugs."

Jeremy regarded me skeptically. His hair longer, the pale curls a little wilder than normal.

I took a chance. "What are you thinking?"

His upper lip rose. "I shouldn't say."

I smiled, puzzled. "No, come on. Tell me."

"All right." He'd gone back to inspecting the window, one of his many irritating traits. Sometimes the ceiling. "I just find all this pretty boring. All these little dull details that don't matter much."

Not many people will insult you to your face so blatantly. I felt like kicking him out, telling him to leave and take his contempt with him. I took a long moment, wrestling for control. Something I learned from dealing with my mom. She has had her perks.

"That's really short-sighted," I finally said, with much less venom than I felt. "Those little dull details can be the critical piece of a medical mystery. And there's another cause of constipation that you never considered. One that's not dull at all."

A suffering expression from Jeremy. "What, like irritable bowel? From stress and depression, like pretty much everything else?"

"No. Like colon cancer. She's the right age. So if she doesn't improve by stopping the Benadryl and changing her diet, we need to look for cancer. A change in bowel habits can be an essential cancer symptom." That came out rather severe, and once again I reined myself back. I wondered how Candore would react if I told Jeremy to not return. That I'd had enough. "I don't think you realize, Jeremy, that you come across pretty condescending at times."

Unexpectedly, that reached him. His face fell.

"Sorry. I get it from my brother."

"The brother who's in training to be a neurosurgeon? The one whose footsteps you're following?" I recalled him mentioning his family's pride.

"I'm not following his footsteps," he snapped. "That's just a coincidence. He's always telling me I can't do it, that I can't accomplish this or that. That I'm not good enough. Not smart enough. Screw him—I'm not a kid anymore. He doesn't rule me."

Okay, so not the proud happy family. I suddenly felt for Jeremy. Normally I would reach and touch him, his arm or knee—that human connection—but I doubted he welcomed contact. Some people radiate a force field.

"Listen," I said. "The top—or the best, or your goal—is a moving target, right? Your ideas and my ideas are certainly very different. And his ideas and yours are probably not the same, even within the same field. Not at all. You don't define each other."

Jeremy studied me and his wintry expression softened.

"No, he doesn't define me." His eyes closed briefly. "You're right, Dr. Waters. Thank you."

Sometimes small steps feel like long strides.

19

"I think your instincts have been right lately," Mom declared over the phone a few nights later. "I think you should quit."

Let me back up. The best thing about my mother is that she always gave me credit for my accomplishments, my grades, my scholarships. Her immense pride when I became a physician.

"My brilliant daughter," she crowed to pretty much everyone. "And she's cute, too! But that's an accident. Must have been a mutation in the family genes."

I don't know why she kept saying that—mostly fishing for compliments, I suspect. The "cute" comment ran against everything she espoused about independent, brainy women. I guess it proved her vulnerability, with flaws like all of us. She wanted people to think her beautiful.

But that's where the support stopped. Scrape your knee when your bicycle crashed? *Don't cry, toughen up.* When I missed first place in the high school science fair by two points? *Move on, life isn't fair.* She hinted maybe I could have tried harder. It's surely a good thing I didn't parent a child, because I probably would have gone extreme one way or the other: either unsympathetic like her, or gushing with too much praise.

"Really? And why should I quit?" My words guarded, for this was likely to end up as a criticism. The October evenings were cooler, and I should have gone outside to enjoy the night, but my feet felt sore so I flopped on the couch. Emcee immediately jumped on top of me. I gasped, not easy to breathe with a sixty-five-pound canine squashing you. But still worth every ounce of discomfort. She laid her snout on my chest and gazed at me with those syrup eyes and the world improved. It had been a good day anyway, with Zane recovering nicely from his surgery and about to go home from the hospital. All good except for the stupid card on my windshield at the end of the day: *Shame On You.*

When I took the card back inside and showed Nellie, her orange hair shuddered and she steamed down the hall, muttering to herself about security cameras. I had no clue how much to worry.

Zane talked to a friend in law enforcement, who shrugged and said to keep an eye out, whatever that meant. Small potatoes to a man in that line of work. He explained these were not actually threats, which muddied the level of concern. They were some kind of insulting, snarky harassment. Motive unknown. Harasser unknown. A pest or a bully, probably not treacherous. Probably.

"You're too serious," Mom railed. "You're almost sixty, and before you know it, you'll be living a boring life like me, picking up your gravel with tweezers for revenge. Most people around here where I live are just huddled inside, waiting to die."

"I'm a serious person. I've always been serious. You never cared before, not for the last fifty years. Besides, I thought there were so many activities there in Sun City that you couldn't decide what to do. Lots of busy people."

She ignored that. "Well, maybe I'm getting smarter. Maybe you have to live past eighty before you see the light."

This shift in direction, suddenly encouraging me to change, annoyed the hell out of me. "I have a mortgage. I can't just stop working."

"Eh. Sell your house and buy a cheap condo. Get an RV and travel the country with your dog. What are you going to do with your things anyway? We all have too much stuff."

A wistful vine crept through her words, and now I understood. Mom indulged in nostalgia for the old days, her carefree rambling. At least a little, she still owned a vagabond heart.

"Let me remind you, Professor, that you never quit your job early." Emcee has the softest ears. Her tongue fell out with pleasure as I stroked them, then she licked my chin and smiled her doggy smile. "You worked until you were past seventy."

"Yeah, but I had summers off. And I didn't start working at the university until after I was thirty." She exhaled. "And I loved my job. It didn't stress me out like yours. It's not like the physical human body changes much, not like I had to study to keep up. There's no new discoveries. Once you know anatomy, you're solid. I'd have to get reincarnated ten thousand years from now to see any evolution in human anatomy. Maybe fifty thousand years. There's no way humans will last that long, not at the rate we're destroying this planet. Or give us one good asteroid. Or a really wicked virus—that's all it will take."

"Come on, anatomy is pretty complex. And the knowledge does change and you know it. Besides, you don't just comprehend the names of things, you get how they work, even at the cellular level. You understand a huge amount."

She used to recite the nerve pathways to me whenever I had an injury. Instead of kissing my elbow to make it better, she explained how pain traveled. She animated the tiny electric impulses that she named Sparky and Twitch, who leapt across synapses and ran to my brain and screamed *Ouch!*

"No, Norah. I *knew* a huge amount, back in the past. It's leaving me. Just the other day, I couldn't remember the sinoatrial node. Couldn't think of the name at all." She spoke quietly, a trace of grief, a shift from her strident voice. Then she rattled back at the usual reckless speed. "So I understand what you've been saying lately. It's demoralizing when you can't stay sharp. So screw them all. Just quit and go have fun."

I was done listening to that, especially since it felt too supportive to be coming from her, and too appealing. Besides, I never said I wasn't sharp. "What's the latest with Johnny Quart? Are you two still fighting? Have you strung a barbed wire fence up between you yet?"

"That old coot. I saw him out there this morning, glaring at my noodle border like he wanted to kick it down. Good thing he didn't or we'd be at war, and I'm telling you right now who would win. He's barely bigger than a jackrabbit."

I laughed, making Emcee bounce and groan. "Maybe he was hungry. Maybe he looked at those noodles and wished he had some lasagna to eat."

"Come to think of it, he might be Italian. Isn't Quarto an Italian name? I bet his family had their name changed to Quart when they came through Ellis Island. You know how they used to do that? What an outrage. He should change it back."

Once she found a wrong to right, no one could stop my mother. She thrived on causes.

"Maybe you should tell him that," I suggested.

"I just might." A faraway tone, already scheming.

I planned to ask about the mailman, but we'd talked long enough.

I rallied and Emcee and I went walking in the soft night, where the sky had evolved from the scorched, ruined gases of summer. As if the air woke up, no longer smothered with cinders. A mockingbird perched high in the eucalyptus tree in front of my house, belting out purloined songs at the top of his liquid voice. I live in a pleasant old neighborhood with white stucco houses, red tile roofs, and quiet streets. Palm fronds clicked in the breeze and glimmered silver under the moon. I could have walked for hours, but it grew late because Emcee likes to mosey while I prefer to march along.

What's the rush? she always complained, planting herself against my tug.

"I'm trying to exercise. Come on."

But there are some really good smells right here. I think that bulldog peed here a few hours ago.

"So what?" I pulled again, dragging her past.

She looked wounded and trotted along until the next good spot.

I'd teetered toward quitting medicine for the last three months, maybe for the last year. Worse since I pushed Austin out. Now that my mother endorsed it, though, the option seemed less attractive.

Thanks, Mom. I think.

I doubted the feeling would last, anyway.

20

Some days the medical student George Clark seemed better. Some days not, still tentative with intimate topics, head down and mumbling into his chest.

When he concentrated, he nibbled his lower lip, making him look like a nerdy squirrel. I probably should have said something, suggested he control that mannerism, but it seemed actually endearing and I let it go. Probably it would fade as he built confidence. I assigned him a variety of simple cases to overcome his reticence and find poise; he tackled them with dogged determination. He saw young men with *tinea cruris*—jock itch—and middle-aged men who needed to lose weight. He saw young women with vaginal candidiasis—yeast infections—and middle-aged women who needed to lose weight. I stepped it up, and he tackled diabetes and smoking and chronic back pain and cancer follow-ups. He spent more and more time with each patient, and sometimes an hour passed before I saw him again.

"You were in there a long time," I commented when he emerged from a diabetic checkup, a thirty-year-old woman who weighed three hundred pounds with a glucose of three hundred.

George nibbled his lip. "She's convinced all these numbers with threes are an auspicious sign. Thirty, three hundred, and three hundred."

"What do you think?"

"I think if that helps her move forward, I don't care. She wants to make changes. That's why we talked for so long." A resolute nod.

Sometimes when I returned to a room with George, the patient's relief was apparent. I could see them think *Thank goodness you're here now.* Don't get me wrong. . .no one minded George because he was respectful and nice, but they saw how he wrestled at times, in over his head. Not drowning, just short of breath and starting to panic.

More often lately, though, my patients commented on what a good doctor George would make. He smiled warily.

I agreed, because they were right. I worry for the future of medicine, of primary care. These patients understood that George actually cared, that a physician must do more than adjust sugars and meds, more than simply juggle the numbers, calibrate pounds and calories. A computer can do that. The physician needs to listen and empathize and discover each patient's roadblocks, devise plans and find a key. Teach the science underlying it all. These complex tasks require both an agile brain and a sensitive heart.

Otherwise let's just design the robots and let artificial intelligence take over. We're headed there anyway.

A robot can ask what's bothering you, your headaches or insomnia. A robot can ask why you're drinking so much alcohol, but I doubt you will gaze back into that sterile LED eye and say *My husband doesn't understand me and he wishes I were someone else. So I'm sad, which is why I drink too much, which is why my blood pressure's up and why I can't get out of bed in the morning and why I'm about to lose my job, which makes me drink more.*

Show me a robot able to unravel that. Maybe they can be programmed to offer placebos. Instead of me worrying about dumb diets like ones based on someone's blood type, I could worry instead about machines giving patients piles of pills when they actually needed lifestyle interventions and empathy.

It occurred to me that Jeremy might be a robot, maybe some sort of cyborg. But he displayed too much facial expression, too much contempt. A robot wouldn't bother. While I knew Jeremy must be deeply broken, I'd made small inroads. He looked happy once when he made a complex diagnosis. He gave me a thumbs-up once when I taught him something he found interesting. Then more sessions came and went, with old aloof Jeremy, tight and unlikable. Disappointed, I couldn't tell if I'd gotten any closer to chinking his armor, any closer to a glimpse inside where a yolk of softness must hide. Then just when I gave up, we'd have another nice moment. I looked for new openings to discuss his brother, who sounded like a bully. Maybe we could get there again.

I ran quite late that morning because a sixty-four-year-old smoker with narrow little eyes and nicotine-yellow fingers complained of chest pain the night before. I pointed out a concerning jiggle on his EKG and recommended hospitalization. He didn't believe me since he felt fine now, and I must be exaggerating because his golf buddy thought he had gallstones. He wanted me to order a gallbladder ultrasound to see. Certainly, listen to your friend who's an insurance broker. You should have brought him along so he could interpret the EKG since I obviously got it wrong.

I made one more fruitless attempt, as his wife tearfully pleaded with him, then I called a cardiologist. Then I waited for the cardiologist to call me back, and somehow I convinced that overworked doctor to rearrange his schedule and see the patient that afternoon. By the time the heedless man left my office, grumbling about the fuss—*women*, I heard him grumble—the visit consumed nearly an hour.

I should not judge. I know that man quailed internally, his bravado a thin veil between him and a terrifying truth. But working around his stubborn defense was infuriating, damn it.

Meanwhile, Ana Merriweather walked in without an appointment and stood sobbing at the front desk, twining her fingers and claiming her life had ended. Betsy hurried back to me with tears in her eyes, sniffled hard, and said I simply must see her.

"Betsy. Can she come back this afternoon? I don't see how—"

"*Please*, Dr. Waters." She blotted her damp cheek with the back of her hand, her face tragic. "She's so desperate." Her voice lowered. "I even offered her to see Dr. Mulch, but she just cried harder. Everyone in the waiting room is upset. I looked up and saw that Dr. Thatcher's new patient and Dr. Cunningham's old patient were crying, too."

Betsy irritated me every day. Rigid, nervous, demanding. Sometimes she seemed like a caged mouse, baring her teeth at nothing. Sometimes she seemed like an angry jaguar—maybe it was her animal-print scrubs. Maybe it was that radio station KSIN that kept surfacing briefly during lunch breaks. Judgmental preacher-tones send me through the roof. And why were they always males, as if they must mansplain Christianity? Sometimes, though, Betsy got it right and sometimes I admitted it. And I could hardly ignore a contagion of weeping in the waiting room. I opened my mouth, but George spoke first.

"I can get Mrs. Merriweather started," George offered, eyes wide at all the emotion around him. "I don't mind."

I ran my fingers through my hair, heard my own stressed-out orders to Betsy, to please reschedule some people if she could. Betsy nodded, jotting it down, her lips stiff because she knew those patients would be upset. Working the front desk is a hard job, often thankless and subject to abuse from patients. Receptionists get yelled at and cussed out for things over which they have no control. Few people want to do that work, and doing it well requires skills far beyond the minimal training anyone gets. The pay isn't great and turnover is high. I grasped Betsy's exasperation, which on some days couldn't be helped.

Every single part of medicine is messy. If you ever catch yourself being mean to a person at the front desk, shame on you.

But George was a reticent first-year student, not really ready for a patient like Ana with her depression and complicated home life and oblivious daughter. Ana's feelings of worthlessness, her possible suicidal thoughts. He'd never dealt with an emotional crisis.

"Thanks, George, I appreciate that," I started. "But I should probably be the one—"

"I can just sit with her until you're ready. So she isn't alone." His benign face calm. We both watched Jo escort Ana into an exam room, Ana's old body hunched, blowing her nose.

Distracted, I glanced at the closed doors, patients waiting. "All right. I'll be there as soon as I can."

"No problem."

He entered Ana's room, quietly introducing himself. "You don't know me, but I'm a medical student working with Dr. Waters this year and she can't see you for a few minutes. If you don't mind, I could talk with you until she..." The door shut.

It took me thirty minutes. Between patients, I heard George and Ana through the door, their murmured conversation. I couldn't make out the words, but they talked steadily, so I left them alone. Finally done, I tapped and went in.

Ana sent me an unsteady smile. No more tears, though. She sat up straight, knee to knee with George, who explained her dilemma.

"Her daughter plans to send the children to boarding school, and it's very upsetting. Right, Mrs. Merriweather?"

Apparently Ana's daughter feared that her girls, only twelve and thirteen years old, had become too attached to their loving grandmother, who now helped with homework and taught them Spanish and how to cook their favorite meals. It sounded like jealousy.

"They're so young for that," I agreed. I readied myself for a long and sticky discussion, about how Ana might sleep and cope, whether I should call her daughter. I needed to assess her despair, her suicidal risk. Inquire again if she still had those potent sleeping pills in her medicine cabinet. But Ana spoke first.

"George here told me we could use some family counseling. That feels right. He said you would know where to send us." Ana grim but resolute, a steely look.

"Will everyone in the family go?" I wondered.

"Yes, I think they will." Ana nodded. "I'll tell them that if we don't try counseling first, before sending the girls off, that I'll be too upset and lonely. And so I'll need to have my old brother Carlos for company. That he'll need to move into the house. They can't stand Carlos. Neither can I, because he's a whiny pain in the ass who never stops talking and he never showers and he smells like cheese, but they don't know I feel that way." She leaned forward and touched my hand. "Don't worry, Dr. Waters. We talked it all out. I see how to tackle this now."

George gave her a quick smile. "You're very determined."

All right then. They didn't need me after all. Good old shy nerdy awkward George. . . . I felt downright proud of him. Because I send so many patients to the family counseling center, I have the number memorized. I wrote it down and Ana dropped it in her bag, snapping it shut with finality.

That's when Jeremy Newell showed up and tried to ruin everything.

21

Jeremy arrived early for his afternoon session. An unusual move, since he often appeared at the last moment with a pained look, as if braced for torture. Having both students on the same day always chafed me because I got no down time. Why they kept changing their schedules was beyond me, but I found it easier to roll with it than resist.

"Hello, Jeremy," I said brightly, feeling anything but cordial. All doctors have cultivated a fake pleasant face, have learned to turn it off and on, mostly for those rotten days where everything goes wrong but your next patient really needs you. You plaster on that face. I doubted this would be the day I breached his barricades, not even close.

Jeremy nodded vaguely my way where I sorted supplies in the nursing station. He zeroed in on George instead.

"Hi there, Clark." One eyelid half-closed, a corner of his mouth turned down as he watched George type. I had offered to finish George's charts since he saw extra patients including Ana Merri-weather that morning, but he wanted to do it himself. Jeremy went on. "Make any brilliant diagnoses today?"

George looked up from the keyboard with cautious eyes, as if used to addressing a tyrant. "Nope. I saved that for you."

Jeremy stretched, arms over his head then out sideways, taking up too much room. He yawned loudly. "All in a day's work, my good man. All in a day's work."

George said nothing and returned to his laptop. Jeremy moved around behind him and peered over his shoulder, reading the note as George tapped along. I saw muscles bunch in George's jaw.

"You misspelled guaiac," Jeremy said, throwing me a look. He must have just been to the barber, his curly blond hair tight against his skull, the skin shining through.

"Almost everyone misspells guaiac," I said lightly. "Don't worry about it."

Jeremy poked George's shoulder. "Missed you at Daggat's party last week. Don't tell me you forgot."

"I wasn't there because I didn't want to be." George gave up and turned to Jeremy. "I don't like drinking parties, and I don't plan to go into any surgical field. So no point in being there."

I barely knew Daggat, a high-powered cardiothoracic surgeon, superb in his work and renowned for his temper and crude talk. Because I have a friend on the hospital surgery committee, I knew they reprimanded Daggat for throwing instruments in the operating room and shouting at nurses. What a jerk. I finished my task and turned away toward my office, not caring to hear this conversation.

"Your loss," Jeremy said to George. "It was a great party. It wouldn't kill you to network a little. What's your plan, anyway? Have you narrowed down your specialty yet, or are you still trying to decide? Are you one of those who's waiting to be inspired?" He fluttered his fingers when he said *inspired,* like it was a prissy insult.

"Yeah. I'm waiting," George replied coldly.

"Well, don't worry." Jeremy laughed. "If you can't decide, you can always get into family medicine. There's always openings."

"Hey," George protested. "That's rude."

I imagined George looked at me, or at my back, as I retreated down the hall. I pretended I didn't hear. If I ever picked a time to have it out with Jeremy, it wouldn't be when George was there.

My mood curdled because of the partial truth in Jeremy's comment. We desperately need family physicians, but bright dedicated students who are inclined toward primary care often find themselves chastened by specialists throughout medical school, told again and again that they could do better. Should do better. Must do better. That only unambitious people pursue family medicine with its lower income. The naïve, impressionable students often buy this distorted advice from prestigious mentors and veer away. Therefore, yes— some less accomplished students do pick family medicine as a last resort. Most family docs, though, are dedicated to their work and enjoy people, trying to make a difference. They like the challenges of front-line medicine and they tackle it with passion.

The fix would be easy: we should cover medical school tuition for any new graduate who pursues family medicine for a decade. The field would blossom overnight. No one listens.

Fortunately, my afternoon with Jeremy seemed routine. Unlike

George, to whom I gave increasingly difficult cases, I assigned Jeremy to simpler ones. He may have been brilliant on exams, but Jeremy struggled with multitasking and only managed one problem well at a time.

So Jeremy saw muscle injuries and simple infections. Nothing that required empathy, not after I watched him talk to a smoker the previous month, his voice thick with scorn. Even though I tried to smooth it over later with that patient, I worried I may have lost him. When I tried to explain compassion to Jeremy as an effective approach, he stared at me with blank incomprehension, as if I spoke an alien language from another galaxy.

"Always give me a differential diagnosis, several possibilities," I insisted, to broaden his thinking. A repeated conversation. "Always list two other conditions that could cause the same symptoms. And likewise with treatments. . .show me a few options, not just one."

"Sure, Norah."

He always sounded bored. He told me he was bored. Nothing I offered compared to sawing open a skull or whittling through a brain. And I'm not certain when he started calling me Norah. I didn't mind much because my ego isn't tied to titles, but no student ever presumed before, at least not without asking.

My patient Bob Holliday appeared with a dreadful sore throat and high fever. Thirty years old, Bob worked for the FBI. Which meant he never told me exactly what he did, but it had to be stressful. His throat looked like an inferno, a swollen crimson tunnel thick with pus—one of the worst throats I'd ever seen. Fevered, hot and sweaty, he looked sick as hell, and bulky tender lymph nodes crowded his neck.

"When a throat is this bad, with all these large lymph nodes," I explained, "it's often mono. Mononucleosis, caused by a mean little virus. We'll do a blood test to know for sure, and I'll swab you for strep, too. Sometimes they travel together."

Bob groaned and wiped perspiration from his face. "Great."

He opened his mouth wide for the swab. I'm normally pretty quick and adept, but Bob was more anxious than I realized. He gagged and jumped, grabbing my hand, and I missed his throat altogether, swiping his tongue instead.

"Oh no, I'm so sorry," he cried in chagrin, dropping my wrist. "Did you get it?"

"No, afraid not. I need to do it again. You've got a very sensitive gag reflex. I can numb up your throat with an anesthetic spray, if you'd like."

Bob shot me a fierce look. "No. I can't believe I reacted like that. Just do it. I won't move."

He swallowed hard and opened his mouth again. His nostrils flared, but when I swabbed his throat this time he didn't move or twitch or even breathe. I realized he conjured up some kind of mind control, something from the ungodly training he'd undergone for torture or who knows what. Wow.

He looked relieved that he'd passed his own test.

"I'll put you on antibiotics until the results are back, in case of strep," I told him. "What's the best way to reach you? Your cell? Your office?"

His face paled. "Never ever call me at work. Nothing's confidential there. . .everyone would know my doctor called. And they'd probably know where you live and where you buy groceries and your dog's name and your favorite color. It's creepy. Use my cell."

I tried to forget he said all that and wondered if he actually knew I had a dog or if that was simply a generic statement. It occurred to me to ask him about the windshield notes, which rankled me more each time. But I stopped myself. Involving the FBI seemed a step too far for those little nasty cards, and it felt inappropriate to pull a patient into my life like that. Especially a sick patient.

Then I asked Bob if Jeremy could see his throat as a learning opportunity, but Bob declined. Perhaps his sore throat might be used against him in some devious world order I couldn't imagine, and the fewer people who knew about it the better. So instead, after Bob left, I simply described his case to Jeremy, a good moment to teach the differential diagnosis for pharyngitis: a cold virus, strep, mono, even gonorrhea. I reviewed the strep algorithm and how to check for a tonsillar abscess and how to manage one. Then we discussed the precautions for mono, protecting the fragile spleen.

Jeremy bridled at the end. "I would have liked to examine that throat. Why didn't you come get me?"

"I asked him, but he didn't want to see anyone else. He's a very private man," I explained, irritated by Jeremy's irritation.

"Thanks for trying."

Innocent enough words if said kindly. They were not.

We wrapped up on time. Jeremy sat with his phone in the nursing area, snickering at a picture.

"What's up?" I asked, attempting to be friendly because I had so many more months with him. Because who knew when the moment might open up, an unexpected breach in his wall. I could hardly imagine it would be that day, not after his earlier comment to George about lowly family medicine, which I'd had to stow away all afternoon.

Jeremy laughed and held up his phone to show me a photo posted on Facebook. A photo of my patient he saw an hour ago.

A forty-year-old mother of three, Annette Bledsoe longed for a different face. That is, for different skin on her face. Patchy dark pigment called melasma spotted her cheeks; it started with her first pregnancy and worsened with each child. Melasma from pregnancy often fades with time, but Annette's did not. On a friend's advice, she scrubbed her skin with lemon juice yesterday, then took the kids to the park.

Lemon juice, facial skin, and sun are a terrible combination. Citric acid irritates skin and makes it react to sunlight, called photosensitivity. And there she was in profile, scarlet skin and bubbling blisters, on social media. Underneath ran his comment: *Patient I saw today. Lemon juice. Can't believe what people do to themselves.*

"What the hell?" I said, aghast. "You can't post that."

Jeremy looked indifferent. "It's fine. You can't tell who it is."

"No, you sort of can. I would recognize her." I'd gone furious. "And even if you couldn't, it's still a HIPAA violation. Didn't you know that?"

"It's just a laugh for my friends. Other students. She'll never see my feed." He seemed somewhat taken aback by my reaction, but not much. Not enough. "Besides, she said I could take the photo. I told her it was for medical research."

"Take it down, right now," I commanded, trying not to raise my voice, not succeeding. "I cannot believe they haven't taught you about HIPAA. Who's in charge of your preclinical training?"

His face changed then. He looked worried and tapped on his phone.

"Okay. There. It's gone—I deleted it." He suddenly turned contrite. "I'm sorry, Norah. Dr. Waters. They did teach us, but I guess I just didn't understand all the rules. I messed up, and it won't happen again. You don't need to call anyone."

"So you do remember it in your curriculum?"

"Yeah, I'm sorry. It's coming back to me now, now that you've mentioned it. It was way back last summer, you know, right after we started. Part of orientation. I should have paid more attention, obviously." He made a little face of regret.

I squinted at him, tried to calculate. Wondered if this might actually be one of those moments I sought. "I appreciate you acknowledging that. I know that's not always easy for you."

He ducked his head. "I'm trying to do better, you know. I know it's hard to tell, but I really am."

Jeremy had never acted humble or apologetic, not ever. So I felt a little bit better, and left it at that. Not my biggest mistake or my last mistake, but definitely a mistake.

22

When I found the bill in my mail from Amigo Veterinary Hospital, I realized I'd never paid for Emcee's care when she had tick paralysis.

I felt bad, for I knew that place operated on a shoestring and barely kept the shelter afloat. I'd been drawn to it for precisely that reason—it reminded me of my old downtown clinic. Gritty and practical. None of those chain-store veterinary wellness plans where you pay in advance then have trouble getting an appointment. Not like those swanky clinics with espresso stations and gourmet pastries, where you can fork out extra to have your pet picked up and returned home by animal limo. No televisions in the boarding suites, endlessly looping Rin Tin Tin and Lassie.

On Saturday afternoon I stopped by to pay. The furnace of summer had dialed way down, now only a mild simmer. I figured it would take about three minutes, and it seemed nicer than sending a check since I hadn't paid at the time like I should. When I picked up Emcee that night, standing at the counter and waiting for the receptionist to figure my bill, Parker annoyed me by harping on about hobbies and dog walking or whatever incomprehensible thing he was trying to say, and I guess I just left. Thinking back, that might have been inappropriate, the way I took off.

Now I blinked at the hefty fee and reminded myself that Emcee's care bordered on ICU-level management that night. The fact that I even thought about my bank balance provided yet another indication that we had to get to the bottom of this financial problem.

"How's Emcee?" the receptionist cheeped, a relentlessly cheerful young woman with purple-tipped hair wearing lavender scrubs. It's hard to imagine, but I suppose some people genuinely feel positive like that all the time. "She was such a sweet patient. Is she back to normal now?"

I reported on her good health and took my receipt. Clients scattered the lobby, waiting to be seen. A massive St. Bernard lay sprawled across the floor, and he raised his head to sniff the air, testing my scent, making me smile. I turned to go and there stood Parker, clean-shaven this time, his straight black eyebrows up. His face appeared more gaunt without the shabby beard, his lab coat clean with neat creases. His messy hair stood in all directions—either just plain sloppy or intentionally untidy, apparently a thing these days. And they say women's hair styles are complicated. I could not imagine how he knew I was there.

"Hey, I just saw you through the door. I'm glad you're here. Come on, let me show you the shelter and all the bums." He beckoned so eagerly that my feet moved on their own, and I found myself inside the blue door before I had time to think.

"Wait. I just came to pay my—"

"Sure, sure. But you have to see what we got today." He gestured me down a row of cubicles with mesh gates. A dizzy parade of dog faces stared at me, long noses and pug noses, hopeful eyes and hopeless eyes, tails wagging like crazy and tails tightly tucked. I reeled, overwhelmed by their need. The yearning, the despair.

What was the dog word for humanity? Caninity?

Parker stopped and pointed into a small open space. A rust-colored retriever mix reclined on blankets, almost the size of Emcee but darker and thin to the bone. I could count every rib, even under the rough hair. Mangy skin, inflamed patches. But she caught my eye, then looked down and prodded her three scrawny pups as if counting. One mewled and snuggled against her, the other two sound asleep.

"Oh," I heard myself say, my hand to my mouth.

He gently plucked up the puppy and deposited it in my arms, where it yawned and its tiny tongue flicked my skin, then settled in against my chest. The pup smelled of wood shavings and milk, while Parker smelled pungent like liniment.

"They found her under an old wrecked car, behind an abandoned house. She had five pups, but two were dead." He took a tube of ointment from a shelf, smeared some on her rash. The dog closed her eyes, enduring. "Took us forever to clean her up, just filthy. She made me think of you."

"Um—what?" Was he trying to be insulting, or did it just come naturally?

"Sorry. I meant she reminded me of your dog. They look a lot alike."

I frowned. "You really could be more articulate. You just called me a dirty mangy dog."

The puppy drowsed in my arms and its mom gazed up, checking. I admit I didn't want to return it yet.

He caught my eyes. "Yeah. I'm not always good at that. Words. If you want to get technical, it was worse than that. I think I called you a dirty mangy bitch."

The last thing I wanted was to encourage him. But a laugh burst from me unexpectedly, startling the pup. I quickly sobered myself and shifted the puppy, cradled it in my hands and replaced it against its mom.

We walked back and he introduced the dogs along the way.

"This is Arf, part beagle. See that lump on his hind leg? Fractured by his last owner, almost healed. That's Snub, a French bulldog who ate a bowl of grapes and had to stay here two days to prevent kidney failure, then they never picked her up. Probably didn't want to pay the bill. That was three months ago. This collie is Blink, lost an eye when someone kicked him in the head. He looks sad because he missed his walk today—our usual walker is sick and none of the volunteers showed up. The staff and I walked as many as we could."

Blink studied us with his one good eye, his long nose down between his paws. The other eye absent, skin sewn over. I felt bad for Blink because he truly did look disappointed, and he seemed annoyed at Parker.

"Don't be oblique. If you want me to walk him, just ask. I can see from the waiting room how busy you are." I scowled, overcome by the dog anecdotes and trying to hide it. I mean, I encountered difficult stories every day, and they were about people, not dogs. It seemed embarrassing to be so moved now, more than I sometimes felt with humans. Was that shameful? My emotions careened strangely out of control, oddly sentimental.

"My apologies." He bowed slightly and cleared his throat, an amused flicker. "Could I possibly implore you to walk this dear dog if you have spare time on a Saturday afternoon? He'd be forever grateful. Well, maybe not forever, but at least for a few minutes, or however long a dog remembers to be grateful."

I must have agreed, because Parker hurried back to his duties, turning me over to Ralph, the young overweight aide. Ralph bent down, grunting, and snapped on a leash, then showed me the back door. He pointed the way to a small park down the street and handed me a poop bag.

"This will be quick," I warned him, testy.

"Thanks. You made Blink's day. I'll leave this door unlocked." Ralph turned away to go help Parker, done with me and my tart mood.

Obviously thrilled, Blink trotted along, tail flagged up as he sniffed every plant and lifted his leg again and again. Unlike Emcee, who stopped for each scent and explored every spot thoroughly before finding the next one, Blink sniffed and pissed without pausing. Just a brief hesitation, a quick sprinkle, and onward we strode. The speedy pace felt invigorating, the late afternoon sun carving through the trees, a light breeze. I learned to stay on his side with the good eye so he could keep track of me, and we briskly circled the park. Twice. A large yellow-and-black butterfly dithered along with us awhile and doves piped and cooed and the whole scene seemed ridiculously Disneyesque.

It got me thinking about butterflies. Most of us are stuck with one configuration, growing into a bigger version of our baby selves, but not these creatures. They're slugs, little wormy caterpillars that shamble around stuffing themselves with leaves until they go hide inside a chrysalis for a few weeks. Then, magically, they emerge as a *completely different insect* with large delicate wings, striking colors, then take off into the sky to flutter hundreds of miles. It would be like a human baby wrapping itself in a blanket in a closet, then suddenly emerging as a sleek whale and jumping into the ocean to swim halfway around the world.

You cannot deny the charm in that. I wanted my own chrysalis. I wanted to emerge as someone else.

No one was waiting in the shelter when we returned. Everyone was working in the clinic. I gave Blink a dog treat from the jar on the counter and put him back in his cage. He flopped down, panting, content. I stole one more look at the puppies, now squirming against their mother as they nursed, and I left.

No one saw me go. It seemed like a stealth move, which felt right.

23

When I stopped by Wanda's office at lunch she looked in bad shape. I wanted to discuss her patient with lupus I'd treated that morning. Lately I'd seen several of her patients when I had a cancellation, because they couldn't wrangle their way into her loaded schedule. Wanda often worked through the noon break, and I didn't actually expect to find her. . . . I planned to just leave a note. Yes, I could have and probably should have sent her a message through the computer EMR, but I'm old and don't always think of that. Turns out it's good I didn't.

Wanda sat at her desk, slumped over, her head on her arms. At first I thought she'd fallen asleep, a quick power nap. But then her shoulders heaved and she sniffed, raised her face and saw me. Startled, she snapped upright and wiped under her nose with a knuckle, sending me a watery smile.

"Hi, Norah." Wanda snatched a tissue and blew her nose. "Don't mind me."

"Are you all right?" I pulled up a chair, put my hand on her arm, aware I just reversed our roles from that day before I went camping, when Wanda checked in on me. I remembered her patting my arm and how I sat back. Or maybe that was Emily.

Wanda didn't pull away. She clasped her hand on top of mine instead, a hot grip.

"I'm so miserable. I'm just so tired I can't think."

"Is something wrong?"

I always counted on Wanda to be the positive force. The peacemaker, the optimist. I'd never seen her distraught like this.

"No, nothing's wrong. I mean, yes. Everything's wrong. Oh, Jesus and Mary. . . I'm not making any sense." Tears brimmed and she grabbed another tissue, dabbed furiously at her eyes. She wiped them so hard I worried about a corneal abrasion and nearly stopped her.

Fortunately she quit, so I gave her a moment to compose herself. Sometimes simply sitting with a person has value. Finally I spoke. "Can I help? Is there anything you can tell me?"

Her mouth wobbled, but she raised her chin. "You had a good

vacation, didn't you? You came back refreshed, right? Maybe I just need a vacation. Like you, off by myself." I started to say something but she pushed on. "I just so desperately need a break."

"Of course, you should take a nice vacation," I agreed. "Why, I can't remember the last time you did."

"That's because I use up all my days off in bits and pieces. I go to school shows or softball games. Church lunches and church charities. Or I stay home when one of the kids is sick. They're always getting sick, because kids do, and what kind of mother doesn't stay home with her sick child? But then my work here piles up, and all my patients want me to call them because they can't get in. I just can't catch up—I'm so far behind."

I opened my mouth to offer help, but she jostled on.

"But you know what's one of the best things about my job?" Her voice rose in a wail. "It's that my job takes me out of the house and away from the kids. I get to escape! What a horrible thing, to feel like that, to even think that—I must be the worst mother in the world." She suddenly crossed herself. "I keep going to confession, but it doesn't help. I keep thinking those thoughts. So then I go to confession again. And again. It's exhausting, just trying to stay saved."

Four children are truly a houseful. Wanda's kids spanned from six years old to fifteen. Her thirteen-year-old daughter hung out with a sketchy older bunch, and her nine-year-old son showed reclusive tendencies, maybe too much time with computers. The other boys seemed normal, which still meant they were often up to mischief. Wanda's husband worked full time, doing something with investments—he shuffled other peoples' money around, after convincing them their money must be shuffled around. Which should have made his schedule somewhat flexible, I thought. Not too long ago Wanda talked about taking a year off, staying home to better sort out the kids, but he talked her out of it because it didn't make 'financial sense.' I had little grasp of him, good or weak.

"I think every mother has those thoughts," I assured her. Didn't they? I hadn't the slightest idea, but it sounded real enough. Heaven knows I would have those thoughts.

"But my patients are sort of my family, too. They depend on me as well. It's too complicated. And I'm so tired. After I get the kids to bed, sometimes I'm up past midnight on the computer, finishing my notes. Then I can't sleep because I worry about whether I missed something important. Or I realize I told a patient that I'd call her back, but then I got too busy or everything else was more urgent. I can't call them at two in the morning, although I've wanted to. That's crazy, isn't it? And little Joey still wakes up at night crying, still wets the bed."

Wanda kept tumbling down the hill and I felt terrible that I couldn't slow her descent.

"Doesn't your husband help?" For the life of me, I couldn't remember his name. Recalling names has always been my weakness.

"Oh, right. Dale can barely do a load of laundry without flooding the house. He has no concept of whites, which is fine if no one minds pink socks." Wanda laughed, a bit hysterical. I seriously grew worried. "And this week he's got a cold and he's dragging around with a box of tissues like it's tuberculosis and he's mad at me because he doesn't think I'm giving him enough TLC and honestly he might be right. I've got nothing left for him. But Lord bless him, Norah, I go to work sick all the time. I put on a mask and I just do it even though I feel horrid. Do you think man flu is a real thing?"

"Probably." I couldn't help but smile.

A sound at the door. Betsy from the front desk cleared her throat, standing there in zebra-striped scrubs—did she have an entire zoo of them?—and staring at us with round eyes. She looked like a shocked porcelain doll when she did that, her pale lips agape, and she did it often. Like we're all nuts. But then, maybe we are. Maybe she's onto something.

"What?" I asked, a bit brusque. Most normal people would have seen Wanda's distress and moved on, come back later.

"Um." Betsy's eyes bounced between us then focused on Wanda, away from me. "Dr. Cunningham. Your patient Tippy Broadhurst says her blood pressure is almost two hundred and she's got palpitations and that you have to see her today. I know you're booked but she said you always squeeze her in—"

"No," I said quickly, before Wanda could squeak. "Who else has any openings today?"

"Dr. Mulch, I think." Betsy glanced at me, then Wanda, but Wanda stared down at her lap, her eyes red. "Tippy won't like that."

"Then she can go to the emergency room. Or she can see Mulch...it's up to her. Dr. Cunningham cannot." I left no room for options but Betsy still stood there.

"What?" I complained. Then I saw it, saw that she held a white index card, stretched it uncertainly toward me. "Oh, crap. You too?"

Betsy made a jerky nod and I took it. *You Little Bitch.*

"This has gotten insane," I exclaimed. Wanda didn't even look up, barely seemed aware—not a good sign. I handed the card back to Betsy because it just wasn't top on my list right then. "Here. Show it to Nellie...this has to stop. And don't throw it out. We'll talk about it later, okay?"

Another twitch from Betsy and she left. Wanda finally stared up, lost, like she hadn't tracked what we said.

"Sorry. I sort of took over." I reached back and shut the door. "Go on, if you want. We've got fifteen minutes, so spill it all. I get the feeling there's more."

A shaky breath. "Well. There's the money thing. You know, how our incomes are down even though we're all busy. Dale is furious and says we're a bunch of financial lamebrains." She winced, apologetic. "He says we should let him look at the books, that he'd do it for free. But that would make Nellie so upset. And it's probably a conflict of interest. I mean, how would that look, for my husband to be seeing everyone else's money and expenses and—"

"It's not a terrible idea," I interrupted. I agreed with Dale, actually, that most physicians were financial lamebrains. Myself included. Physicians find themselves placed in authority over things they know nothing about, and business management is often part of that. "It would save us money because we wouldn't have to pay a stranger, and he'd be highly invested in the outcome. So he would try harder. And Nellie's already upset. She's worried we think she's embezzling—which would be pretty easy for an office manager like her to do. It happens all the time. She's terrified we'll fire her. Let me talk to the rest of the docs."

"Really?"

"Frankly, I don't care who does it. . .it should just be done. But I can't speak for how the others might feel. And you need some time off, don't you think?"

"Oh, Norah. I feel so pathetic. I should be able to do this. I'm not stupid. I think I'm a pretty good doctor, and my patients mostly like me. I mean, there's a few patients who. . .well, you know how that goes. But I love my children to pieces and need to be there for them too. And right now I just want to go sit on a beach and do nothing. I'm just a wreck. How did I become such a failure?" A sob snagged her throat.

"You're not a failure, and you are a good doctor. Don't worry, I wouldn't say that if I didn't mean it, because I'm not a very nice person. Unlike me, though, you're just too nice."

Not many could make "being nice" sound like a malfunction, but I managed fairly well. And I steeled myself for what I must say, even though it was the last thing I wanted. Sometimes you just have to suck it up.

Women physicians cannot win. If they cut back work for their kids, they're chastised for wasting part of a career that a full-time man could have filled. If they decide not to have children, they're considered self-centered and overly ambitious and there's something wrong with them. They're not "real" women. They might be shrews. I quit counting the times people inquired when would I get married, have children, lead a normal life. Asked by friends, family, strangers. People who wouldn't dream of soliciting my religion or politics or even my favorite book—they somehow found this a proper thing to probe.

News flash: doctors don't lead normal lives, male or female. Most of the time they carry on. But they constantly worry and stress about mistakes and they can't keep up and they sleep poorly and sometimes fear catching a deadly infection. They constantly want do-overs, triple-thinking what they might have done better. Half the work is below their qualifications, yet sometimes they are not qualified enough for what walks through the door. They enjoy many of their patients and really dislike a few. If you are a patient and wonder if you're the one your doctor dislikes because of how you behave, then you might be. We're neurotic as hell and we probably all need counseling but don't dare go because what if someone found out and thought we were mentally ill? You could lose your license.

Meanwhile husbands of women physicians travel along, wanting to be cared for as well, pursuing their usual lives. Some rise to the occasion and do their share; some don't. Show me one male physician who truly felt he had to choose between children and career, or who did as much around the house. Never mind the studies finding how female physicians' patients have better outcomes and higher satisfaction.

Some statistics show that over a quarter of physicians retire early—both males and females—exhausted by stress and fed up.

"After today," I asserted, sounding bold but sinking a little inside, "I think you should take a week or two off. Refresh yourself. Make some new strategies. I'll cover your patients. The others can help too. What do you think?"

Strained, desperate, her wet eyes beseeched me. "But Zane is already out because of his surgery. We're seeing his patients too. And my patients really don't want to see a man like—well, they don't want to see a man. Your offer is so very generous, but you don't have time for that."

"Nonsense. No one is indispensable. What if you got hit by a bus?"

That should not make someone feel better, but it did. Wanda's look of gratitude pierced my heart. Almost as much as Blink, maybe a little more. Maybe I've still got a little bit of humanity left, every now and then.

But don't count on it.

24

A week went by. I lowered my head and slogged away, seeing Wanda's patients, seeing Zane's patients, seeing my own patients. Routine visits for healthy people got delayed, much like during an influenza epidemic.

Arriving early, staying late, we pulled together with battlefront mentality. Emily, Brian, and I actually bonded together over the situation. Yes, even Brian Mulch. He pitched in on Zane's and Wanda's patients with unexpected good humor. It just goes to show that nobody is one-dimensional, and even annoying people have their good sides. I constantly try to remind myself of that. Humans are complicated.

Some nights when we all worked late on our charts and made calls, we ordered pizza and fired jokes back and forth, up and down the hall from our offices. I managed to bite my tongue when I heard Mulch peddling supplements and using steroids for too many simple problems. This seemed a new kick for him, handing out short bursts of steroids like special treats.

"Steroids are natural hormones," he once said into the phone. "Your own body manufactures them, but sometimes not enough."

There is so much wrong with that statement, because the human body does make enough, almost all the time. Sometimes extra steroids are truly necessary when the body is overwhelmed with inflammation, like with rheumatoid arthritis or lupus. Steroids can break up a bad asthma attack or dangerous allergies. And there are uncommon endocrinologic diseases where the body actually can't make steroids. Among the downsides, though, which are considerable and too lengthy to list, steroids raise blood sugar and blood pressure, and lower immunity to infections. Long-term steroids weaken bones and cause fractures.

At least Mulch's vitamins could be a useful placebo. While excessive amounts of vitamins A, D, and E are dangerous, most doses don't cause problems, and we all know that placebos often work. Placebos can help even serious conditions, like depression. Humans yearn to get better.

But I let all that go while Wanda stayed home and Zane recovered from surgery and the three of us oversaw the entire practice. We worked hard and generated a bantering camaraderie.

"You should have seen this patient, Norah," Brian called out to me one night, playful. "He's nearly homeless and needs a new place to live. Don't you have a spare bedroom?"

"You should have seen this one, Brian," I shot back. I avoided the steroids. So far. "She's well-adjusted and as healthy as a horse, so obviously someone should convince her to take ten supplements."

"Hey, you two. I can't take all this sugar. Quit spouting rainbows at each other," Emily snickered. Sometimes her daughters dropped by and studied out in the waiting room, textbooks and papers spread on chairs, quizzing each other and laughing.

Because I felt bad about neglecting Emcee on those late evenings, I often ran home and brought her back with me. She wandered between us, visiting and soliciting handouts, investigating the curious scents in the hallways. Then she flopped at my feet.

Are you going to eat that pizza crust? she asked.

"Yes, of course," I said, "that's one of the best parts."

Then will you give me some cheese?

No one could resist those maple eyes, and Emcee gained a pound or two.

Of course, the med students kept coming. And now I second-guessed myself, worried that I'd been too hard on Jeremy about the online posting. By showing my temper, I hadn't reacted constructively. As much as he'd provoked me, I should not have gotten heated, which made him defensive and tense. A defensive person cannot listen well and the interaction becomes unproductive. And I worried that his contrition was insincere, just to placate me. Then I worried how suspicious I'd become and couldn't let even a good thing feel good.

Actually behaving the way we know we should is not always easy.

So I kept trying to chip away, to flake off Jeremy's smug veneer. Because apparently I needed more unattainable projects.

"What do you do for fun?" I asked him during a lull between patients. I'd grown tired of my subtlety not working and took it up a notch.

"Fun?" One eyebrow up, incredulous, like I'd asked him to fly to the moon. His blond eyebrows nearly white, invisible.

"You know. Hobbies. Sports. How do you wind down?" In a minute I might have to explain what hobbies were, define relaxation. He remained mute, so I oddly found myself supplying examples. "You know, like movies? Are you a runner?" He frowned, so I dove into the deep end. "Do you waterski? Play billiards? Knit sweaters? I know—you're a juggler!"

Jeremy laughed. Someone stop the planet. Jeremy laughed. Out loud and amused, not derisive. I felt dizzy.

Though he restrained himself quickly, a trace of smile lingered. "Dr. Waters. Can you see me *juggling*?"

He quit the "Norah" after the social media incident.

My chin raised. "Jeremy Newell, I can imagine you doing anything you want."

"Well, trust me. I don't want to juggle." Still slightly amused.

Encouraged, I pushed for more. "For all you know, you might be the world's greatest juggler, but you'll never find out because you never tried."

Jeremy retreated quickly, his cold eyes accusing. I'd hit a nerve, easy to do because he had so many exposed nerves. I'd crossed some toxic, invisible line by talking about choices and I triggered something painful. Backing off, I tilted my head toward a closed exam room door, where Jo stood waiting.

"Go on ahead," I said quietly, sad for him. "That patient's ready."

One step forward. One step back. Running in place. Maybe I'd gained an inch or two.

Every few days, I received an email from Wanda at home as she tried to reorganize her life. Brief notes, cautiously upbeat. Were we managing? Could she take off one more week? I told her to do what she needed and refused to answer when she inquired about specific patients.

Part of Wanda's problem became clear. She called too many patients on the phone, and now they expected it. She called them a lot, instead of sending a quick note or email. I mean, we all called our patients when necessary. I never let a woman wait for results on her breast biopsy—the minute that report hit my desk, I'd be on the phone, whether it was normal or abnormal. She just needed to know. Anything serious with a patient, any major shift, I'd call.

Occasionally a patient conversation took five minutes, but often ten minutes or more slipped by while you had a discussion and they remembered something new, or their symptoms changed a little, or their grandmother had worries. Phone calls could be dangerous time-drains. Emails and snail-mail letters were safer, with the added bonus that a patient would be less likely to forget the details because it stood there written in black and white. Or often a medical assistant could call the patient and briefly outline the situation until the next appointment.

If Wanda made just four or five calls a day—and she clearly made more—that would consume nearly an hour by the time she reviewed each file and counseled each patient and charted each conversation. The process took longer than the talking itself. One extra hour a day, five hours a week, twenty hours a month, two hundred forty hours a year, the equivalent of over twenty workdays a year.

Unlike lawyers who capture a small ransom for telephone advice, physicians don't get paid for phone calls. It will take a deadly plague to change the landscape, to transform virtual visits into legitimate doctor encounters worthy of reimbursement. Apparently I'm enough of a sociopath to imagine such things. I don't want a truly deadly plague, just one that's contagious and socially terrifying enough to prompt change. Maybe a plague that makes everyone go bald. A fair amount of medicine is conceptual and exams are not always necessary.

No wonder Wanda staggered under this load. Her kind and noble instincts were incompatible with sanity. She couldn't say no and buried herself in an avalanche of yes.

"Holding up okay?" Emily asked me Friday evening as we walked to our cars. A magnificent night, cool and crisp, the stars sharp. For once her red hair looked limp, her eyes tired.

"Hey, all I've got at home is a dog, not two teenagers. How about you?"

"I don't know. It hasn't been that bad—the girls take things in stride. And I like working with you. Even Brian has stepped up, which I never would have predicted. But I'm really glad Wanda will be back on Monday."

I hesitated, then pushed on. "Is it just me, or is Brian prescribing. . . ?"

"Too many steroids?" she snapped. "Damn right he is. And I told him so. I told him if I ever caught him giving one of my patients steroids for minor symptoms, he'd have hell to pay."

This was a first, me feeling I'd been too diplomatic.

Glad to have survived the ordeal, I looked forward to normalcy the next week. And as much as I enjoyed Emily, and as much as Brian did his best, I felt like I'd spent far too much time with medicine and physicians—again. I needed to branch out to save myself.

No one but Emcee knew about my escapes, how I slipped over to the shelter when I could and walked Blink. He looked for me now, gazed along his narrow collie nose and sort of nodded when I appeared, solemnly stood and waited, a slow smile. Occasionally I walked a few others while I was there. While not exactly a hobby, it was apparently the closest I could get. Occasionally I saw Owen Parker, and sometimes he walked a dog with me, too. He looked a little better these days, neater, no more stubbly beard. But his cynicism outpaced even mine, so it felt fairly destructive to talk with him.

"Save any lives today?" he asked, a flare of dark eyes.

"No, I wasn't in the mood. Maybe tomorrow."

It made him laugh, a rare moment. Then he retreated.

"Just like here—they don't make it." He turned dismal. His stories of animal abuse and neglect, of owners who couldn't or wouldn't pay for life-saving treatments disheartened me. Even when he cut the rates and offered them payment plans, sometimes they still said to put the pet down. Sometimes dogs contracted parvo because their owners didn't bother with vaccines, then couldn't afford the pricey treatment. Thus the euthanasia at his hands of healthy or potentially healthy animals. The shelter overflowed with the ones he salvaged anyway, treated at his expense.

Emcee seemed to understand my trips and appreciated the extra treats when I got home. As long as I walked her, too.

25

Mom demanded to know if I was any closer to quitting my job, any closer to living my "real life." For some reason my transition became urgent to her.

"Mom. I can't do it right now. Everything is too complicated at the practice. Besides, running off across the country is your dream, not mine."

Of course I lied because I might quit. I might not. It might take a disaster to push me over the edge; it might only take a small disappointment. Straws accumulating on the camel's back. I'd rarely felt so equivocal, so ambivalent. I knew I would go to Zane first, and I imagined weathering his predictable disappointment in me. Then the clamor from Emily and Wanda. The indifference of Mulch. But maybe I'm wrong. Maybe they would be glad to shed themselves of my gloom, maybe they would secretly celebrate. Little notes to one another. *Probably for the best.* Plans for my replacement, looking forward to someone new, more upbeat.

My mom goaded me to hook up with a sexy man and pursue wild adventures because she wanted that for herself. She didn't really care about my disillusion with medicine, or my dismay over Austin. I never told her the rest, Grace's downfall or Zane's cancer or Jeremy's arrogance. Not to mention lonely Blink or desperate Wanda, and certainly not Owen Parker, so sullen because veterinarian medicine was as bad or worse than human medicine.

When I considered that list, I wondered how I got out of bed every morning, put on my shoes.

"My dream is everyone's dream!" Mom cried. "It's patriotic!"

Next she would start singing Simon and Garfunkel, looking for America. Emcee put her head in my lap, sensing my exasperation, and I toyed with her delicate ears, scratched her neck. We sat out back and watched a full moon climb through the sky like a monarch over Earth, dappled clouds illuminating its path like spotlights. The trees stood motionless, the lawn slathered in creamy light. I wondered what living on this planet would be like without a commanding moon, that odd ethereal timepiece floating over us, marking the months and tugging the tides.

"What about your mailman?" I asked, deflecting. "If you're so up for excitement, why haven't you asked him over yet? And does he even have a name?"

Her laugh cracked, almost a cackle. Something happens to our voices with age; the fragile vocal cords turn brittle and stiff. The elasticity deteriorates. I imagined my tissues drying up, creaking and frail, and felt more depressed.

"I like calling him The Mailman, with caps," she said. "You know, like The Highwayman. It's more romantic than a real name."

"I bet a million dollars that you know his real name." She never let a fact like that escape her. For sure by now she had searched him out and knew his shoe size and what car he drove. Her affinity for details was a signature trait. It's what made her so good at anatomy, and I inherited some of it.

"Yes, I do." A little miffed, a little hesitant. Something else there, too. "His name is Archibald Prendergast. So you can see why I prefer The Mailman."

"Well, why haven't you asked him in?"

A long silence. I finally grasped it.

"Oh my god," I exclaimed, startling Emcee. "You have, haven't you?"

"Maybe." The word drawn out. I swear, I could hear her smile.

"What happened?"

"He came in, of course. All the way in, if you know what I mean."

"Ew, Mom. Please. Those are not details I want to think about."

"Good grief, Norah, get a grip. You're a doctor. And the details you should be asking me are all the important medical questions, like whether I used protection."

"Ew, Mom. Stop. Daughters don't want to hear this stuff."

Now I comprehended her vision. She wanted to escape with this man, her new fling. Leave staid, groomed Sun City with its pristine pebble yards and grids, embark on exciting journeys again, go somewhere akin to Woodstock or Burning Man. Make her life messy again, unpredictable. Trying to persuade me, she wanted to convince herself.

"Oh, grow up," she said. "And I did, just so you know. Use protection. Any man who's not willing to put a rubber raincoat on it can go find someone else."

I ignore a lot. "So why don't you run off with him? Quit obsessing about me and what I do."

"Uh huh. So now you're trying to get rid of me." Sounding irked.

"Oh, please. I offer to come visit you all the time, but you're usually too busy."

"Not true! I love it when you drive out. Why don't you, this Sunday?"

I thought a minute, but I had no plans. Besides, even though we talked all the time, I hadn't seen her in a while. And although she was perfectly capable of driving to see me, it felt safer for me to do the traveling.

"Sure, Sunday would be good. Shall I bring Emcee?" I asked. The dog loved road trips.

"No, wait. The Mailman and I talked about having a picnic in the park. Champagne, strawberries, all the romantic jazz. Let me check with him first and see what he's thinking."

Typical.

After we disconnected, I listened to the mockingbird, not quite so loud because he clung to the eucalyptus tree out front, and I sat in the back with palm trees and the moon. I rested my head and tried counting his songs, wondered how many tunes that mockingbird had stolen from other birds and claimed for himself. After a dozen it got confusing and I gave up, putting my mind back on Mom.

Her life had turned into a geriatric love romp. Meanwhile I had Emcee, and some days I had Blink. For right now, that felt good enough.

I sensed that the day approached, though, when I might crave more than dogs in my life.

Thanks again, Mom.

26

On Monday at noon, the last person I expected to find waiting in my office was Zane Grayson.

"Norah." A big bear hug. He'd lost weight and his skin seemed oddly transparent, like an infant. As if he had been reborn, but as a more frail, damaged version of himself. I heard a faint synthetic crackle from his colostomy bag and tried not to look at his belly. Then I caught myself sniffing for fecal odor and felt ashamed.

He reported getting better every day.

"Are you coming back?" I asked with mixed feelings. I both dearly wanted him there and I dearly hoped he would retire, for his own sake. But what did that mean, for his own sake? Forced relaxation? Maybe he would be happier working. Not my call.

Many physicians struggle with retiring, when to stop. If they're not practicing medicine, they don't know who they are. Where to go, what to do. I saw them in the hospital doctor lounge, old men shambling and slightly disheveled, in worn blazers that no longer fit. Still coming in for grand rounds, listening to cases, craning to hear and nodding to themselves. They seemed lost vessels, trying to rig their sails in a changing sea. I suspected they needed to find something else to love besides medicine.

At one time, I imagined that would be me, still practicing until an advanced age, working on and on until I collapsed and they pried my stethoscope from my cold dead hand. Now I couldn't be done fast enough.

"Maybe I'll come back. Maybe not." Zane dropped into the chair, a heap strangely without form. The human body devolves quickly when inactive, loses muscle and shape. "I can't quite pull the trigger either way."

"You probably just need more time." It sounded lame even to me. Step up, Norah, I commanded myself, and say something meaningful. My brain stood aside, oddly helpless.

"Time." He held my eyes a long while, but it didn't feel uncomfortable. Almost as if we communed that way. His eyes a little watery, making me think of blue oceans. He blinked and went on. "Time keeps shifting. I keep getting focused on what's happening this second. Like when a tree drops a leaf, or a lizard zigzags through my yard. This morning I drove past a little lake, a golf course pond. . .a duck glided across it, leaving a perfect ripple, a perfect trail through the smooth water. Water like glass, a mirror, all green and gold. I pulled my car over and stopped to watch, like it was the most beautiful thing I'd ever seen."

I sat speechless. Impossible to reply to that. Then he laughed, slapped his thigh.

"I'm losing it, right? But that's not why I'm here. I came by to see what little money is coming in for me these days. Of course, I haven't been seeing patients, so I'm not getting much now except what's already been billed. I'll try not to rile up Nellie and Betsy too much. But I never thought I'd have to worry about this practice, not like this. I don't mean me so much, but the rest of you. It's keeping me up some nights, to be honest."

"How does everyone feel about having Wanda's husband look at the numbers?" I knew Zane had been discussing it with each partner.

"We'll probably do it. Dale seems solid, seems ethical. And no one wants to pay a fortune to a stranger. It'll take a while."

"Good." I felt relieved. The budget nagged me like a bad tooth-ache, and not the kind that faded away on its own. The kind that made it hard to concentrate, impossible to relax. We needed a financial dentist.

He squinted at me. "And we had a bargain, you know. You and me. I held up my end, since I seem to be alive."

"Zane. I've barely had time to think, what with both you and Wanda out. Surely you have better things to do than worry about my mammogram."

"Nope. Turns out that I don't." He leaned back in the chair and smiled.

An awkward silence while I glowered. "All right, I promise. But quit pestering me. You're being inappropriate."

"Sometimes you have to be a little inappropriate to get things done. Sometimes I relish that."

"Maybe you should keep practicing, then. You don't sound ready to stop."

He looked thoughtful. "Why do we call it practicing? That makes it sound like we don't know what we're doing. Like we don't have it right, so we have to keep practicing. Like we're rehearsing. It's kind of insulting. Both to us, and to the patients. It makes us seem incompetent and makes them sound like guinea pigs."

I laughed. "What should we say, then? That we're *performing* medicine? That we've got it nailed, like some gymnastic feat? That we've learned how to stick the landing?"

"That's a good one. It sure feels like gymnastics some days." His face amused. "But I think we know better than that. No one ever gets it perfect. Maybe now and then, but not often." Then his expression turned serious. "Hey. Are you still getting those cranky cards on your windshield? Or has that stopped now that I'm not around? I started wondering if it was some family member of one of my patients. You know, someone who didn't like how I treated their mom. Or grandma."

I winced. "No, they're still coming. And now Betsy's getting them, too. Always the same, white index cards with black borders. Thick cursive writing."

One for Betsy this week: *Get a new job*.

Two for me: *Another day, another mistake* and *Snake oil salesman*.

That last one ticked me off. I'm not a man, and that snake oil message should obviously have gone to Brian Mulch. I'd been collecting the cards and handed the stack to Zane.

"Did Nellie put up a security camera? We talked about that." Zane shuffled through them, his mouth twisted. "No actual threats, though. Just insults."

"Yeah, she had the camera put up." Discomfort washed through me. Truthfully, I'd been too busy and preoccupied to manage this and left it to Nellie. Maybe I took my cues from the younger docs, Emily and Wanda and Brian, who were more used to trolling, more used to nasty social media. They paid less heed when I asked for their reactions. Now I worried that I hadn't given it enough attention. "Then later on Nellie found a piece of duct tape on it, blocking the lens."

Zane scowled. "I don't like this at all. The cop I talked to suggested we hire a private detective. Do you think we should?"

I had no idea. A stakeout in our mundane little parking lot? I imagined surveillance cars and men in trench coats with low fedoras and shifty eyes. Probably we'd find an adolescent who had been refused a narcotic prescription. The audacious deeds were likely already posted online with daring selfies. "Maybe we could try putting the camera somewhere else? Where it can't be reached?"

Zane handed back the cards. I flipped through them, haphazardly noting the dark ink, the left-slanted words. A few odd letters, the tightly tied Os I'd seen before. Most of the Os were actually double-looped, a small o inside the bigger O, which looked quite peculiar.

"I'll talk to Nellie." He left then, with a chary glare. "Keep your promises, Norah."

So I did it and saw my doctor, however grudging and ungracious I may have been. People seriously needed to leave me alone. First my elderly mother and now my senior partner, trying to micromanage my life and tell me what to do, where to go. What the hell kind of vibe was I giving off now? I think I liked it better when everyone thought I was suicidal.

Mammograms must have been conceived by a sadist. I followed the minimum guidelines, every two years, but it approached three years. The most recent Pap rules said every five years if your Paps had been normal, but probably six years had passed. And the colonoscopy? Hadn't done it yet. I didn't have time for that.

"You look familiar, but I can't quite place you." Helen Hensley, my personal family physician, is a sarcastic woman. Tall, with short coffee-brown hair, many years my junior. Friendly, but no nonsense. I loved her and her practical approach; never mind that she was one of my students long ago in that downtown clinic. I knew quality when I saw it.

"Very funny," I replied. "I didn't realize you were a comedian now."

"Only when indicated. You know us family docs, we have to stay nimble."

I could view her laptop well enough to see her ordering the mammogram and a referral to the gastroenterologist for my colonoscopy. Sitting there in my birthday suit, with only a light cotton gown, I grew cold.

"We can be fast," I said, "because it's about thirty degrees in here.

And I'm sure you have more urgent things to do than chat with me about how healthy I am." Not to mention that I had about a million better things to do. Fortunately, even though she didn't see me often, Helen coolly handled my cranky attitude.

She made her exam thorough but quick—we were fairly like-minded. I never mind the breast exam, but no woman embraces a Pap. At least speculums have come a long way, being disposable plastic now instead of cold hard metal. Those old metal speculums were gathered up and sterilized at the end of the day, to be used again, over and over. Gross. I'm all for eliminating most plastics in our daily lives, but the speculums can stay. Why human evolution kept the cervix hidden so far up inside the vagina is anyone's guess, especially considering how vulnerable the male genitals are. I mean, they just hang there in the breeze. It's beyond me how men even walk around with all that dangling stuff. That they can ride horses is quite a feat.

Once I dressed, Helen handed me the mammo slip and the gastroenterology referral.

"Don't put these off," she instructed sternly. "You're a little late on the mammogram, which is bad enough, but you've never been screened for colon cancer. That should have been done eight years ago, when you turned fifty."

"Right."

I must have sounded indifferent, because she opened a drawer and pulled out a test kit for guaiac, which checks for blood in the bowels.

"Here." Helen handed it to me. "I don't trust you to schedule the scope."

I actually felt relieved. Even though it's a nuisance and disgusting to collect a stool sample, it only takes a few minutes and I can do it in the privacy of my own bathroom. Getting a colonoscopy involves an aggravating, diarrhea-inducing prep that keeps you up all night, and necessitates taking a day off work. You have to be sedated so the doctor can slide a thick scope up your colon without sending you through the ceiling. Then, because of the sedation, you can't drive yourself home, and you spend the rest of the day in a bloated fog.

The only good thing about a colonoscopy is that it's done only every ten years, and the stool test should be performed annually.

But I'll stick with that. If I take a day off, it will be for something way better than scoping my colon.

I endured the mammogram. Even though technology has improved and radiologists can now better see all sorts of blips and fuzzy blops that might mean cancer, the method still involves standing half-naked in an arctic room while two cold heavy plates squash your breasts as flat as possible, one then the other. My breasts are ample-sized and I used to be curvy, so flattening them out enough for a good look is painful. And I think I'm seeing more droop these days, which doesn't help. Since I passed fifty, everything started changing. My waist has thickened and the curves of my torso are less like a hourglass and more like a glass.

I admitted to myself, though, that I felt better after checking off those preventive duties. It's stupid not to take care of yourself, not to undergo a few simple tests to catch cancer early and save your life. Otherwise what a waste.

When I completed all my tasks and got normal reports, I sent Zane a small note.

Obligations fulfilled. You can get off my back.

He knew I was kidding. I'd do anything for that man.

27

I'm not inherently against office birthday parties. . .I just worry that they're fodder for discontent. If that seems too melodramatic, you haven't worked in an office with complex hierarchies and way too many egos and drama. The perception that perhaps one person got a better cake, or a more-clever present, or a bigger bunch of balloons, can derail the best intentions. Never blatant, never given voice, bearing a wounded heat that rarely rises above a simmer, these microhurts still cause pain. But eliminating the parties seemed even worse, so there they were.

I came up with the idea for Betsy's little gift the week before. When I left the parking lot at dusk, Betsy leaned dejectedly against her faded brown Pinto, her lunchbox resting on the hood.

"Do you need help?" I offered, lowering my car window.

Betsy startled, obviously lost in thought. Her head swiveled, glancing around nervously. She looked at her watch and her teeth caught her lip. "Oh no, Dr. Waters. My car won't start again. That's all. I'm just waiting for Dickie. My husband."

I realized I'd never heard his name before. "Will you need a tow truck?"

"No." She turned and looked up the street, anxious. "Dickie has a friend who'll come fix it tomorrow. Or the next day. Is it in the way?"

"Not at all. I just feel bad for you, waiting out here. Is he coming soon? Can I give you ride?" Every now and then I remember to behave nicely. And Betsy did seem forlorn.

Her eyes widened, almost panicked. "That's very generous, Dr. Waters. But you should go. He's almost here. Really."

Clearly she wanted me gone, so I went off. More drama, I thought sourly. I tried to imagine what she didn't want me to see. An ugly husband? Maybe he had no front teeth. Maybe he drove a half-wrecked car, dented and scraped, the windshield cracked, a bumper missing. I'd never met him. . .no one had. Now I felt curious and wondered how I might casually ask to see a photo. Sometimes I truly dislike my human side and I quickly vowed to never ask such a thing.

And talk about timing. That week Zane managed to garner a white card during his one afternoon visit: *Bungling Old Docs Should Leave.*

Women are more wary than men, predisposed to watch for threats, to worry about their safety, and for good reasons. My latest card directed me to *Go Back to the Kitchen.* So this person knew I was female, likely did know our cars. What else did they know? Where I lived? Betsy's recent note said simply *Incompetent.* When I prompted her to talk about it, how it made her feel, she whispered "horrible" and looked away and wouldn't say more. I tried to reassure her but likely failed. She scurried away as fast as she could.

"Is your husband upset about the cards?" I asked later that day. Dickie. How appropriate.

Silent, Betsy stared at me like I'd grown an extra head.

"Dickie, right?" I prompted.

"Oh, Dr. Waters. He's always upset anyway. About pretty much everything. That's nothing new." She smiled, somewhat inappropriately considering what she revealed. Which made me suddenly concerned in a new way.

"Betsy." I peered around quickly to make certain no one overheard. "Is everything all right? He doesn't he harm you, does he?"

Her face shocked. Offended. "Dr. Waters, what a terrible question. Of course not." Then she looked at the floor, then the ceiling, then down the hall. "Don't you worry, everything is fine."

"I'm so sorry. I'm not prying. I just—"

"I'm sure you have more important things to concern yourself with." She straightened and tossed me a proud look, then abruptly turned and stalked off.

Her outrage seemed staged. I vowed to stay alert.

Anyway. We celebrated her birthday at noon with pizza and a nice bakery cake. Jeremy happened to be there and he sat in the background, happy enough to eat some pizza but otherwise not engaged, studying a medical journal balanced on his thigh. He didn't look up when we sang Happy Birthday, so I sat down beside him and tapped his shoulder.

"You should say something to Betsy," I murmured.

"Excuse me?" he said too loudly, sidetracked from his article and frowning at me.

I gave him a stern look and inclined my head toward her. "You know. Tell her happy birthday."

That familiar critical squint.

"To be nice," I explained, since apparently I needed to. Perhaps he'd been partly raised by wolves. My heart sank as I sensed the enormity of this Jeremy project, the likelihood of failure. I kept wanting to regain that fleeting moment of lightness we had about juggling.

Jeremy slowly rose and set the journal on his chair. Wiped his mouth with a napkin. Walked almost sullenly over to Betsy and waited for her to notice him. Pleased with her small party, Betsy turned his way with a smile.

"Happy birthday." Jeremy's words monotone, painful.

"Why, thank you!" Betsy beamed, oblivious to his funk. She reached over and handed him a slice of cake on a paper plate.

Jeremy accepted it silently and returned to his chair, took up the journal and sat. He cast me a suffering glance and resumed reading as he picked at the cake with a plastic fork.

I knew I should give up because Jeremy seemed a lost cause. Then I remembered Grace. Then I remembered what Clarence Darrow said, nearly a century ago. I became a fan of Darrow after my brother Ben and I read the play *Inherit the Wind* when I was about nine, him thirteen. I mean, we were defending science—you couldn't get much better than that as far as Ben and I were concerned. We took turns with the voices and created magnificent drama and performed parts for Mom. She even praised us.

Lost causes are the only ones worth fighting for, Darrow said. I watched Jeremy not look up at a funny joke as lively laughter ran around the room. My lost cause.

Zane gave Betsy the present that I suggested—and he mentioned it was my idea—an Uber gift card for when her pitiful car stranded her again. A modest amount, in keeping with the usual parameters so no one else felt slighted. Her mouth fell open as she grasped what it meant and she stared over at me, apparently dumbfounded. I admit our relationship had never been exactly cozy, but come on. I'm not a monster. Then her eyes filled and two fat tears rolled down her face. It felt kind of uncomfortable. Her breath stuck and a sob escaped and she ran to the bathroom.

A clumsy silence ensued until Wanda started chattering and Emily told a story and Nellie began picking up to prepare for the afternoon. Wanda slipped out to go find Betsy and check on her. Jo and the MAs had been deep in conversation about a troublesome patient and never saw it happen.

Jeremy read through the whole event, running his finger down the text so our distractions didn't make him lose his place.

Perhaps I should just let him skate, do the minimal, pass the rotation with mediocre marks. I would detail my concerns soon at the midterm evaluation and maybe he would try to improve. Maybe not. I fretted how to present my thoughts in a way which might convince him that patient engagement, that seeing the whole picture, would help him be a better doctor, whether he became a neurosurgeon or anything else. I had been coaching him as we went along, told him where he came up lacking and where I expected more effort, so he shouldn't be surprised by my feedback. Still, his bland performance, as disconcerting as it felt, did not warrant a failing grade. We would likely keep muddling along.

I didn't know it yet, but a bigger doom already marched toward us.

The fact that I kept overhearing his interactions with George didn't help. I didn't mean to eavesdrop. Maybe my hearing is abnormally sharp, maybe I'm easily distracted. Maybe I'm nosy.

Jeremy was about to leave the clinic as George arrived for the afternoon. Usually they spoke minimally to one another, but for some reason Jeremy lingered and started needling George. They didn't notice me in the lab taking inventory. Or maybe Jeremy knew I was there and didn't care, just as likely. I could see them at the edge of my vision.

"Seeing any hot girlfriends this weekend?" Jeremy asked George, leaning against him, prodding him with a finger.

George opened a laptop and logged in, glanced up briefly. "Nope."

I happened to know that George just started dating a fellow classmate, cautiously excited about it because he really enjoyed her company.

"Or maybe you just like guys." I could actually hear the sneer on Jeremy's face.

"So what if I did?" George glared at him now.

"Oh sure, that's fine, nothing wrong with that." Jeremy chuckled. "Might explain a few things."

George wearily swiveled back to him when he didn't leave. "How about you?"

"What about me?" Jeremy snipped.

"Your love life. Any romantic plans?" George almost sounded clinical, rote, like he was interviewing a patient he didn't like.

"What's it to you?"

"I'm just making conversation," George replied mildly. "Like people do. You know, you say one thing and then I answer, then I say another thing and you—"

"Geez, Clark." Jeremy interrupted. "And no, I don't do romance these days. I don't have time for that. Just some quickies, nothing serious and no commitment. Helps with stress. You should try it."

"Right. But no thanks." George bent back over the laptop and said nothing, so Jeremy finally left.

Clarence Darrow or not, lost causes or not, something shifted inside me away from Jeremy, a seismic clunk. We can rebuild a home destroyed by an earthquake, but we can't put the fault line back in place once it moves too far. For the first time, I felt something alter, some irreversible change with Jeremy. I quickly smothered that unstable sensation, refused to believe it.

And maybe my emotions should have gone other places, but I felt quite pleased that George could take care of himself.

28

A few weeks went by. I had talked a little with Betsy but not as much as I'd wanted, despite my best intentions to stay in tune. I went to her desk because I needed a yellow marker for an article I wanted Jeremy to read, all about doctor-patient relationships and lawsuits. Maybe I could appeal to his practical, defensive side. He would never read the entire study, so I wanted to highlight the most salient points. This author encouraged the physician to maintain eye contact, to show an approachable demeanor, and to always ask about any concerns. If Jeremy saw this advice from someone besides me, he might believe it more. The fact is that a patient who likes you, who thinks you care about them, is much less likely to sue even if you screw up.

I waited for Betsy to get off the phone because I didn't know where she kept the yellow highlighters. A messy little pile of notes caught my eye. As if she'd been sorting them, a mix of phone messages, patient comments, reminders, and a memo from Nellie. Then I suddenly flinched when I saw a short sentence written in blue ballpoint pen. A sentence bearing three letter Os with double-looped knots.

Betsy hung up as I stabbed the note with my finger. Upside down to me, a little hard to read, I craned my neck. *Don't you forget.*

"What's that?" I exclaimed. "Who wrote that?"

"Um." Betsy glanced at me with concern, like I'd finally jumped off the deep end. She carefully picked up the note and cocked her head—her ribbons of silky hair fell forward and she looked like a spaniel. She shrugged. "I have no idea."

"You don't know what it means? Why it says that?" My voice more strident than intended. But those letters were unmistakable, those odd-coiled Os like on the windshield cards.

Betsy gazed at me guardedly then away, as if wondering who to call for help.

"No, Dr. Waters. I don't even know how that got there. Where it came from. There's no name on it." Her words slow and hesitant. Maybe how you speak to someone who's deranged. She took a long look at the note, turned it over and back and shrugged again, then proceeded to carefully crumple and wad it up into a tiny, wrinkled ball, which she dropped from her fingertips into the wastebasket.

She finally looked back at me and smiled. "Weird, huh?"

Not as weird as you, I wanted to say. Why not just throw the paper away without all the production? Nonplussed, I returned to my office and resisted the impulse to hurry back and snatch that little wad from the trash, to study it again.

You're losing it, I told myself. There must be hundreds of people who made their Os like that. Millions. I scribbled a few sentences on a notepad and scrutinized my Os. Just one loop. I told myself sternly to move on or I would drive myself crazy, dissecting everyone's writing.

My participation in the admissions committee reeled along.

I felt bad about Peter Calloway, the radiologist who asked us to join him for dinner that day, which seemed so long ago. He probably craved socialization, working in his dim cubicle, stuck in the dark chilled cave of the hospital basement and staring for hours at hundreds of stark images on film. Radiology departments usually get sequestered below ground, windowless, to better contain the radiation and to eliminate distracting daylight. When you enter those areas you feel some trepidation, passing through tightly sealed doors with black-and-yellow hazard labels, those deadly triangular wheels of radiation warnings, and you can't help but think of Chernobyl.

Or maybe that's just me and my rampant imagination. Maybe I never should have read *On the Beach* with Ben back in those days. After that book, he and I spent a few months devising plans for what we would do if a nuclear apocalypse came breathing down our necks. . .whether to perform good deeds or throw caution aside and recklessly start skydiving. Then, seeking some warped sense of balance, we read *Hiroshima*. I was around eight years old. No wonder my father disapproved of our literature choices. Mom called us enlightened. Dad came and went in between Mom's boyfriends, absent-mindedly affectionate to us, paying most of the bills. I'm not sure how to categorize their relationship, but it worked for them. Twenty years older than she, he died long ago. I missed him, but not like a usual daughter-father connection. More like a favorite uncle.

At any rate, I had originally offered to dine with Calloway the next time the committee met. But then it didn't happen because his partner got sick and Calloway had to return to work that night.

Calloway projected a relaxed vibe, definitely geeky but not awkward like George Clark. More like technical, contemplative. His thick ginger-brown hair dropped down a little ragged, a little wiry, his fair complexion peppered with freckles. A few of those freckles even sprinkled his lips, sort of cute. An Irishman for sure, with the first threads of silver in his hair but hard to see unless you looked for it. No wedding ring. Although he seemed to appreciate my occasional acerbic comment, quick to smile, he never made such statements himself. Evidently a genuinely nice guy, though not saccharine like the internist, who reminded me of Wanda Cunningham. Those two women acted fond of pretty much every person on the planet, would give any soul the shirts off their backs. They wished the whole world too much goodwill to suit me—you know not everyone deserves it.

Then when I covered for Wanda, I missed the following admissions meeting altogether. I still fulfilled my duties and assessed my fifteen applicants. I emailed my ratings to the group, my yes/no/maybes, but sent regrets about not attending in person. I couldn't make it because no one has figured out how to cram thirty hours into one day. Most responded with a little note.

FROM THE INTERNIST: *Oh, sorry you can't be there! We'll miss you so much. Hope you have a good day.*

FROM THE PSYCHIATRIST: *Take care of yourself, too.*

FROM THE COUNTY NURSE: *It's always something, isn't it?*

FROM THE ENT SURGEON CARTER BILLINGS: nothing.

FROM PETER CALLOWAY: *The things people do to get out of a dinner. . .*

Calloway's note made me laugh, and he clearly still wanted that meal. Whether that meant with the group, or just with me, wasn't certain. I felt a mild current stirring there, for he did look at me quite a bit, in a pensive sort of way. I mean, so did the psychiatrist but he scrutinized everyone, methodical and clinical. As if he planned to write a book about the mental disorders of physicians. He'd have to create a pretty thick tome, but I would read it for sure and hopefully learn something about myself.

I couldn't decide what to do if Calloway asked for more, because this felt like a first date. Starting over seemed inevitable, but also depressing. Not exciting, like it used to be. Maybe a point comes, a certain age or a certain number of abandoned relationships, when it's time to slow down or stop. When you give up. Like a menopausal uterus, time to close up shop. If my mother taught me anything, it was that I did not need a man to complete me. Which felt ironic now, since she'd gone misty over The Mailman. I also knew she'd kick him to the curb if he crossed her. I can't recall when she ever gave a man a second chance. Unlike me, regrets never plagued her.

This committee session presented the usual thought-provoking applicants. We finally agreed on nearly everyone except the last two. I wanted Melanie Hernandez, a dedicated young woman whose volunteer efforts filled pages, mountains of work at youth detention centers, an advocate for teens in juvenile court. She nailed the interviews, and her warm personal statement made me want to adopt her. Her pedestrian grade-point average held her back a bit, along with a non-outstanding MCAT score. A decent score, just not dazzling.

We toggled between her and Josiah White, a young man with similar grades and scores who amassed hundreds of volunteer hours with his church youth group. Except the hours he spent mostly consisted of "bonding" and "sharing" by playing basketball and organizing complicated fundraisers to build a new basketball facility—for the church and its members, not for the community. He raised tens of thousands of dollars, no small feat. He also spent a month on a proselytizing mission to a downtrodden bush community in east Asia, though I don't remember exactly where. Not the point.

I didn't see how the discussion was even close. Which meant Carter Billings did.

"You must have liked his personal statement," Carter insisted, pushing at me. "I thought his analogy of life as a basketball game was inspired."

"His whole application seems very basketbally," I observed. "A pretty limited focus. And don't you think he went a bit too far when he implied that Jesus played point guard for him?"

"It's a metaphor, Norah. Do you have something against religious applicants?" Everything about Carter looked sparse: thinning hair, rimless eyeglasses, small ears, minimal lips. A narrow neck.

He scowled at me and the psychiatrist perked up. The internist looked stressed at our exchange. The county nurse rolled her eyes and Calloway appeared thoughtful, unreadable.

"Of course not," I said slowly, choosing my words. "I don't care what religion a person follows. But his volunteer efforts feel self-serving."

"Oh, come on." Carter slapped the table, making everyone jump. "He spent a month in a jungle, eating monkey meat and fried beetles—that's a little more challenging than a county courthouse. That's dedication to an impressive degree."

My eyes narrowed and my jaw clenched, not my best look. Everyone stared at me, waiting.

"He went there to convince them to change their culture," I said. "To abandon their own religion. Not exactly a mission of mercy."

"Maybe he would call it that." Carter crossed his arms. "Does it really matter? Or does it just matter that he's a well-meaning person, a good soul, wanting to make the world a better place? We can always use people willing to make sacrifices. That's what good doctors do."

My blood pressure rose about forty points. "Good doctors are also tolerant and humble. He thinks his god chose him for medicine. He said so during his interviews. Four or five times."

Carter huffed. "So what? He's dedicated because he thinks like that. And who are we to say he isn't right?"

Time to shut my mouth. Or to nicely offer up neutralizing words, like *we'll just have to agree to disagree*. But Carter felt like a bully and I thought of George, taking Jeremy's abuse.

"Then maybe his god should have given him better study habits so he'd get better grades." I wish I could say I regretted that, and I guessed I probably would before long.

Everyone startled me by laughing. Even Carter. As if I'd made a good joke. A group wisdom must have taken over, diffusing the argument. The only one not laughing was me.

It goes back to brother Ben. A surprising array of my feelings all go back to Ben.

He grappled with the idea of deity, of why he'd been singled out for punishment with his cystic fibrosis. Because of his warm, considerate personality, Ben rarely complained or bemoaned his fate. Stoic, he suffered in silence. He never deserved the living hell of chronic dyspnea, that sterile medical word for breathlessness.

First our father, then our mother, tried on religion as comfort. Ben gamely wore it for a while, talked about higher purposes and salvation. But it never really made sense, never really fit, and eventually the effort faded. A few people attempted that solace at his funeral wake, but I turned away from their mysterious ways. I couldn't even watch sports when athletes offered prayers just to win a worthless damn game that no one remembered a few days later. What kind of god cared about that and let a sweet, generous young man die?

So no, I didn't laugh. I perhaps marshalled a crooked smile.

As always, we voted. Both Melanie Hernandez and Josiah White landed in the "maybe" pile, waiting to see if anyone more impressive came along. I just felt down. I really should not let Ben show up in my head during daylight.

"How about that dinner?" Peter Calloway stood beside me. He looked wary, as he should, but he spoke only to me and didn't even glance at anyone else.

"Sure, sounds good," I lied. I wanted to go home and hug Emcee, not make small talk. But it was early enough and I'd promised. I could do it; I'd done worse.

We walked down the hallway together and here came Dr. Angelo Candore, the assistant dean who asked me to take on Jeremy.

"Hello, Norah. So good to see you," he exuded, smiling too big. A shift of his eyes, back and forth between Peter and me. "How's that Jeremy Newell working out?"

Candore meant well. He had a difficult job, keeping students and attending physicians happy with each other. That meant dealing with egos and obsessive personalities, with people who were often stressed and tired. He brokered objections and passed along compliments, balanced on a slender line between demands. I wouldn't take his job for a million dollars.

"Give me just a minute," I said to Calloway, turning to Candore.

His insincere smile seemed off base. "Why are you asking? Did Jeremy complain about me?"

"No. Of course not." The way he said that made me doubt him, an odd twitch in his neck and another glance at Peter, but he moved on. "It's just nearly time for midterm reports. So when I saw you, I thought I'd get it straight from the source. I worry about him."

"Worry? That's interesting." My radar pinged. "I thought you said he was a brilliant student, no problems. That his first attending was the problem. You said he'd be an easy ride."

Candore's face fell and he looked again at Peter, as if he might need bailing out. As if another man might understand, which ticked me off. "Well. I don't remember exactly what we discussed. It's been months."

Peter leaned forward, listening closely.

This was partly my fault, but only partly. I blamed myself that I hadn't asked more questions when Candore first called. Maybe he did try to tell me and I didn't get it, too thick-headed, too quick to criticize other physicians. Maybe I really was too bitchy for my own good and it served me right. But Candore presented Jeremy as the innocent piece of that equation, I was quite certain.

"Are you saying that Jeremy made problems for his original preceptor?" I asked bluntly. A perilous heat climbed inside me. "Is that really why you moved him?"

"Well, he—"

"Because he's one of the least compassionate students I've known." I lowered my voice and looked around. My mind teetered on an edge, a treacherous place, crowded with images of Jeremy's patronizing face. I saw Peter's eyes go flinty, his hands clasped together. "If you knew Jeremy had issues, you should have prepared me. Given me some word of caution, what to watch for. Any hint would have helped."

"Some things are confidential." A stern face from Candore, as if I should appreciate that. "We can't just go gossiping about—"

"Gossiping? We're colleagues, Angelo, discussing a student under our tutelage. That's called evaluation, not gossip. What happened with the first preceptor? You need to tell me." For the second time that afternoon I felt my blood pressure soar. At this rate, I'd have a stroke before we got to dinner.

Candore tucked his tie in his shirt as if preparing for a procedure, finally met my eyes. "Jeremy was just a bit indiscreet."

"Was it online, on social media? About a patient?" I felt incredulous that Jeremy might have done this before. He had acted so unaware, so contrite, when I called him on it. I believed him, which made me feel duped. And stupid.

"No, no, of course not. Not a patient—they all know better than that. Trust me, we cover patient confidentiality a great deal. But it was about the preceptor, his attending, online. I guess that first attending vented to Jeremy about his ex-wife. Then Jeremy poked at him a tiny bit in his post, about his personal life. His divorce. Of course, Jeremy never thought it would get back to the attending. He was remarkably naïve."

Until this moment, I'd planned not to rat on Jeremy about the incident with my patient. We all make mistakes, and he'd apologized nicely, although that was apparently an act. Something cracked inside me, something not pretty.

Candore had big soft eyes and reminded me of Emcee when she's in trouble, and now he pleaded. "I shouldn't have told you that, not at all. That was completely confidential. Very private. These incidents are not for discussion. Please forget I mentioned it. Please."

"This is very disturbing. I'm not certain I can keep working with him now. I've lost my objectivity . . . I don't feel I can trust him in my practice." I forced down my anger, not really succeeding. Even Candore's plea felt calculated. Quietly fuming, I explained about my patient with the rash. "Set up a meeting with him, right away. Don't worry, I'll write this all down and I'll be there to discuss it."

"Over just one incident? Surely—"

"He's got more problems than deceit and lack of compassion. As if that isn't enough. He also can't multi-task, and he's not thorough. I have to give him simple cases. His ability to apply practical knowledge seems below average. I've talked with him about this, ways to improve, what to read, how to present his cases, and he doesn't try. And I've seen him browbeat George Clark. He's a bully."

"Norah. Surely we can—" Candore started to reach for me, to touch my shoulder or something, then thought better of it. His hand hung oddly in the air a moment, then he rubbed his jaw.

"Set up a meeting," I repeated. "I'll talk with him honestly and I'll give him a chance—I really will—but you need to be there and you will probably need to find him another preceptor. It's extremely unlikely I can continue."

Candore grimaced. "Let me check my calendar. I'm afraid I'm leaving on vacation in two days. Could you possibly put up with him for one more week?"

I can't even imagine my face, when Calloway suddenly stepped in. He hooked my arm.

"I'm so sorry, Angelo," Peter said firmly, "but we're quite late for dinner. We really must go. Can you two talk about this tomorrow?"

"Of course," Candore sputtered.

"Thanks. That okay with you, Norah?" Peter so pleasant, drawing me gently down the hall. We were already ten feet away.

I resisted, hanging back, more to say. I started to glare at Peter, but then I recognized something wise in his carefully calm expression, and I nodded as we hurried off.

29

We pushed out through the big glass doors of the medical school into an exquisite evening.

In October, the desert recalls it has seasons and wakes up. As if suddenly remembering those days when the sun retreats and stops beating the land with its fiery sledgehammer. The nights sigh with relief and people emerge cautiously from their dens, feel the fresh breeze. After the long cruel summer, it's magical.

Peter Calloway and I strode a block away and stopped. The soft air helped; you'd have to be dead not to notice the sweet twilight.

He turned to me, his troubled eyes direct. "I probably shouldn't have done that. I can be too impulsive and that was not my best moment. If I came across as demeaning, I apologize very much. Obviously, you can handle yourself. I was just afraid that I couldn't handle me."

That threw me. "What?"

"I've never liked that guy. He's slippery. You can't constantly play both ends against the middle. It's like he has no standards, just makes it up as he goes, no matter what he says." Peter's eyes cut to the heavy street traffic, the congestion and rumble of early rush hour. He gestured ahead and started walking. "Come on."

We ducked into a Mexican restaurant, a quiet retreat. Dim lighting, candles in purple jars, guitar music. Quite a charming place.

"Peter," I began as we sat in a booth. I temporarily sidelined my messy day. Peter Calloway was impulsive? This guy, who wore composure like a cloak? "What did—"

"Wait." He held up his fingers. "First things first. This place makes exceptional margaritas. . .you want one?"

"After today? Absolutely."

He held off talking much until the drinks came, that tangy tickle of lime and tequila, the sharp salt. I sighed, lost for a moment. Maybe I'd changed with age and was simply no longer cut out for this work, my tolerance gone. Flexibility, gone. I'd seen too much of medicine's dark side, too much of peoples' failings. And now I had to meet with Candore and Jeremy. That ugly dread flooded me so I took another gulp of my drink and looked up, found his eyes on me.

"Explain yourself," I said.

He fiddled with his glass, wiped at wet rings on the table. His hair more brown than red in that light, the freckles faint. Comfortable crows' feet crinkled by his eyes.

"It's kind of embarrassing. I doubt I know you well enough. . .this might shut the door for ever seeing you again." He made a funny face, uncertain.

"Okay," I conceded. "Let's do this. Tell me about yourself, then you can ask for something humiliating or revealing about me. That's fair, right?"

"Deal." He laughed. He looked down to gather himself, then his eyes leapt up. "You see, I've had a terrible temper all my life, starting when I was a boy. You can't imagine the profanity I could fling! Because of that, as a kid, I spent lots of time in my room. Which, by the way, was not punishment because that's where all my books were."

"Ha," I agreed. "How do you discipline a bookworm? Make them watch television?"

"Right." He nodded. "There's something about my Irish genes— my dad had it too. That temper. He still does, at ninety years old. Our home life felt like riding a bucking bronco, hanging on through all the twists and turns. Falling off, climbing back on. I had so much hidden anger."

"Anger?" I said mildly, pretending innocence. "I wonder how that feels."

He gave me a look. "Very funny. My mom left him when I started college. The day I left, she left too. My older sister had already gone." His mouth turned. "Before long, out on my own, I saw how anger worked against me. People didn't trust me, not emotionally. I was a friendly guy in spite of the temper, so it hurt to see my friends step back, turn away."

I wondered how many people I'd turned away in the last few years without realizing. Not so much with anger, but bitterness.

"I always apologized, but the damage left scars," he went on. "Luckily one friend had the courage to suggest I try to change. A brave man."

"Is he still a friend?"

"Yes. The best. Of course, I railed at him for that at first, but then I started working on it. Really hard. Mostly through exercise, mostly running. Counseling. A little meditation. And after a while—quite a while—my fits faded away. Not all at once, nothing's that easy. But I found this place, almost like another room inside of me, where I could go and be myself without flipping out. I like that room. . .it's my home now. When I'm there, I think more clearly. I'm myself, my better self."

I stared at him. I wanted another room. I thought of my caterpillar in its chrysalis, quiet and snug. Peter saw my expression, allowed me a smile. "I'm not perfect, not even close. I'm not fond of Candore, and so when you and he were talking. . .he obviously was lying to you, disregarding you. That was disrespectful, and that pissed me off. My old temper flared up and I nearly snapped at him, nearly told him to shut up and cut the bull."

"That would have been interesting."

"No, it would have been ugly, because it has a way of escalating. Sometimes I feel it coming, feel it building up, and sometimes it strikes like lightning. You didn't notice, but I do this thing, where I rub my left palm with my right thumb." He held up his hands to demonstrate, briefly closed his eyes. His light eyelashes a pale screen. "It interrupts the impulse, quiets me. That's when I pretended like we had to go. I'm really sorry."

"Fascinating," I murmured, holding up my own hands and trying. I pushed really hard on my palm, but I only annoyed myself and possibly bruised my hand. I guess I expected some sort of quick alchemy.

"You have to practice when you're on the cliff," he admonished. "It's not like pushing a button."

"Not my best skill, teaching myself a skill like that." I wrinkled my nose, giving up already. It seemed too close to meditation.

"Give me a break. You work hard at everything, or at least you do once you decide to. Besides, you don't really lose your temper, not like me—you sink deeper and get more cynical. An escape I admire, by the way, especially since you're funny about it. And honest."

"You shouldn't compliment my animosity," I complained. "Don't make me feel proud. It might encourage me."

"Oh, I doubt you need encouragement."

"Hey. Be nice." I squinted at him.

"I am being nice." He grinned. I did like those freckles on his lips, just two or three.

Our food arrived and we talked about other things, the normal stuff. Families and backgrounds and education. Then he abruptly changed topic.

"Okay, your turn."

"All right. . ." I scrunched my face.

"What are you fighting? Or who?" He sat back, not confrontational. Just inviting.

Even though I'd made this bargain, I did not want it. I didn't know whether to trust him. Our relationship, if that's even what one called it, remained a hatchling in a nest, nowhere ready to try its wings.

"Nothing, Peter. I'm not fighting anything." He shook his head once, kept waiting. I may have glared. "Or maybe everything."

"Ah."

"Okay, I am. I'm fighting everything. Medicine and how frustrating it's become. Electronic records. Private practice with impossible budgets. Egomaniacs. People who don't listen. People who don't care. Mean medical students. My mother. My ex-boyfriend. Myself." I leaned over and sucked up the dregs of my drink, now mostly melted ice, no relief there. "I probably left out a few."

His eyebrows rose. "There's more?"

"No, that's enough." I laughed, self-conscious. I felt empty now. But oddly, it felt like a good empty, not the hollowness that usually echoed inside me when I thought such things. It felt like a purge, as if I'd thrown the garbage out. At least for a while.

"All right then." He seemed satisfied, although I couldn't imagine why. Not after I dumped that miserable lot in his lap.

I noticed his eyes looked green in the subdued light. I'd thought before they were blue.

"Are your eyes blue or green?" I blurted.

He gazed at me for a while, considering how it was a straightforward question.

"They change," he said at last. "Like a chameleon."

On that note I made my regrets, for I needed to get home to Emcee.

He walked me to my car and we agreed to have dinner again after the next session.

I spent some time that evening, considering the pros and cons of chameleons.

I couldn't tell if he only meant his eyes.

30

"I have a confession to make," my mom announced on the phone.

"Heaven help me." I took a long breath of cool night air and braced myself. This could be anything, from another irritating encounter with Johnny Quart to new exploits with The Mailman. Or maybe something entirely fresh and disturbing.

"You might not like this, but I've been talking with Austin lately." A dramatic pause, giving me time to react.

I reclined out in the back yard again, my favorite evening oasis now that summer had retreated. A new-moon night, as dark as Phoenix skies ever got, a brave spangle of stars fighting for visibility. The air nippy enough to contemplate a jacket, but I had Emcee.

"I'm not surprised. Austin loves talking with you." Emcee lay on my abdomen with her elbows digging into my liver. Ouch, I mouthed, pushing her over. She shifted a fraction, still painful. *I'm comfy,* she objected.

"He's lonely." Mom sounded reproving.

Always good to be supported by your parent.

"Maybe he should have thought of that when I asked him a few thousand times to contribute to the household." I felt unsympathetic. "Besides, he has that male advantage—young women will be interested in him if he gives them half a chance. Younger women who are much more appealing than me. What's more attractive than an aspiring author? He's an expert at that shabby, sexy look. He should go hang out around college campuses, be all moody and romantic. Lots of swoony little fish swimming around in that sea."

"Norah. I remember once upon a time when you used to be a nice person. When you used to take care of others. I'm telling you that Austin's hurting, and you make snide remarks."

Maybe she was right. Maybe I should be kinder, maybe flick that chip off my shoulder. A lot of maybes gummed up my brain. Maybe I should tolerate failings better, both others' and mine. The radiologist Peter Calloway suddenly appeared in my mind, surprising me, and I thought of his quiet, peaceful room. It made me want to call him, ask him to help me find my own room. Quite a peculiar impulse, which I quickly shoved away.

"Maybe," I conceded. "But try spending over thirty years in medicine and see what happens to your nice side. I'm planning on handing my job over to a robot soon."

Perhaps I should. Perhaps this was simply too hard, year after year, decade after decade, seeing people stumble and fall despite my best efforts. One promising treatment after the next bit the dust. The false hope of so many pharmaceuticals, the hype and lies. Medicine still hadn't found a reliable or safe way to help patients lose weight, other than removing part of their stomach or giving dangerous drugs. I got excited at first when tobacco sales started dropping, then along came vaping and a whole new generation became quickly addicted to nicotine in scented plastic dispensers. And because people now lived longer, we saw more dementia, more cancers, more heartbreak. Band-Aids for everything, trying my hardest, then people accused doctors of being in it only for the money.

So let's do it. Let's charge up the robots and program them to express sympathy, to prescribe placebos, to extend their metallic claw and hold their patients' hands. They won't get tired, won't shed tears of frustration, won't try to pull their own plug when they can't imagine their futures.

That went dark pretty fast.

"Hey, not a bad idea," Mom said. "I hear those robots are getting so smart, they know way more than any human. I wonder what that will be like, the first time I see my robot physician. Will I call it 'doctor?' And do they examine you, too? That could get weird."

I sighed and tried to remember the bright star gleaming over my head, a spiky twinkle. Maybe Arcturus.

"Mom. I'm kidding about the robots. Half of what I do is counseling, and I don't think robots can handle that."

But maybe I'm wrong. Machines could likely be taught facial recognition, could learn to identify sadness and anxiety. We humans think we're impossibly intricate, but perhaps we can be reduced to a string of formulas. Imagine the programming: one forehead wrinkle on a patient means depressed, two wrinkles mean suicidally depressed. The software would include an algorithm for calling 911, which the robot could perform internally. A knock at the exam room door, and there the attendants would be, ready with a straitjacket to cart you off to the nuthouse.

Nuthouse? Who says nuthouse these days? What was wrong with me?

Emcee breathed slow and deep, asleep on my belly. Her feet twitched, a dream of running. She brought me back, made me smile.

"All I'm saying," Mom carried on, "is that it wouldn't kill you to show Austin some charity. He said you hardly talk to him when he comes to visit the dog."

"It wouldn't kill him to apologize or explain why he didn't step up. You wouldn't have put up with that for a second. We'd still be together if he'd bothered to try. And I'm not sure how much longer he needs to come around—it probably makes things worse. I mean, we can't do this indefinitely. It should have been a clean break." I wondered why I went along. Did I feel bad for Austin, or the dog? Was I experiencing humanity, or caninity? Let's be honest. . .maybe I put up with it because I hoped he would change. That was a trap and I should know better.

"Oh, honey, he's a man, and you hurt his pride. You can't expect him to be very discerning. A man wants a woman, for obvious reasons. A man wants a dog, for a friend. They're usually not much deeper than that."

I laughed. Growing up under that attitude, it's no surprise that I never married. She was wrong, of course. I thought about the vet Owen Parker, a complicated man with more layers than the Grand Canyon who I'd probably never understand because he kept so aloof. And now Peter Calloway, another complexity. Or a chameleon, whatever he meant by that.

"Does The Mailman know how you feel about men?"

"I'm sure he doesn't care. He's a man, so he wants a woman. He'll have to get his own dog."

This was the place in the conversation where we tired of one another and I usually asked if I should visit next weekend, and where she came up with better priorities. I stayed silent and let her take the initiative, which meant nothing happened.

I knew the day approached when she would decline with age, her memory slipping, unable to accomplish the daily tasks of living. Her home dirty and disordered, a refrigerator empty except for moldy bread and limp celery, wearing her clothes inside out. By age ninety, over a third of humans suffer dementia. But whenever I tried to discuss this, which I did periodically so we could make a few plans that lined up with her wishes, she cut me off.

"Just let me rot in my home," she would declare. "If I've forgotten how to shop or eat, I'll wither up and die. When I quit answering my phone, wait a few more days to be good and sure I'm dead before you come check. Maybe you'd better wait a week."

"That's practical," I agreed. But on this particular night, we didn't go there.

"Just give Austin a chance," she insisted. "He's afraid to push, so maybe you should try opening the door. Just a little crack."

"I'll think about it," I said.

That's the best way to get her out of my hair.

31

Jeremy, Assistant Dean Candore, and I met right before Candore left on his vacation to Mexico. Bound for the beaches of Cancún, he would head to the airport after we finished. Candore seemed the cautious type, someone who packed light to keep an eye on his carry-on bag and avoid luggage fees, and he probably wore his swim trunks under his khakis.

I had no reason to think such thoughts. They came from my bad mood because I had to cut my workday two hours short for this uneasy encounter. Let me repeat that teaching medical students is volunteer work, no compensation. It actually cost me, since I saw fewer patients when teaching because it takes time to do it right. You volunteer for the love of learning and mentoring, to stimulate your brain and make meaningful connections. To give your life more purpose, for what that's worth. I'm not sure anyone has ever convincingly proved that human life actually has a purpose. Evolution just does its thing. Sunrise, sunset.

I chided myself for hostile thoughts about Candore. He was probably a great guy with an impossible job. Then I remembered what Peter Calloway said about Candore being slippery.

I could have avoided this. I could have done it by phone or email, even video. But feedback in medical education is terribly lacking. It often comes late, and sometimes not at all. Preceptors put it off, too busy to fill out the forms, too nice to make important but tough suggestions. Most students and residents perform extremely well because they're bright high achievers who want to learn and who care about people. So when someone exhibits problems, the preceptor feels awkward. Delivering critical comments effectively takes both skill and nerve, because it feels like confrontation and no one enjoys that. On the flip side, some physicians behave overly brusque and brutal, because that's how they were treated and it feels normal. Like most forms of abuse.

An intern once told me she received a marginal pass three months late. It nearly wrecked her. If she'd been told on the spot, she could have implemented changes. Another student received biting remarks on a written form—*too quiet, doesn't know much, doesn't seem to care*—from a physician he worked with for twelve minutes in a frantic emergency room. He was so frustrated he wept.

I hated to perpetuate that. Students deserved honest feedback, on time and in person. And part of me wanted to give Jeremy an opportunity to redeem himself, some sort of second chance. I secretly still hoped he might see a light, however dim. I wouldn't kick him out if he met me halfway, or if he even took a few steps toward me. We'd done it before and perhaps we could again. If he could just *pretend* to care, pretend to engage, that façade might be an accomplishment and a way for him to navigate.

Jeremy arrived five minutes late, which irritated me. He dressed formally, a dark blue blazer and red tie, like he would for a job interview. That felt bizarre, some sort of power move, and his acid eyes told me something had changed for the worse. I realized too late that I should have asked Candore exactly what he'd told Jeremy about this meeting. I unexpectedly saw that Candore might not support me. I comprehended that Jeremy had complained about me after all, and possibly made his case convincing. I supposed it wouldn't really be lying because Jeremy saw his view as the truth.

Of course, I had already scrutinized Jeremy's handwriting for looped Os.

Candore hemmed and hawed: how nice that we were able to meet, sorry about the short notice. It felt artificial and evasive. I cut to the chase.

"Jeremy. Dr. Candore brought us together because some problems have risen to the surface." I looked at him squarely; he held one eye squinched nearly shut, the other a cold chip of ice. "We were talking about your progress a few days ago, and I expressed some concerns. I've discussed them with you as we've gone along, and I had planned to summarize them with you at our midterm evaluation next week, but we've stepped it up."

I glanced at Candore, to see if he wanted to jump in, but he nodded and waited. His face vapid.

I reviewed the last few months. My concern that whenever I asked Jeremy to be more thorough, to take a deeper history, he barely made an effort. How I repeatedly must prompt him to form a wider differential diagnosis, to name several possible conditions instead of only one. He never asked patients about their emotions, never identified any mental health issues, even though nearly ten percent of adults suffer depression and almost twenty percent combat anxiety. He never once mentioned a concern about alcohol consumption, a problem for one in ten of our population. I'd coached him frequently about this. I also pointed out his progress, how he could generally give logical presentations and create decent chart notes. I mentioned how I'd seen a gentler side a few times, some glimmers of engagement. I didn't say *glimmers*. I made it sound better than it was.

I presented this in a supportive way, and although I expressed my frustration, I behaved considerably kinder than I felt. That's what teachers and physicians do. You separate your personal emotions and try to be objective. I carefully slid the whole package back to him, asked him why he thought we weren't synchronizing. I gave him plenty of room for reasons, and suggested maybe it was me as much as him. Oil and water, opposing magnets, pick your image for incompatibility. Some people just grate on each other, I implied.

"Jeremy and I have had some good interactions," I went on, seeking a more positive tone. *Very few*, I thought without saying it. "We've learned from each other. He has high aspirations and plans to go far, to work very hard." I turned to him. "I feel that to get there, though, you must build a solid foundation first. I believe that's where we clash. I think we must find a way to work around that, and we need to be honest with each other from now on. What do you think, Jeremy?"

I kept my face open, tried to be inviting. Maybe we could salvage this.

Candore still sat quiet. Not a peep. His face now tight. He shifted once, like he would speak, then nothing.

Jeremy blew out a long breath, staring at me, then moved his gaze to Candore.

"This feels like retaliation," he said curtly.

"Excuse me? Retaliation for what?" Me being caught off guard. "We've reviewed all this, so it's not new information. We need—"

"There's several things." He cut me off, his lip crimped like tasting sour milk, his eyes still fixed on Candore. Disconnected, because he spoke to me but looked at him. "You know I don't like family medicine. You overheard me say it to George Clark. It's mostly trivial work, and most family doctors are weak intellectually, and you know it. Why else would they pick such a demeaning career and work for peanuts? The patients are whiny over nothing and they're a waste of my time. I'll never need to know this boring primary care rubbish."

He finally turned his hard gaze on me. "Besides, I think you're still bent out of shape about that rash I put online. No one would have seen it, and you couldn't tell who the patient was, no matter what you say. You just want to get back at me. You bear a grudge, and that's what I told Dr. Candore here. You don't like me, and I hurt your feelings because you're oversensitive about family medicine. So now you're attacking me. Trying to malign me."

I sat stunned by his venom, this savage assault. And he obviously had complained to Candore about me, even though Candore denied it earlier when I asked. The silence went on and on...someone else would have to break it. It seemed like an hour. Staring at Jeremy, I remained icy and mute.

"Well. Well. My goodness, Jeremy." Eyes darting, Candore's hands flapped, empty fidgeting. He looked my way then jumped back to Jeremy. "I hardly think you should say—"

Jeremy interrupted again. He sat very straight, almost military. "You asked what I thought the problem was. So I told you. I'm just being honest."

I took my time, debated leaving. I stared him in the face and waited until his wintry eyes connected. "There's a difference between being honest and being malicious. We'll let that go for now. But I imagine that you grasp the difficulty here. You've just made it clear that I can no longer participate as your mentor. But you must pass this first-year rotation to be promoted to the next year, correct?"

He shrugged, silent, but I detected a slip in his defiance. He hadn't grasped that.

He looked like a stranger. No, worse than a stranger. More like an extraterrestrial, someone never seen before on this planet. A small part of me wanted to ask Candore to leave so Jeremy and I could speak alone, so I could maybe grab our old elusive link. A fool's errand.

Candore remained paralyzed, so I went on.

"Please excuse us, Jeremy. I need to speak with Dr. Candore privately. You can wait in the foyer by the stairs." My face immobile, a mask.

Jeremy stood uncertainly. I don't know what he expected, but he looked at Candore and got nothing. He exited before I had to ask him again.

"I don't know what game you're playing," I said quietly to Candore, my lips taut. Though incensed, I also felt sad and tired and old, and dearly wished I wasn't there. "You said Jeremy didn't complain about me, when obviously he did. You didn't disclose that to me before this meeting, which I find unacceptable. As a colleague, you owed me that. I am formally requesting an investigation of this situation and of Jeremy by the student progress committee. As soon as possible. I trust you will initiate that in a neutral way, and keep me informed."

He climbed to his feet, his face blank, which seemed ridiculous. "It's all about confidentiality and privacy, I'm afraid. It's all—"

I cut him off. "And I wish you luck in finding him a physician preceptor who cares less about their patients. But you probably can."

When I left, Jeremy did not wait in the foyer and was nowhere to be seen.

32

Needless to say, the rest of the day crashed and burned. I'd finished seeing patients by mid-afternoon in order to meet with Jeremy, but left many tasks hanging and needed to return to work. Impossible to focus, of course. A thousand retorts and rebuttals flew through my mind, things I could have said. Being nicer. Trying harder. Being crueler. Making threats. Resigning my faculty position. Leaving without a word.

Nothing would have helped. I kept seeing Jeremy's haughty ruthless face, Candore's stupefied distress. I wanted to shake them both.

Somehow I accomplished my most urgent duties. A blunt headache gnawed at my forehead, and I couldn't make my leg stop jiggling. I am not normally a leg-jiggler, so this new phenomenon apparently came as a bonus side effect from the Jeremy encounter. I wanted to run or scream, pound on inanimate objects, throw things. I snatched up a pen and hurled it against the wall, where it made a small pathetic smack and dropped to the floor with a tiny tap, which only made me feel more ineffective.

The office had closed but everyone still puttered around, an unusual and tremendously aggravating development. I craved space and privacy, so I could rave and shout. Then I discovered why: Dale, Wanda Cunningham's accountant husband, had arrived to begin his inspection of the financial records. Everyone fumbled and hovered about, as if they should keep an eye on him. Not that Dale behaved in a menacing way. He's a pretty mild person. But everyone seemed anxious, worried he might find errors that implicated them.

Physically, Dale and Wanda appeared utterly mismatched. He stood tall and portly, a high forehead, with heavy, black-rimmed glasses and thick-soled shoes. He dwarfed her tiny frame. If I compared Wanda to a hummingbird, Dale seemed an ostrich. He settled himself in her office, looking too large for her petite desk, and spread out his notebooks and ledgers, opened a spreadsheet document. His precision, the way he lined up his pencils and his yellow legal pad, signaled he would not be leaving anytime soon. Exactly the sort of person you wanted for this kind of job.

Nellie stalked up and down the hall, pausing grimly at Dale's door to offer help, as an office manager should. Her spiky orange firecracker hair practically sizzled against her dark skin. He politely declined her assistance. The medical assistants smiled too much and brought him cookies, which he politely accepted. Dour-faced Betsy ruled the front desk like a five-star general in green-and-yellow cheetah-print scrubs that made her look like an angry cartoon, practically daring anyone to mention her bill collections. As for the physicians, Wanda had already left to parent the children. Brian Mulch seemed unaware as he stood in the nursing station, unpacking boxes of supplements that smelled like cat litter and stacking them neatly in a cabinet. Emily looked amused as she sat on the phone in the middle of everything, chatting with a patient in Spanish and laughing now and then while she typed into a chart at the speed of light. My Spanish is weak, but I gleaned they were talking about potty training for a toddler. Emily and her practical advice helped bring me back on planet Earth. Between Jeremy and Candore, I felt like I'd been to Mars.

I just wanted solitude and fled.

I swear, if I had found a white card on my car just then I would have gone homicidal on the perpetrator. Fortunately no cards or card-bearers appeared and I didn't spend the rest of my life in prison.

I couldn't face going home yet. While I didn't want to be around people, I also didn't want to be alone. I felt like a hopeless seething mess.

Instead, I ended up at the Amigo Veterinary Hospital. I hadn't visited Blink in three or four days. I missed him and our energetic walks. Dusk descended, cool shadows, so the park would be pleasant. When I arrived, the lobby hardly had clients, a quiet night. I waved at the receptionist and hurried across through the shelter's blue door.

Blink rose quickly when he saw me, his tail waving. He let out a happy woof, a first, which warmed my heart. I never meant to get close to him, but clearly I underestimated something about both of us. Maybe I should have been a veterinarian, for I never quite felt this same deep flush of satisfaction with people. Then I remembered the troublesome human owners, as bad or worse than patients. I remembered the euthanasia—not the appropriate times, but the unnecessary times for cost or convenience—and quickly backed out of that fantasy.

As I clipped on Blink's leash, Owen Parker materialized beside me. We had developed a kind of friendship since he occasionally accompanied me when the clinic ran slow, sharing our frustrations and sometimes laughing. His scruffy beard had reappeared, the same tousled hair, only this time instead of wet fur, he smelled like hamburgers. He wiped his mouth with his thumb, as if he'd just taken a bite.

"I need a break," he announced, pulling another leash from the hook. "I'll go with you."

"Don't you have patients to see?" I asked shortly, not in the mood.

"Not really. Nothing that can't wait. Why are you all dressed up? Why are you wearing that to walk a dog?"

Truthfully, I'd forgotten I wore nice clothes, my outfit a little better than usual because of the formal meeting with Jeremy and Candore. A black skirt and tailored jacket, low heels. The poster child for business casual.

"I didn't plan this out. I had a day from hell and right now I pretty much hate everyone. Especially stupid worthless men. And I worry about Blink and I need fresh air. Alone. No offense." Though I technically apologized, I obviously didn't mean it.

"Ouch." His face went long. "*All* worthless men, or only specific worthless men? Asking for a friend."

"Very funny." Then Blink frolicked and rubbed against me, leaving a swath of long pale dog hairs attached to my skirt. Frustrated, I swiped at them but they clung tight.

"Here." Parker reached in a drawer and pulled out a set of green surgical scrubs. "I can't help with the shoes, but these will probably fit you. Save your good clothes."

I did thank him for that, ducking into the restroom and changing quickly. Few men would have even recognized the problem, much less tried to solve it, so surprise bonus points for him. When I returned, he waited with Blink and another dog, an eager young Dalmatian.

"Owen. I appreciate your help, but I truly want to go by myself. I'm terrible company right now and I'm warning you—you'd do well to steer clear." I tried to act nicer because of the scrubs.

"Yeah. Sorry, but that's not a good idea. You apparently haven't noticed, but this is kind of a borderline neighborhood. No problem during the day, but it's sketchy after dark. I promise not to speak, and I'll walk five feet behind you."

I glared at him.

"Okay, six feet behind," he conceded.

That made me laugh. Under the circumstances, an accomplishment.

I gave in. "Come on then, let's go. You can walk next to me because you got me to laugh."

He introduced the impish bright-eyed Dalmatian, called Barf. Barf's appetite included essentially everything, and twice he'd needed costly bowel surgery after swallowing indigestible items. First a rubber toy, then half a shoe. Barf showed no signs of changing his tastes, and his family could not afford the vet bills, so here he was.

"He might grow out of it," Parker said doubtfully.

True to his name, Barf puked once during the walk, but it was just a small slimy bunch of grass, nothing illicit. Four or five men lounged across the street, gathered around a rundown truck with broken fenders, coarse laughter. Passing a bottle. I sensed their eyes and felt thankful that Parker came along. He actually owned a better soul than he often displayed.

"Blink is such a nice boy," I commented. Our shadows stretched and shrank as we passed under streetlights, a little dizzying. Half a moon glowed yellow, listing sideways in the darkening sky like it was drunk. Or maybe I was sideways. Or maybe I should get drunk. "Why hasn't anyone adopted him?"

Parker reached down and scratched Blink's head. "He's a large, older dog—bound to have health problems sooner or later. People want cute little dogs these days. And he's disabled with that eye. It puts some people off."

Contented, Blink trotted along, his tail flagged, snuffling and spritzing. Every now and then he turned his head back to me and licked my hand, a quick swipe, which unexpectedly choked me up. I suddenly wanted to sit down and cry. I wanted to throw something at Jeremy, something heavy and sharp. I managed to mask my emotion and pretended to sneeze.

Parker's hand touched my back, there and gone.

"Do it," he urged.

"Do what?" I swear, no one could follow this man's train of thought. His mind hopped around like a rabbit. We stood under a huge old pine tree, the kind that shouldn't grow in the desert but got planted in the park decades ago and survived. Long fragrant needles and pinecones littered the ground.

"Do whatever you need to do. Run, scream, go kick something. I don't care. I'm just along for the ride." Deeply shadowed by the tree, I couldn't read his face.

But that released something inside me, outrage at Jeremy and Candore and medical education and a thousand more injustices. I felt cruelly betrayed, cheated, dismissed. Spurned, rebuffed. Dozens more desultory synonyms jammed my brain. My jaw set and I handed him Blink's leash. I picked up a few pinecones, then bent and scooped up more until I held an armload.

Fifteen feet away, a small innocent park sign stood on a post. *Please Pick Up After Your Pet.* I'm a lousy aim and not very strong, but I hammered the poor sign with a savage barrage of pinecones. That's not accurate—half of them missed, but each time I slammed that metal plate with a satisfying twang, I wanted more. Again and again, panting and swearing. I hurled dozens, uttering a few oaths, stomping over and picking them up when I ran out. Parker stood watching with the dogs.

Eventually I wore myself out. My fingers prickled smartly from the rough pinecones. I stood huffing, arms hanging down, hands empty. The sign now slightly scarred. Blink tipped his head at me.

"You done?" Parker asked, matter of fact.

"Yeah." I brushed off my stinging hands, sticky with sap.

He handed me the leash like it was nothing and we finished the walk. Somewhere along the way he got the story out of me. He didn't say much, just winced and jerked his head a few times, almost like a tic. Some sympathetic words, but not going on about it. I appreciated that, for I didn't want to be soothed, and he grasped that. Calmer, I thanked him and went home.

Emcee didn't care that I seemed wrung out. She carefully smelled my legs and feet, then my hands.

Who's the other dog? she asked, a plaintive look.

"He's a sad case," I explained. "He's homeless and needs a family. He's nice. You'd like him."

I'll be the judge of that. Sniffing my legs again. *Maybe you should bring him home.*

"I've already got a big dog. Not sure I need two, you know."

She sat at my feet and gazed with those soft eyes. *I'm lonely sometimes.*

"I'll think about it." My usual disclaimer.

Sleep didn't even enter my mind, not yet. Emcee and I ate together, then I walked her, because that only seemed fair. Slowly I wound down and nearly talked myself into moving on from Jeremy. Into feeling good about moving on. I'd tried my best, but Jeremy had turned out unfixable. I still had shy George Clark, who continued to improve, and my life would be so much easier with only one student. I still liked many of my patients. I thought about the physical release of throwing those pinecones and contemplated taking up something violent, like kickboxing. Or maybe tennis, slamming a ball with all my might.

I sat at my computer and opened a new document, labelled it *Stop Practicing*. Just to see how it would go. The first version came out too angry, then I overcompensated and the second one turned out too sweet. So I abandoned that, for a while.

Just after eleven, as I thought about showering, a tap came at my front door. No woman alone wants to hear that, and my pulse jumped. I thought of the windshield notes with sudden alarm. But Emcee, who usually fills the house with ferocious barking at any knock—never mind that she'd only lick someone to death—stood at the door with her tail swinging, anticipating. It was so unusual that I wondered about a neighbor, maybe someone needing help. I crept nervously to my door and peered through the peephole.

Owen Parker looked back at me, the ghost of a smile, his hair a heap. I opened the door, saw he wore comfortable jeans and a black T-shirt.

"What the hell, Owen," I said.

"I saw your lights were still on." He leaned against the door frame. He noticed Emcee beside me and raised his chin at her, a sort of "what's-up" motion, and I swear she mimicked it back and lifted her snout. You can't make this up.

"How do you know where I live?" I demanded. He seemed out of line. Beneath the porch light, with his shadowy beard and moody eyes, he looked like a hoodlum under a streetlamp. James Dean had nothing on him.

"Um. We have a file on your dog, you know." Like I was naïve.

"Is that ethical?" I began to understand what was happening and started to panic. I had no idea what I wanted.

"Ethical? I don't know—I don't care. Do you care?"

I stared at him. "Why exactly are you here?"

His eyebrows quirked. "I came to get those scrubs you borrowed. You forgot to return them."

"I'm still wearing them," I pointed out.

He studied me, those dark eyes.

"I can fix that," he said.

33

My silence stretched out way too long, but Owen seemed willing to wait. I wanted to ask *What do you mean?* but of course I knew what he meant. Not that long ago, talking with my mom, I knew the day approached when I would crave more than my dog for company.

"I didn't expect this," I finally said, trying to read him. Serious? Playful? Presumptuous? Nothing fit.

"Good. I like to surprise people." His black T-shirt looked soft, his jeans faded and frayed. Worn leather loafers without socks.

"Mission accomplished," I said. That felt too flippant, but my brain apparently had checked out, as if waiting behind me to see what I would do. I had to make a decision, and pretty quickly. Instead, what absurdly came to me was the admissions selection protocol: yes/no/maybe.

Get a grip, Norah.

The moon lay low, lacy light through the leaves. My porch light, which runs on a motion-activated timer, suddenly clicked off and dropped us into gloom. I could have reached behind me and switched it back on, but I didn't.

"That's better." Owen glanced at the bulb as if he'd asked it to go dark. His fingers brushed the hem of my scrub sleeve, just above my elbow. Only the fabric, nothing else, then he withdrew his hand. A minimal gesture, basically nothing, but it felt intimate.

I collected myself. "We should talk about this. Maybe not out here. You want to come in?"

"No. There's...rules that you should know." He slouched deeper against the frame. "Well, not rules. Conditions."

"What?" I bristled, thinking *No thanks*. I should have guessed he would be weird or kinky. I started to retreat, ready to shut the door. "Sorry, I don't want—"

He laughed, a slice of smile that came and went. "No. What I mean is, this would only be once. Just tonight, not again. I'm not ready for more than that, and you do not want a relationship with me. Not right now. Trust me."

I'm fifty-eight years old, closing in on fifty-nine. I've been around a long time, and I've been with quite a few men over the years. All kinds, all shapes, all sorts of personalities. There were lost chances and mistakes, and while none turned out to be a lifetime fit, most were worthwhile, mostly interesting and satisfying in their individual ways. At one point I thought Austin would make it to the end, that he and I might grow old together. But looking back, the signs were there all along. Subtle at first. The problem is that we often don't notice those signals, or don't listen to the warnings, even when they clang in our ears. Perhaps someone should study that phenomenon. Or maybe I'm the problem, and I'm just deaf when it comes to men. Or maybe just stupid.

Still, I'd never had a discussion like this.

"And why is that, that you're so unworthy?" I mirrored him, leaned against the door myself. "Have you done terrible things?"

His mouth slanted. "Yes."

My late-night mockingbird suddenly pitched in, brazen and annoying near the top of the tree, belting out birdsong into the sky. A disjointed soundtrack to a surreal conversation.

I decided to lighten it up. "Okay, let's start with the worst. Have you killed someone?"

"No." A slow smile, then he switched. Bleak eyes. "Just animals."

"Oh, crap." I felt bad, grabbed his hand. "I'm so sorry. That was supposed to be a joke. I wasn't thinking."

He gripped back, a calloused palm. "Don't worry. But I won't tell you about my past. It got ugly, and I've done some shameful things. Believe me, you don't want to know. And full disclosure—I'm moving to Colorado in a few months. An old friend and I plan to open a new practice. A fresh start. You don't want that story, either."

He touched my hair, up by my temple. The backs of his fingers grazed my cheek, and I tilted toward him without thinking. How long had it been now since Austin? Six months, maybe seven.

I trapped his hand and stopped him.

"Don't. We're still at the talking stage. And it's late and I'm tired of standing." I moved from the door and sat on a low stucco wall that runs along my porch. He eased down beside me, as if not to startle me, and I went on. "But. . .why me? Why right now?"

I wasn't being needy. I wanted to know. He didn't hesitate.

"Because I'm drawn to angst these days. I've become like a moth to that flame. I can't help it." He stared up at the moon, like he might find an answer there, then back. "You've been troubled for quite a while. Then today it was worse, a whole new level."

The mockingbird, who had paused, let loose again with a river of song, high in the eucalyptus. The broken moonlight flicked back and forth across us.

"Hey!" I looked up and called through the branches. "Pipe down! We're trying to have a conversation here."

"Dinosaur," he said, dismissive.

"Excuse me?" That hardly seemed warranted. We were about the same age, I guessed. Yelling at birds didn't make me a prehistoric crank, or did it?

He laughed. "No, not you. The bird. He's a dinosaur. An obnoxious one. All birds are dinosaurs."

"Oh. Sorry." I felt like an idiot, but it was his fault. "You can be hard to follow, you know. You leave out a lot. Our conversations always feel like there's pages missing."

One corner of his mouth deepened, maybe amused.

"And you've got a sense of humor." He leaned against me. "You're humble. And you care too much, even though you try not to care. I mean, you try really hard. And. . .you're sort of cute."

I wondered then if he might be drunk, or maybe stoned, although I couldn't smell either. At this point I hardly cared, because something had shifted. We felt more relaxed together.

"Come on," I insisted. "Tell me what bad things you did. Alcohol? Drugs?"

"Worse. But I'm not telling you."

"Insider trading, I bet. You look the type. One of those eccentric computer geniuses, working out of your basement. Or out of your garage, since houses in Phoenix don't have basements."

"Actually, I am a computer sort of guy. But not the stock market, not even close. Quit guessing."

"You've been in prison?"

"Please. I'm smarter than that."

"Exotic bird markets? Is there a rainforest parrot up your sleeve?"

He folded his lips, half humor, half annoyance. "Stop."

"Male prostitute?"

"You *wish*."

I laughed, the way he said that. We'd gotten louder, just to hear ourselves over the damn bird. The avian repertoire was truly amazing, one raucous tune piled on the next, hollered into the night.

"How many songs can they learn?" I wondered, suddenly curious and staring up again.

"*Mimus polyglottos*. Some of them have been recorded at over two hundred songs. You're changing the subject." His hand around my shoulder, drawing me to him.

"You know the scientific name? I'm impressed." My face against him; his shirt smelled like clean laundry. "And why do they shout so much in the middle of the night?"

"Of course I know the scientific name. I've studied animals for years—remember?" He pulled back a little, squinted at me. "Nocturnal mockingbirds are single. Unattached man-birds, looking for available woman-birds."

"Man-birds? Woman-birds? Are you hearing yourself?" He could be so inarticulate.

"Hey, you professional females are a tough audience." He touched my hair again. "I don't want to step on your toes. Should I name the birds correctly, then? Cocks and hens? I hardly want to call myself a cock, or call you a hen. I mean, I already once called you a bitch. I shouldn't dig that hole any deeper."

"You're right," I agreed. "You can't win, can you?"

"No. I've never won." His face somehow both melancholy and hopeful at once.

Without warning, he kissed me. No gradual nuzzling, no gentle start, suddenly forceful and full on the mouth. Wolf-hungry, consuming.

I discovered that I was famished too.

34

Even when something startling occurs to me, I've come to understand that the rest of the world doesn't change. Even after an unexpected comet streaks through the sky, the sun rises and people eat breakfast and everyone goes back to work. So do I.

The mood at the office rose and fell. Everyone remained edgy about Dale, Wanda Cunningham's husband, as his careful eyes trudged through the accounts, searching for our missing income. He spent increasingly more time with the bills and receipts, and he no longer appeared so placid. His expression had turned cautious, hooded. Something was up.

Dale and I developed a fairly good rapport because he knew I wasn't helping myself to extra money. I suspect Wanda put in a good word for me. Dale found something else about my finances, though, and produced a list he'd compiled just for me, of all the visits and procedures where I should have charged more.

"This doesn't explain your drop in income," he clarified. His voice came out oddly wispy for a large man, as if ordinary conversation made him winded. "It looks like you've always done this, Norah, right from the beginning. You should be charging higher fees. You see a lot of complex patients, which means the visits should cost more. You see the most patients who have no insurance, and the most Medicaid patients, who often have more chronic conditions. Your undercoding can actually get you in trouble, get you audited. Not as much as overcoding, but you shouldn't do it. Especially since you could be making more. Significantly more."

Insurance fraud and Medicare fraud cause huge problems in our warped healthcare system. Unscrupulous physicians bill for services they never perform. Bigger and more organized crooks collect sham medical bills from sham practices in empty buildings. Billions of dollars in waste and deception. It made me sick, and apparently it made me financially self-destructive. Another major reason why I should not have entered private practice.

"Okay," I allowed. "I'll try to do better."

He peered dubiously at me and turned back to his ledgers. "At least you're not overcharging."

"Someone is? I mean, consistently?" That set me back. Dale's face went deadpan, though, and I realized I should shut up. "Sorry. I shouldn't ask. But do you think you're getting to the bottom of this?"

He slowly swiveled his head toward me. Dale never moved with any sort of urgency. Heaven forbid if the place caught on fire...he'd probably perish.

"Well," he said. "Too soon to tell."

I was dying to learn more, but his guarded expression stopped me. I wished Dale good luck and returned to my patients and my new task of trying to charge them more.

In the meantime, Wanda made changes. She arrived earlier every day—breakfast with the kids was now Dale's job—and she left at four o'clock on the dot each afternoon. Only a few extra phone calls, less lingering over her computer. She seemed happier.

This particular day I saw more than my share of men. Man-patients, I thought wryly, recalling Owen Parker and his man-birds. Not something I should do in the middle of my day, thinking of him. Not if I wanted to stay focused.

Women go to physicians more than men. Partly that's having a uterus, because menstrual periods can be flighty, and because women control fertility. A man can't take a pill or implant a device in his body. He can't get hormone injections or have hormone rods put under his skin. There's no monthly calendar for him to monitor, for none of his days are "safer" than others. His anatomy offers no natural pouches for inserting creams or gels or rings or sponges or rubber cups. If he wants responsibility, he has two choices: condoms or a vasectomy.

Of course, female patients see physicians for many concerns besides periods and reproduction. They tend to be in touch with their body-mind connections, and feel comfortable pursuing answers. I'm biased, of course, but much of the time men just don't seek the same kind of help and advice.

Anyway, that day I saw more men than usual. Minor complaints like foot fungus and sore hamstrings from lifting too hard at the gym. Potentially serious complaints like chest discomfort and testicular pain. A weed aficionado who wondered why he couldn't get it up. No surprise, probably because of the weed. And finally, Niles Gomez, with the opposite concern—he could hardly keep it down.

Twenty-five-year-old Niles usually saw Brian Mulch, the last time two years ago. Young adult males rarely visit doctors. I felt curious about his switch to seeing me, for Mulch had openings most days. Maybe Niles felt uncomfortable seeing a man about his genitals. I could imagine, though, that talking to a woman nearly old enough to be his grandmother might also be odd. It felt like a compliment, anyway, so I quit over-analyzing. Always a tough task for me.

"This is pretty embarrassing," Niles admitted, looking at his hands.

His black hair stood up in a short crewcut, his skin broken out in scattered pimples. He seemed young but sincere. We'd already talked about his work, writing for a small community newspaper, the kind of rag that shows up in your driveway and you toss without reading. He also translated the Spanish-language version. I remembered the work Austin turned down, a job remarkably like this, and wondered if it might actually be the same.

Because of my harping mother, I'd finally agreed to sit and talk with Austin the next weekend, which I now regretted. But maybe Mom knew something she didn't say. Maybe Austin planned to apologize; maybe he found a decent job. A disorienting thought. Did I even want him back? Between Austin and Owen Parker, staying centered at work could be downright demanding.

"Don't worry," I assured Niles. "I've seen or heard just about everything. Nothing is off limits here."

"Okaaaay." A long exhale. "I just. . .I mean, I'm worried about. . .Okay. It's normal to masturbate, right?"

"Of course. Completely normal. For both men and women." I nodded to bolster him, but he looked down again and picked at a cuticle. "Is there anything else you wanted to ask about that?"

"Okay. Here goes." He looked wretched. "Can you masturbate too much? Is it dangerous or anything? I'm kind of worried."

This seems like a strange time to mention it, but one of the best things about family medicine is how you just never know what might happen next. It could be mundane or complicated, life-threatening or sad, or as simple as pie. It could involve ears or toes, hearts or kidneys. One minute you're laughing with a patient, and five minutes later you're crying with another. It's a splendid roller coaster, and it's rarely boring. Some days, in fact, I could use a little boredom. Then I remembered sore throats and penicillin reactions, which made boredom quite appealing.

"Why are you worried?" I asked.

"Because I do it a lot." Niles flushed. "What if there's something wrong with me?"

"First of all, there's probably nothing wrong." I paused until he looked up at me. "There's no right or wrong as far as numbers here. Let me ask you some questions, and then we can see."

He nodded tightly.

I ran through my list. He never missed work, or a meeting, or a deadline, because of it. He never avoided friends to stay home instead on a porn site. He had a girlfriend last year, and now hoped to ask out a new prospect soon. He never masturbated to the point where his skin turned painful or raw or bruised—he looked aghast when I asked that.

"I'm not finding any concerns," I concluded.

"That's great." he said. Partly relieved, he still looked tense. "Does that mean you don't need to examine me? I mean, down there? My friend said you would."

There are times when I want to smile but I do not. "No, absolutely not. It sounds like your parts work just fine. You just needed a consultation because you had concerns."

"Will it. . .I mean, it won't. . ." He stopped and started over. "Does it mean I won't get turned on by real women if I keep doing it?"

"Not at all. Just let me know if anything changes or you have other questions. I'm always here."

Now he relaxed and grinned, slightly crooked teeth but a nice smile. He shook my hand, pumped it vigorously, one foot already out the door.

"Thanks, Dr. Waters. Thanks so much."

When he walked down the hall, he had a jaunty spring in his step. That's when I could smile. That was a huge scary step for Niles, and I respected his courage. In his heart, he knew he shouldn't rely on his friends with their misinformation, so he did something about it. Niles Gomez grew up a little with that visit.

Then I thought about Dale Cunningham and his diligent investigation, and clinging Austin, and nasty Jeremy Newell, and devious Angelo Candore, and my smile disappeared. I thought of my partially written letter of resignation. Perhaps I should not have told Niles that I would always be there.

35

A week had passed since my meeting with Jeremy and Candore, and I'd heard nothing. Candore probably still lounged on a Yucatan beach, crusted in golden sand beside a swishing surf, drunk on rum from dawn to dusk. I actually had no reason to imagine him as a lush...I just liked that vision. I also liked picturing him brightly sunburnt, his skin charred crispy.

I'm a defective person, as if anyone had doubts.

Not having Jeremy lightened my load more than expected. Sometimes you don't realize the weight of a burden until you set it down and straighten your back. When his usual day came and went without him, no superior comments, no snide looks, I wanted to celebrate. A hollow revelry, though, since I felt such a failure. I couldn't stop myself from revisiting our discussions, trying to recall the trick that unlocked his better parts. I kept thinking about his brother. I wondered about his parents. Then it maddened me to discover I actually still worried about what happened to him. But once upon a time he thanked me for helping him. That ability to relate crouched somewhere deep inside him.

George Clark continued improving, less timid, more assertive. My expectations for George were modest. I hoped he would become relaxed with patients and somewhat at ease with most topics. He got there sooner than anticipated, and then he surprised me by passing those goals and moving on.

"I've got an idea," he announced at the end of the day. He seemed eager, if hesitant, waiting for me to respond.

"Let's hear it." I put down my work. Something about quiet George, still prone to chewing at his lip when he turned anxious, made me want to act like a cheerleader for him. Go, George, go! You can do it!

He shrugged, even though he had nothing to shrug about. As if preparing himself for rejection.

"As you know, I've been working with a few smokers lately. They want to quit, but they can't quite get there. Have you ever thought of putting together a support group?" His nose wrinkled, teeth on his lip, that amiable squirrel. "We'd have to do it around five o'clock or so, at the end of the day, so people who work could make it. And of course, you'd have to be here, too. So I guess that's really too much to ask, isn't it? I'm sorry. I didn't think that through."

He turned away, already defeated before I'd opened my mouth.

"George," I said quickly. "I like it. It's an excellent idea. To tell you the truth, I've thought of it myself, but never got around to it."

"Really? You wouldn't mind?" His eyes lively, excited.

"I think it's brilliant. This could be your patient project—you can track your results, your successes and failures. You'll need to write it up first, and get all your permissions in place. It's a lot of work."

"I already have!" he nearly chortled. He hurried away, then reappeared with a folder of papers, thrust it at me. "Here. See what you think."

Betsy appeared suddenly, tapping rapidly on the open door, her face livid. She didn't even wait like anyone normally would, didn't apologize for interrupting. Unfortunately, George often seemed invisible to people, so maybe she didn't notice.

"Dr. Waters. I cannot tolerate this. That man keeps meddling with my schedules." She wore black scrubs with bright yellow tiger stripes, like a caution signal. George stared at her, still holding his papers out to me.

I took the folder, pointed George into a chair, then looked at Betsy. A bit coldly, for being rude to George. "What man are you talking about?"

"That Mr. Cunningham. Dr. Cunningham's husband." Her lips turned white, pressed together, and her eyes glittered. "He has no business tinkering around with the patient schedules. I thought he was here to look at the bills. I'm afraid he'll ruin my templates— that program is very tricky. It took me forever to set all that up."

"Maybe you can show him—"

"He won't listen to me," she moaned, then stamped her little foot in frustration. Something else, too. Some kind of misery. "Please make him stop. He has to leave me alone."

For the life of me, I couldn't understand why she came to me. "Betsy. His work isn't personal. You should talk with Nellie. That's what office managers are for. If something is out of line, I'm sure she can talk to Mr. Cunningham."

"Nellie doesn't get it," Betsy snapped. "Take my word for it, you all will regret turning that man loose in this practice." Breathing hard, her nose flared. "And I don't understand why we're so worried about this stupid problem with Mr. Cunningham when someone out there is threatening us. Threatening me. Those terrible notes! Aren't you worried for your safety, Dr. Waters? What if something happens to us? What then?"

"Betsy." I felt badly, not realizing how this weighed on her. When I asked her before, she barely engaged with me about it. Not the time to point out that no one had threatened us, since it clearly felt like that to her. "You should have talked to me. I didn't understand how frightened you were."

"Well, of course I am! What is wrong with you people?"

She whirled and stomped away.

Maybe she was right—maybe something was wrong with us. Maybe we should be more concerned. Maybe I should have shared with Betsy how I'd talked with an attorney friend of mine, who explained the difference between threats and harassment. Threats were more of a felony, the attorney explained, so the perpetrator probably understood that and stuck to merely harassing us. More of a misdemeanor. Probably not someone who planned real harm, but who knew for certain?

I promised myself to tell Betsy that. Maybe she would feel better.

I looked at George, who sat there, surprised.

"I'll talk to her later," I sort of explained, feeling a bit lame.

And what was all that about Dale Cunningham? Always fierce about her scheduling, Betsy owned it like a wildcat protecting its young. Maybe when you were Betsy you took some pride, got defensive when questioned. If Zane was right about her home life, this might be the only place she felt in control.

Nellie usually handled her, but maybe Nellie had had enough.

I think Zane soothed Betsy. I'd seen them talking in the past when she looked upset. Since right now he only came in once a week, perhaps she was melting down a little. My conversations with Zane still had a dream-like quality that I rather enjoyed. He made no decisions yet about practicing. Or performing, or whatever it is that we do.

George and I shook Betsy off and dove into his project.

We decided that once every week at five-fifteen, George would conduct a forty-five-minute group session about quitting tobacco. He wanted to give brief talks about nicotine withdrawal and behavioral modification. He wanted to explain how pesticides and fertilizers, those noxious chemicals sprayed on tobacco plants, soaked into the leaves and eventually landed in their lungs, poisoning their cells and starting cancers. The group would practice relaxation and imagery and share their stories. Most impressively, he already had five patients ready to sign up. I needed to be there, but he would run the show.

This cannot be emphasized enough. Hands down, tobacco is the single most worthwhile mission for a physician. Nothing saves more lives. Within days after quitting, a patient's risk of dying begins to drop. Nicotine does not belong inside us—the plant manufactures it to kill off predators who try to eat it. Why anyone ever imagined it a good idea to vape nicotine in pretty little scented plastic tubes remains beyond me.

I'd never seen George happier. When I praised his idea again, his face shone like a nova. He thanked me over and over for my support, until I practically had to shove him out the door. Internally I worried if he could pull this off, likely to stutter and freeze in front of the group, but his earnest desire disarmed me.

I had to get going. I hadn't seen Blink in days, and I knew he watched for me, missed me. Not a situation I meant to create. But if I went right away I could still be done before dark and get home to Emcee at a normal time. It was to Owen's credit that going to Amigo Veterinary Hospital barely seemed awkward at all.

Just before leaving, as I closed down my computer, a new email appeared in my inbox. Something from Peter Calloway. I shut it quickly, before I could be tempted, and I'm not sure I'd ever felt so confused and pleased and guilty, all at the same time. But it was a nice feeling, saving that email for later.

36

Why I let my mother talk me into visiting with Austin remains a mystery. Family gets under your skin in ways that can never be completely shed, no matter how much you try.

About four years ago, I first met Austin in a bookstore. Maybe that's a trite scenario, or maybe it's romantic, or maybe trite and romantic are synonymous. I neared that crossroad in my career, about to leave the downtown clinic and contemplating whether to join this private practice on the edge of Scottsdale. I sought a book for those nights when I woke at three and couldn't sleep. With *Sapiens* in one hand and a Nevada Barr mystery in the other, I looked back and forth at the covers, unable to decide.

"When I'm not sure, I always go by weight," Austin had said, stretching his arm over my shoulder to pull a book from the shelf above me. Slightly brushing against me. "That way, if you don't like it, it works better as a doorstop."

He admitted later that his reach was a ruse to get near me. He wore a full beard then, neatly trimmed—I thought he might be a college professor. I remember laughing, thinking him funny and possibly wise. His good looks didn't escape me, either, dark brown hair that blended nicely into his beard, glints of gray. Distinguished. Soon we sat in the coffee shop, discussing the merits and dangers of post-midnight reading.

Ultimately, I bought both books. Kept my options open, enlightenment vs. entertainment. Call me reckless.

"Good contingency planning," Austin agreed, flipping through the pages as we shared a tiny table, then considering me with those deep brown eyes. Earthy, lingering. "And two hardbacks. You must be a tycoon. Or maybe a wealthy baroness?"

And there it was, that first warning which I ignored. Day one, hour one. I didn't expose my profession yet, but I blithely sidestepped his comment about my supposed affluence and gave him my personal email address. I actually almost never pay full price for a book, much less buy a new hardback. . . . I usually troll the sales tables and bargain bins.

Revealing yourself as a physician to anyone who doesn't know is a precarious move. When I was younger, people thought I was joking. They literally did not believe me. Even in the hospital, riding an elevator in my white coat, friendly well-meaning people asked me *Oh, what kind of a nurse are you?* Now that I'm older, I sometimes get deference and respect. Some people clam up, others let their medical problems gush out like a fire hose. A few regard me with horror and cringe away, like I'm going to attack them with a flu shot and take over their minds. A few of those pounce, aggressively determined to convince me that vaccines are hoaxes and only the paleo diet will save humanity from extinction. So you get cautious.

Now at eleven o'clock on Saturday morning, prompted by Mom, Austin and I sat at my kitchen table with the coffee I'd made and scones he'd brought. No beard now, but his hair hung longer, nearly to his shoulders, making him look both younger and older at once. I always liked his soft changeable hair that flipped over his collar, but this style seemed too lank. The tips of his ears poked through and made me think of elves.

I looked different, too. Right after I sent him from my life, I had my long-ish wheatfield hair chopped into layers, feathered and fluffed into soft waves. It made me feel like another version of myself—or at least made me look like another version—one that I hoped would be better and wiser. So many times I grilled my conscience to see if Austin's relationship crimes were really so bad. The fact is, they were not. But what they represented was disrespect. He blew me off, and I couldn't take that. So maybe it was all about my ego. I've tried talking to myself about that for months and it appears I cannot be convinced about any other options. Which brings up the question of why he even wanted me back, stubborn bitch that I was, and made me wonder all over again if it was my money. Full circle.

Now Austin acted borderline comfortable and a little witty, but I didn't trust it. I could manage being friendly, but friendship is usually a pipedream, because the two halves of an ex-couple rarely want the same thing.

Emcee lay between us, alert for crumbs or offerings, her eyes shifting hopefully back and forth.

"How's your writing going?" I asked. A loaded topic, but safer than inquiring about employment. Besides, I recently knew from Mom that he'd taken a part-time job at a grocery store. A temporary position, just for the winter, when the Arizona population swells with snowbirds.

"Good. Really good. Incredible progress." His eyes shone and he put his hand on top of mine, gave a squeeze. "I could use someone to take a look at it. See how it flows."

"Me?" I pulled back, uneasy. A terrible idea, because what if I didn't like it? "You must have better readers. Readers who understand literary feedback. You know, style and plot development, all that. I don't even have the vocabulary."

Not a true statement. I had the vocabulary because when brother Ben and I read to each other, we discussed those books at length. I just didn't want to go there with Austin.

Austin wrote fairly well. He created intriguing characters you'd like to meet, people you wanted to track to their triumph or doom. His settings came to life in exquisite detail, with striking language. But he also got carried away, going on too long, dazzling descriptions that careened out of control. His plots and characters lost focus, too, drifting off into dead ends. Sort of like him.

"Don't worry." He retrieved my hand again, confident. "You're going to love it."

My hand wasn't happy about being held. I stood up to get more milk for my coffee, and when I returned I kept my fingers firmly around the cup.

"I'd rather wait till the manuscript is done before I read it. At least until the first draft is done. How soon do you think?" I asked. Based on history, that would be never.

"Soon, soon. Maybe a month." He laughed, his deep chuckle that made me smile in spite of myself. His eyes lit when I reacted. "Your mom is helping me, you know."

"You're kidding, right?" I wondered how much he'd been calling her.

"Her stories are a riot. She gives me all kinds of ideas. I've added a character like her to the novel, and she's stealing the show. There isn't all that much fiction, you know, about lively eighty-year-old women. There's other new characters, too." A mischievous spark.

"She's eighty-six years, no less. Who else have you added to the book?" I had a bad feeling. I put down my cup and slid my hands into my lap.

"This is why you're going to love it." He leaned forward intently, his hair swinging. His eyes locked in. "There's a woman doctor in it now."

I should have felt flattered. I should have given him a chance to explain how this book had somehow morphed into something so completely different from before. The story used to champion a diner waitress with two kids who discovers her artistic talent as a sculptor. Obviously absurd, highly unlikely, but it harbored some lurking potential because of the gritty protagonist and Austin's vivid descriptions.

This new physician character didn't please me. I felt exploited, without seeing even one word on a page. Maybe the doctor had a tiny part, or maybe she inspired people, a stirring role model. Not likely. It felt too personal.

"I see." I stared at him, tried to control my face. Tried to act mildly curious instead of suspicious. I failed. "So, this woman doctor. Is she also a neurotic shrew, like me?"

Near the end of our relationship, during one of our quarrels, that's what he called me.

"Norah. I never meant that. I was just upset and wounded. I just lashed out." His expression reproachful, probably trying to make me feel bad and pretty much succeeding. "I did apologize. I hope you remember that."

"I know. I'm sorry," spoke the neurotic shrew. Maybe I should add the term *neurotic bitch* while I was at it. After all, I'd recently been more or less called a bitch by Owen Parker.

Whoa. Not the moment to think of that man. I truly should live alone for the rest of my life. Regardless, this switch of inserting "me" in the story did not feel safe. Otherwise why didn't he leap in and assure me, explain this fresh character so I would trust him?

I appealed to my better self, whoever that was. I wanted to be kinder. "Austin. Why are you here?"

"Because I miss you. I want to try again. I've got a job now." He looked so forlorn.

"I'm just not there right now." My words soft and sad. I really didn't want to give him more pain, although that felt impossible. Unfortunately, he misinterpreted my hint.

"I understand. You need more time. . .your emotions travel at a different pace than mine." He gave me a gentle smile, bordering on indulgent, which annoyed the hell out of me. "I'm more impulsive. But I can wait. I'll wait a long time for you, Norah."

That did it. I knew this phase of the argument, the plea, the pledge. Nothing had changed.

"Don't," I said abruptly. I avoided his eyes for a moment, brushed crumbs from the table into my palm, then connected again. He looked bewildered. "I don't really see how we can go back. I've thought about this a great deal, and I need to move on. I hoped we could be friends, but I'm afraid it's too uneven."

We were both standing. Emcee felt the tension and stood too, her anxiety clear.

Is this happening again? she asked. *I hate this.*

Austin's expression reluctantly shifted to one of tolerance and he put his hand on my shoulder. It took every fiber of my willpower not to jerk away. The crumbs still clutched in my hand.

"I'll go now," he said wisely. "I do want to be your friend. Let's talk again, all right?"

We were at the door when he picked up my fisted fingers and pecked the back of my hand, a quick kiss. Chivalry? A peace offering? A sense of lost romance? I couldn't imagine what he was thinking.

"I'll call you next week, okay?" His eyes deep.

"No," I replied evenly. "Wait until I call you."

He sent me another disappointed glance. As he retreated, I opened my hand and brushed the crumbs into the empty air.

37

My mom and I never established a routine for our communications. A few times a week, more or less. Sometimes I would call her, or she might leave several voice messages about almost nothing. I usually let a few pile up. This delay became a habit on my part, not really a calculated plan. Maybe my way of controlling her, which of course I could not. Besides, I think she enjoyed sending me little cliffhangers.

Saturday, 12:30 P.M. "You won't believe what Johnny Quart has done now. I almost called the cops on him because he threatened to call the cops on me. Because of my music, my hard rock. Everyone knows you have to play the Scorpions loud or don't bother."

Saturday, 1:45 P.M. "I filed a complaint with the homeowners' association against my neighbor across the street. She just planted an aspen sapling in her yard. An *aspen*. You know it won't survive one summer here, poor baby. That's plant abuse."

Saturday 2:20 P.M. "Have you heard of this new food called chocolate hummus? Healthy *and* chocolate? I think it must be an aphrodisiac, based on what happened last night."

These calls began shortly after Austin kissed the back of my hand, when I sent him out with a trail of crumbs. Curiously, Emcee did not linger by the closed door like usual, hoping he might return. Instead, when the door latched, she followed me around as I cleaned up and tried to wipe Austin out of my mind and off the kitchen counters. Then Emcee trailed me to the back yard and settled with me on the lounge, which I dragged into the sunlight. I needed a hot cleansing blast of ultraviolet rays.

Mom knew Austin had been to see me and she wanted a report. I wasn't quite ready.

The sun washed over me for an hour. I lay there and attempted to nap, Emcee sprawled on my legs, as I kept shuttling Austin out of my head. Easier said than done, because he crept back again and again. I thought about going to walk Blink, just to distract myself, but I didn't want to talk with Parker about Austin. That surely would happen, because Parker's laser beam of perception would highlight my discord in seconds. As he said, he flew like a moth to such flames.

Owen Parker, DVM. Man of mystery. About a hundred times, I almost searched him online to unearth his past. Maybe I could find complaints, arrest records, court documents, divorce filings—something might turn up. Perhaps his past misdeeds weren't really that egregious, only in his mind. Maybe they were horrid. Ultimately, I didn't look. He didn't want me to know, and I decided I would rather not know, either.

After that night with Owen, I went to see Blink two days later, because waiting any longer felt wrong. I had no idea what to expect, but I walked in like usual, waved to the receptionist in the busy lobby and slipped through the blue door.

Blink jumped up and woofed at me, wiggling and happy. Standing nearby, the aide Ralph grinned, missing my disquiet as I pretended not to glance around for Owen.

"He's starting to think you're his human," Ralph said, handing me the leash.

"I know." I saw Ralph's eyebrows climb up his wide forehead, waiting for me to say it. I was almost ready to take the plunge and adopt Blink and I nearly said so, and then I didn't. I fell back instead on my lame excuse. "I'm thinking about it."

Ralph shot me a frustrated look. "Things are going to change around here when Dr. Parker leaves. The shelter may not stay open."

That set me back. "What do you mean?"

Ralph raised one shoulder and turned away, heading into the clinic. "This shelter loses lots of money. It's pretty much funded by Dr. Parker. The new vet probably won't do that."

I wanted to ask about the new vet, but Ralph was done with me and my indecision and the door closed behind him. I opened Blink's gate when suddenly Owen appeared beside me, his radar operating with its usual precision. He swept an arm around me, a strong hug, kissed my cheek and released me, all in one quick sequence.

"Great to see you again," he said enthusiastically, as if I'd just returned from a long voyage.

"Likewise," I remarked, more cautious. Blink tilted his head to see me better with his one eye, waiting. I could almost hear him say *Come on, humans, let's go.* But I went on, "I thought I'd better see how things stand."

Now Owen tilted his head, remarkably like Blink. "Things stand like always. Better than always."

I studied him, took my time. His face open, waiting. Part of me wanted to drag him to the closet and attack him. Our crazy night, just two days before, still felt fresh and wild. Another part of me, the prudent part, wanted to never see him again, to pretend it never happened.

Instead I nodded.

"Good," I said.

"Good," he echoed, returning my nod. His smile broadened and his dark eyes blazed. As if we shared the best secret in the world.

Maybe we did.

Now I lay on the lounge chair with Emcee, recovering from Austin. For some reason I couldn't figure, thinking of Owen helped, left me feeling clear-headed and only a little bit unsettled. That's when Mom called again and I answered.

"How did it go?" she demanded before I'd hardly said hello.

"How did what go?" I played clueless. "I want to hear about your neighbors, and this new aphrodisiac. Chocolate hummus."

"I'm telling you, that's like a magic potion." She's easily distracted and temporarily forgot about Austin.

"I don't know. That sounds kind of rank. Like broccoli dipped in chocolate."

"Not at all. They really make it work—whoever invented it should get a prize. I went back to the store and bought ten big tubs of the stuff."

"Mom. Did you check the expiration dates? That hummus will go bad before you can ever eat that much."

"Not at the rate I'm using it." She made a giggling noise, which came out screechy, a fairly disturbing sound.

I sighed so heavily that Emcee, resting on my feet, opened her eyes and gazed up at me. *I was sleeping,* she said.

"I'm changing the subject," I announced. "Do you really have to play your music so loud that you're upsetting Johnny Quart?"

"Nonsense. It's not that loud. I can't help it if the weather's gorgeous and my windows are open. He's so repressed. I bet he's peeping in, watching me dance. I don't wear much when I dance. What a pervert."

I gave up. Even talking about Austin had to be better than that.

"Austin came by today," I said. "You know, your best friend."

Her voice lowered, wary. "No, he's not. What did he say about me?"

"He said you're collaborating with him on his novel. He said he's adding you in as a new character in his plot, and that you're stealing the show. I think he's immortalizing you."

Silence. I sensed her wheels turning, grinding that information. "Mom?"

"I don't like it." Her words carried a new sharp edge. "No one can capture my essence, least of all a man. Can you imagine what some of my old consorts would think? Most of them are dead now anyway, but still."

"Consorts? No one says that." Where did she come up with this stuff? And clearly, Austin had been telling her something different than he told me.

"I like *consort*," she insisted. "It sounds dignified. Something a king or queen would say."

I steered her back. "I thought you would love being the archetype for a character in a novel."

"He calls me too much and it's hard to get him to hang up. Doesn't he have better things to do? How can you write a novel if you're on the phone all the time? Besides, The Mailman might get jealous. He's a little possessive." The knife back in her voice. "Please tell me that you didn't make up with him. You're not back together, are you?"

Typical.

"Mom. The only reason I sat down with Austin in the first place is because you asked me to. Because you thought I was being too hard on him and I should give him a chance. *You used to be nice,* you said. *Open the door just a crack*, you said." There's no point in sniping at her, but it's hard to control. I can mostly stay calm and tolerant with her because I've had a great deal of practice. Putting her on defense only riles both of us up.

"Well, I changed my mind. I'm starting to think he's kind of a mooch. Not just financially, either. Intellectually."

It always feels strange when your parent fires your own words back at you, as if they had the idea first. I nearly told her how he also inserted a woman physician in his novel, but I decided we'd talked enough. Small doses of Mom go a long way.

"So it sounds like you and The Mailman are getting along well," I noted, preparing my exit. "I'm glad that's working so far. But what do you mean that he's possessive? Jealous?"

"You sound different." She said it like an accusation. "What's going on with you?"

"Nothing. Same old me," I said. It would be a cold day in Phoenix before I told her about Owen Parker. And I noticed that she didn't answer my question about jealousy.

"I've got a sense about you, you know. Something is changing."

"Nope. I'm still grumpy and bitter and considering quitting."

We disconnected and I caught myself smiling. It turns out that sometimes I can be mysterious, too.

38

I admit I'd grown mildly obsessed with handwriting, with the double-looped Os, after Betsy so deliberately threw that note away. I couldn't decide whether to believe her claim or not, that she didn't know who wrote it. I was dying to see her Os. Finally she left a handwritten message on my desk about Ana Merriweather. . .just fat round letters, nothing intriguing.

I had to quit fixating on the cards. It seemed they came less frequently anyway. The writer might be getting bored.

Around mid-morning I realized I'd left my cell phone in my car. I didn't need it because the office is of course full of landline phones, but I hated to miss a text from Peter, which often got me through the day. More and more, I counted on his clever wit to keep me running, a development both pleasing and disquieting. So between patients I popped out the back door to grab my phone, armed only with my keys.

And there he was.

A small man in a dark gray hoodie stood five or six vehicles away with his hand on Zane's roof where the car stood parked by the block wall. The man's head whirled around at the noise of my exit, and I glimpsed a razor-thin nose, a narrow black moustache. The rest of his face shadowed by the hood.

"Hey!" I cried.

Furious, without thinking, I started toward him. He crammed both hands in his pockets and dropped into a crouch, a glint of veiled eyes. Trapped between cars, caught with the wall at his back and my glowering advance, he tucked his head and barreled out straight at me. I gasped and halted, arms raised—I thought he meant to bowl me over. Maybe he did, maybe not. He missed me by inches as I ducked and cringed away. By the time I opened my eyes and recovered enough to look behind me, he'd run around the building and disappeared.

A little shaky, heart knocking, I plucked the card from Zane's windshield and found another one on mine. Nothing for Betsy; her weather-beaten Pinto wasn't even there. Probably stalled out at home. I quickly retrieved my phone and retreated inside, where I sought out

Zane and Emily, the other two docs there at the moment. Wanda had the day off with a sick child, and I guess Brian Mulch was working too, but I rarely thought of him as a real person.

Zane and Emily were beside themselves. Zane distraught, Emily enraged. Overly solicitous, they kept asking if I was okay, brought me water and snacks. But I was fine and before long I found myself calming them down. I mean, I never was touched, never truly menaced. I shouted and the man ran off. End of story. We all had to resume seeing our patients, a nearly impossible task but unavoidable. Zane decided to call the police, who appeared at lunchtime. I had little to offer them: a small, shrouded man, a sharp nose, and a pencil moustache, like a thin line at the edge of his lip. I couldn't estimate his age. He sounded almost like a cartoon villain.

Zane's card: *Enjoy your dementia.*

My card: *You broken clock.*

Which I assumed was a reference to the proverb that even a broken clock gets the time right twice a day. The officer looked at the messages then at me. I could practically hear him thinking *What the hell?*

"So you're the clock?" Almost amused, but he knew better than to show it.

"Apparently," I said narrowly.

He suggested a security camera.

Two weeks earlier Nellie and Betsy propped a ladder against our one-story building and secured the camera to the unreachable edge of the roof. Nothing happened for a while, no snide notes, then five days later we found a pillowcase over the camera and new rude cards. He must have used a pole to put the pillowcase up there.

I suspected that my close encounter would end it. Maybe he would be scared off now, afraid of being identified. It seemed unlikely he was dangerous, for he could have done so much worse, real damage to our cars, real threats to our safety. It felt more like creepy sport.

I would talk with Betsy again. If she remained truly unnerved, we could follow the cop's suggestion and hire a private detective. Because that's what I needed, a new expense.

39

George Clark's first tobacco support group went better than anticipated. I worried George might be clumsy as a speaker, might stam-
mer and lose his place. And let's face it, people trying to quit smoking
are a tough crowd, for good reasons. Almost all have tried before
and failed, and they're looked down on for it. They doubt anyone
can help them, and they doubt they will succeed. At least a small
part inside them wants to keep smoking, because tobacco relaxes
and comforts them. Divorcing nicotine can be a brutal and confusing breakup.

Nine people came for a forty-five-minute session. Nine people
stayed for an hour and a half, listening intently, sharing their expe-
riences, asking questions. Within the first ten minutes, George had
them laughing, and at the end they shared phone numbers. They
called him Doc George and promised to return.

He and I straightened the chairs in the waiting room after people
had gone.

"I don't know what just happened," I proclaimed, "but you've
apparently become some sort of anti-tobacco ninja."

A big smile claimed his face. No wrinkled nose or nibbled lip,
nothing squirrel-like about him. George displayed real confidence.

"That was so interesting, wasn't it? I mean, it actually seemed
fun." His eyes a little startled in a good way.

"You showed some skills." Giving specific feedback is important,
and I piled it on because it was true. "Great use of lay language,
excellent listening. Good eye contact, and very respectful. You did a
nice job of normalizing concerns. You've come a long way this year."

"Right? Thanks to you." He looked a little playful. "Can I con-
fess something? I've been doing an informal experiment."

"Oh-oh," I said. "On me?"

A troubled flicker crossed his face and he turned awkward. "Um.
I do need to talk to you about something personal. Not related to
this. Maybe later."

"Okay . . ." I had no idea what he meant. Personal about him, or
me? "Maybe now?"

George reverted, looked cowed. He looked away. "I'm not sure it's my place."

So, about me. I waited, he waited.

"Tell me about your informal experiment first," I suggested. I wanted to regain our camaraderie.

"Okay." George nodded, as if readjusting his thoughts. "You know how you always tell me to ask patients if there's anything else they want to talk about? Before they leave?"

"Of course."

"Well, there's often some other thing. Sometimes really minor, sometimes really major. Sometimes that little something-else at the end was the actual reason they came in." His face shone again with discovery. "So if that happens, I'll say *Why don't you tell me a little more about that?* You know, an open-ended question, just like you recommend."

I nodded again and George grinned, discomfort forgotten.

"So I shortened that phrase, just to see if it made any difference. I said *Tell me more about that.* That worked just as well, so then I tried *Tell me more.* Always in a friendly, inviting sort of way. It still worked."

He paused to see if I had questions, and I gestured him on. George looked a little excited, like he was savoring this.

"So I shortened it even further. I started saying *Tell me.* Same results. Finally, I just said *Tell.* And guess what? Same thing! Now today, for the first time, I didn't say anything. I just gave the patient my friendly look. You know, where you sort of raise up your eyebrows like you're saying *tell me more*, even though you say nothing." He mimed the face.

"And?" The suspense was killing me, even though I suspected the outcome. His flair for drama surprised me.

"Same thing! All you need to do is be open and pleasant, and people will talk to you. You hardly even need words." He sat back, pleased as punch. "Isn't that wild?"

I regarded George affectionately. It seemed so odd, because this year I was having maybe my best medical student experience ever, right alongside my worst.

"You've come a long way," I repeated.

"Thanks to you, Dr. Waters," he repeated. Then his face fell. "Okay. I have to show you something."

We moved to the back office where he sat down at a computer. I looked over his shoulder as he brought up one of those physician review sites, places where patients can make comments and score their doctor's performance on a one-to-five scale.

Physician online ratings are problematic. Many complaints attack appointment issues, or waiting on the phone, or billing. Not actually the doctor. Many of these sites cannot verify whether the writer is actually a patient in that practice. The worst reviews come from angry people who got denied excessive narcotics or some other inappropriate request. I've had frustrated drug-seeking patients threaten me. . . . *I'll post bad reviews and ruin you,* they said.

Yes, being a doctor is endlessly rewarding these days.

I'm not saying that some bad reviews aren't warranted, because of course they are. But either way, a physician cannot respond. Publicly acknowledging a patient's condition, or even a patient's existence, is a breach of confidentiality. It's a monstrous ethical blunder that a state medical board will pursue. Unlike a plumbing service, I can't write back. I can't say *You're upset because I didn't give you oxycontin for your minor back pain, even though I offered you a referral.*

No one said life is fair. Still, my reviews were strong enough and my average hovered around four-point-seven.

George stopped scrolling and frowned, pointed at the screen. "These just showed up recently. You can see how they're all dated within the last week or so."

I actually gasped, making George wince. I stared at five new reviews about me: four scored at 1 out of 5, one scored with a 2. George tilted the screen so I could read the comments.

Rude, unfriendly. Refused to answer my questions about diabetes, acted like I was dumb.

My worst experience ever with a doctor. She told me I was "really fat" and to come back after I found some willpower. I went home and cried.

Rushed, disorganized. No eye contact, she spent whole time looking at keyboard and typing.

Will never return. Waited 2 hours to be seen and the office smelled like feces.

Dr. Waters didn't care that I was really depressed. She said to toughen up and quit whining.

"What the hell?" I said. Nothing rang true. Of course I never said any of that crap, and no patient ever waited two hours. But my stomach sank anyway. It felt like a public flogging, tied naked to a stake, for everyone to see.

"I just thought you should know," George said dully.

"How did you find this? What made you even look me up?" I sat down, overwhelmed at the slander. Truthfully, my knees went a little weak. On top of the windshield cards, this simply was too much. Was it the same person, a new method of attack? I felt trapped in a toxic, furtive world of anonymous loathing that I didn't begin to understand. I reached for the keyboard, to explore my other partners' reviews, when George reluctantly spoke up.

"I heard—" George stared at the screen instead of me. "I heard someone talking."

A kick to my head. Jeremy, of course. I looked closely again, saw that each notation had a different electronic signature. Each patient name sounded androgynous, could be either male or female. Pat. Jamie. Andy. If Jeremy was smart about this, they probably all came from different servers.

"Is it who I think it is?" I asked. George had to know. Jeremy probably bragged about it. I could see his sneer, his uneven face. I imagined him laughing, felt myself go hot then cold.

"It—it's hard to prove," George stuttered. He looked miserable. "I'm really sorry, Dr. Waters. I'm going to check, see how to get these taken down."

I took hold of myself. I was bigger than this, and it was simply stupid. My patients knew better, and I hardly took many new ones, so few people would be checking me online. Deal with it, I told myself. Like everything, it would blow over, because things almost always do. So much for hoping Jeremy retained a miniscule scrap of sentiment from our association. For that time he thanked me.

That time he laughed at my teasing. This attack felt a step too far, absurdly vicious. Part of me wanted to call him, demand that he cut out this garbage. A smarter part of me knew I should not. And I asked myself for the millionth time why any physician still practiced medicine these days.

40

The next admissions meeting went smoothly. For once, most decisions were straightforward.

We knew each other now, understood our strengths and prejudices. The internist seemed too sweet and forgiving, but she could find hidden gems tucked inside an application, issues that occasionally made a difference. While the psychiatrist said little, he seemed smarter than any of us. The county nurse could be dismissive but had a keen nose for honesty. Even Carter Billings, who showed little patience for "touchy-feely" students, sometimes championed underdogs who had depth. Peter Calloway saw both the big picture and noticed important details; he never let trivial nonsense distract him. I hadn't yet discovered his downside.

I hesitated to think how they saw me. I probably came across erratic and a bit unbalanced, because that seems accurate. My year felt like a carnival ride: fast then slow, down then up, sideways half the time.

Every now and then, Peter sent me a text.

HIM: *Tough day today. I think half the people in Phoenix had something inside them that wanted out.*

ME: *Physically or mentally?*

HIM: *Physical. Appendix, gall bladder, cyst, tumor. I'll leave the mental stuff in your camp.*

ME: *My camp is a messy place.*

HIM: *Messy makes life interesting.*

ME: *Be careful what you wish for.*

After the admissions meeting, he and I had dinner again. First I furtively scanned the halls for Dean Candore, but he wisely laid low and kept to himself. Three days earlier, the student progress committee finally sent me a form, requesting my version of the events with Jeremy. I spent hours on that report, trying to get it right. Wanting to be fair but accurate. I would rather have talked to someone but understood the need for documentation. I tried very hard to be objective, balanced. I stuffed down my fury and searched my brain for positives, something to temper the critique. Of course what I actually wrote and what I wanted to write were unrelated.

What I wanted to say: *Jeremy is unfeeling and rude, but he dresses well and always has a nice haircut. Once he arrived early and cleverly used his extra time to bully another student.*

After carefully documenting the details, I summarized. "Jeremy presents himself professionally. He never missed a session. He displayed progress with writing chart notes and his knowledge showed improvement over time. His physician-patient relationships need more expressed empathy and expanded histories to include wider reviews of symptoms and mental health concerns. He should beware premature diving and must show an ability, or at least an attempt, to develop differential diagnoses and alternate treatment plans."

Then I detailed how he put my patient on social media and claimed not to understand HIPAA. The sordid events with Candore, the overheard conversations with George. The policy about "confidentiality" (whether an actual policy existed or not) that undermined support for preceptors.

Likely nothing would come of it. They would assign Jeremy to another mentor who either tolerated him better or didn't care. Or didn't notice. My careful treatise about his performance would be discussed once with him and he would deny it, then he would disparage me in a convincing way. Old, out of touch, incompetent, sour. That report would then sit in his file, a one-off disregarded forever on, unless he piled up more concerns and complaints. He would likely grow more cunning and learn to hide himself better. I didn't mention the bad online reviews about me since I lacked proof. Simply knowing the truth didn't count.

And he didn't stop. Every week more negative reviews appeared. I tried not to look, but I'm human and prefer to suffer. A few patients noticed, commented about it to me. They blinked with concern, as if trying to understand how I could have slipped up. I muttered some nonsense about online trolls and assured them it would go away soon, while my guts twisted and turned upside down. Sometimes I awoke at night thinking about it, and it took a long time to find sleep again. Fatigued, I forced myself not to check the site every day and occasionally succeeded.

At least the windshield cards stopped coming. For now. As if fate understood I could only manage one attack at a time. My parking lot encounter must have scared him off.

Peter and I returned to that Mexican restaurant. The one with a comfortable aura, friendly soft candles, and excellent margaritas.

"That may have been our least contentious meeting yet," I remarked, enjoying my drink.

"I know. Boring." His amused eyes looked green again.

"Peter." I didn't want my stress to show, but between Jeremy and budgets and an especially trying week with a few rude patients, this suddenly felt important. I desperately needed to find someone in medicine who enjoyed their career. Someone I respected, that is. "Are you actually happy? I mean, do you like your work?"

"Um. Yes," he nodded. His eyes wide, like it might be a trick question. "It's good. It feels like exactly what I should be doing."

"Why?" Forlorn, I wanted to know how to get there, even though the duties of family medicine and radiology stood continents apart on the planet of healthcare.

He sat back and thought. When his lips came together, the freckles vanished, then slowly reappeared. Sort of mesmerizing, until I realized I was watching his mouth and made myself stop.

"I like solving a problem. Often I'm the first one who knows what's really going on. I get to look inside that patient and put all the shadows together and say *Look, it's THIS*. Sometimes I'm the one who calls the surgeon, telling them they need to operate. And even when the diagnosis isn't certain, I know what we should do next, what other studies to order. We strategize. We're all invested, together."

"So it's like having power?" I might have felt potent a long time ago.

"Maybe a little. Not really." His light eyebrows gathered and he looked unsure. "Hm. I've never analyzed myself this way, so bear with me. It's more like having this ability, this skill, to contribute. Interpreting all those shades, all those shapes and silhouettes. It takes a long time, years and years, to know what you're seeing. I've analyzed thousands and thousands of films and scans. Millions. To read just one CT scan, I have to put my eyes across hundreds of layers. If it's a major trauma case, there can be thousands for just one patient."

I tried to imagine his job but could not. It felt like working with phantoms, analyzing wraiths. "Do you miss people?"

He smiled. "That's a misconception. I work with lots of people. Especially techs—they make or break my day. And I'm careful, because I can make or break theirs. We're a good team. And I interact with patients more than you'd think, getting consents and performing procedures. I explain scary stuff and make it less scary. I walk them through it, sort of hold their hands." He took a long draw on his drink and his eyes went a little faraway. "But it's not just decoding the pictures. You have to understand the equipment, the radiation, how tissues absorb the beams and create the light and the shade. How the images get generated, all the physics. Why one part glows and another goes dim. It's like being Marie Curie, discovering hidden things, except for her dying part. Sometimes I feel like I'm playing with magic. Potentially dangerous magic, maybe dark magic—I mean, it *is* radiation—but still magic."

"That's kind of beautiful," I admitted, caught up in his vision. I remembered wanting to be a wizard. "And here's a funny thing. My dog is named after Curie."

"That's definitely weird." He gave me a look.

"Hey, I wanted to inspire her with the name of a strong woman scientist." I stirred the remains of an enchilada on my plate, then looked up. "You may be the most well-adjusted physician I know."

Peter laughed. "Sure, when I'm not worried about overlooking some teeny tiny dot the size of a nanoparticle that turns out to be a cancer. It just takes one second of distraction, a blink or a yawn, and I've missed it. Someone steps in the reading room to ask me a question and I lose my place, my focus. Sometimes I have to start over. And the subtleties drive you crazy, what exact words to use. How specific to be, how vague. No second chances. I have to get it right the first time."

That brought me back down to earth.

We talked about Jeremy and the reviews. We talked about George and his tobacco group, and I compared George to an emerging caterpillar, stretching and opening his butterfly wings. I'd given up on my own metamorphosis but happily gave that image to George.

When we returned to our cars, he slipped his hand around mine as we walked along. An early November chill penetrated the night, a delicious bite. After enduring the summer, anything resembling coolness seems incredibly marvelous, almost amazing. The warmth of his hand good, just the right firm grip. Comfortable.

The next meeting in two weeks felt a long way off. But we were busy people with much to do in the meantime, and neither of us seemed inclined to rush. By our age, maybe we'd borne too much, tried too many times. Maybe we were afraid to know each other very well and have to give up whatever this was. While philosophically aligned, we knew nothing about the details that derail people, the clothes on the floor, dishes in the sink. The volume of television. The unfinished novels or their equivalent.

I looked forward very much, though, to the texts and emails.

HIM: *Tough day today. Nothing seemed black or white.*

ME: *I thought everything in your world is black and white.*

HIM: *Nope. Fifty thousand shades of gray.*

ME: *Is that a suggestive reference?*

HIM: *Never. And by that I mean: maybe.*

ME: *Now you really do sound like a chameleon.*

HIM: *Chameleons don't make sounds.*

ME: *Very funny. Or is it funny? Ambivalence consumes me.*

HIM: *I've seen worse. Besides, I respect ambivalence. It's usually where the truth lies.*

ME: *Where truth lies? I think you just made an oxymoron.*

HIM: *Proud moment. Aren't you glad to know me?*

ME: *Hm.*

ME: *Let me think about that.*

41

My patient Janet Hancock ruined her heart with alcohol. Even now, she talked about drinking with nostalgia and recommended spots where I might enjoy an indulgence. She loved beer and wine, whiskey and rum. Tall drinks, stubby shots, frothy mugs, and delicate flutes of champagne. She loved noisy bars on busy streets and mellow bars on beaches. Her formal diagnosis was *congestive heart failure due to alcohol cardiomyopathy,* and it would shorten her life considerably.

When it comes to drinking, usually we worry about the liver, that rubbery organ under our ribs. It filters alcohol from the blood, a thick sponge. But from a liver's viewpoint, alcohol is a toxin that damages the cells, a condition called cirrhosis. The liver doesn't care if you drink when you're happy or sad. It shrinks to a small hard stone and quits working.

Alcohol doesn't stop there. It streams all around the body and spoils cells in the pancreas, the stomach, and the nervous system, including the brain. And the heart. After decades of marinating in alcohol, Janet's cardiac muscles sagged. A flabby heart cannot beat very well.

Her symptoms worsened for a week before she came in. I examined her that day, then the next, and the next. I increased her diuretics and monitored her potassium, but she didn't improve, remained short of breath with swollen legs. Instead of dropping weight as I intended, she gained another pound.

"This isn't going in the right direction," I told her, worried.

"No kidding. I'm propping up on pillows to breathe at night. And look at my poor legs," she groaned. Sixty years old, her sparse mouse-brown hair stood up in back like a child's, as if she'd forgotten to comb it. Her legs dangled, doughy with edema.

"You're not drinking again, are you?" Unlikely, but over the years you learn to question pretty much everything.

Her mouth dropped open, appalled. "Dr. Waters. I would never."

"I know, I know. I'm sorry, but I had to ask."

"That's all right." She looked sad. "Sometimes I think what the hell, maybe I should just drink anyway. My heart's already wrecked, and maybe I'd be happier. But don't worry," she added quickly, seeing my face. "I know better."

"Nothing different in your routine?" I inquired for the third time. "No salty foods, no change in how you take your medications?"

"No, nothing different," she puffed. "Just those pills for my sinus infection last week."

My electronic mouse skimmed quickly through the chart. I feared dementia must be encroaching on me, for I did not recall that visit. Whenever I can't remember something, I start panicking about Alzheimer's.

"Did I see you then?" I asked.

"No, you were booked. I saw another doctor, that young man. Dr. Mulch." Her eyes closed, weary from talking.

"Oh." I found the encounter and looked at the meds.

"What's wrong?" She read my expression, which I'd failed to hide.

"Well." What do you say when another doctor maybe harmed your patient? I kept my voice neutral while my brain seethed. "You might be having side effects. From either the antibiotic, or the prednisone."

"That's possible?"

"It's always possible, I'm afraid. Nothing is ever simple. How long were you sick before Dr. Mulch treated you?"

"A day or two. I felt really bad, all achy and tired. Those pills helped right away."

"I understand."

I did not understand. I read Mulch's note as a slow burn stoked inside me. Janet clearly had a cold last week, a virus, but on the second day of her symptoms he gave her a fluoroquinolone, a potent antibiotic which sometimes worsened heart failure. And prednisone, a steroid. Steroids make people feel better almost immediately because they reduce inflammation so rapidly. But they also cause fluid and salt retention, swelling and elevated blood sugar. They raise blood pressure and hamper the immune system. Steroids have uses, but not often and not for Janet.

I looked back up at her, at her bloated legs and feet, at her anxious, exhausted face.

"I'm really sorry," I said slowly. "We've tried hard, but I think you need treatment in the hospital for a few days. You need IV medications and close monitoring to get better."

She nodded and closed her eyes again, as if she might fall asleep where she sat. Her skin gray, unhealthy. "I don't want to, but I know you're right."

Janet left, driven to the hospital by her sister.

Maybe the meds had nothing to do with it. Maybe her congestive heart failure flared up on its own. We don't always understand why. Maybe she spent last week bingeing on potato chips and didn't want to tell me.

Probably not.

I headed for the other side of the office, hot and angry. I needed to talk with Brian Mulch about steroids. My steam rose as I stalked down the hall. I wondered if Mulch read her chart at all. Did he not see that she had heart failure? Did he not grasp the side effects?

Then it came to me, stopping me short. It knocked my breath, like running full speed into a wall. I stood there in the hallway, feeling sick and embarrassed. Fortunately no one came along to see me stuck there, clutching my laptop, my mouth wilted with chagrin.

I recalled my bad day, not so many months ago, when I treated Clara Farrell. I ordered a penicillin injection she didn't really need and set off a dangerous allergic reaction. I had my weak excuse: I ran late that day, worrying if Ana Merriweather might be suicidal, so that distracted me.

None of it mattered. Doctors aren't allowed excuses. They have to rise above it all. If that sounds unrealistic, it is, but it's part of the package and justifications don't count. I let myself get sloppy and I did a hasty, easy thing. Was that so different from Mulch? His actions seemed worse, more recurrent and systemic, but I still flushed with shame at my hypocritical outrage. My face went pink and moist, blushed with regret.

I stood there at Brian's open door, deflated. I rarely thought about him lately, hardly looked at him or talked with him. He sat stiffly at his desk with his back to me, a medium-sized man with medium-brown hair. Nothing about him stood out except that he groomed himself well and dressed well and kept carefully manicured hands, small and soft, immaculate nails with clean white moons.

He must have heard me and turned suddenly, gripping some official-looking papers with crests and seals, his eyes startled behind tinted designer eyeglasses. He looked stunned, and I hadn't even attacked yet.

"Brian," I began, sorting through my muddle. I fanned my warm face with my hand. "I want to—"

"I'm being sued," he blurted in dismay. He thrust the pages toward me. "For malpractice. By my patient. By his wife. I can't believe it."

"What? Why?"

Nothing stabs a person in the gut quite like a subpoena.

For a physician, a lawsuit can be career-changing. The doctor becomes defensive, withdrawn, professionally stunted. I'm talking about normal doctors, grinding away every day, trying to handle their workload and take care of people. Sometimes bad things just happen, things that no one can foresee or prevent, and other times mistakes are made. Even when you try your best, medicine is slippery and unpredictable. Some lawsuits are warranted; many are not. Only about five percent ever go to trial because most get dropped or settled out of court. But the road to that settlement is rough indeed.

Let me be clear. A truly wronged patient's road is much rougher.

And I'm not talking about the few physicians without a conscience who dupe patients into unethical treatments, or doctors who utterly screw up because they don't care or cut corners. Who don't keep up. Nor those who blithely prescribe life-shattering doses of opioids and benzodiazepines like Valium and Xanax. Who knows how they sleep at night. Wait, they probably take Xanax.

Brian nearly wailed. "She says I never told him to eat less salt for his blood pressure. Last month he had a stroke, and he's only sixty-three years old."

"How bad of a stroke?" I hated to ask.

"Bad. Really bad. I went and saw him in the hospital, and he's a disaster. He can't walk, and he barely talks. Food dribbles out of his mouth. He'll never be right." His shocked eyes beseeched me. "I went there to support them, because he's been my patient for years.

I didn't charge for the visit or anything. I was being nice, on my own time, and she's suing me!"

I sat down. "There must be a misunderstanding. You must have talked to him about salt and diet and everything else. You're all about such methods, right? That's got to be in the chart. I don't know if you can even be sued about such a thing. It would be impossible to verify the harm. It sounds bizarre."

"Of course I talked to him about it. I mean, I'm sure I did. I must have. But it's not documented. I just looked up every visit for months. I don't know why it's not there. I just don't always put it in the chart," he moaned.

This felt ridiculous. Brian surely addressed this—he was the king of natural remedies, after all—but his equivocation concerned me. And perhaps a patient held some responsibility, since everyone knows this about salt. It's everywhere. Still, the documentation would have solved the problem.

I tried reason. "His wife can't know every discussion you had with him."

He threw me a black look. "She always came in with him."

"Did he have other risk factors? Diabetes, tobacco? High cholesterol?"

"Just the blood pressure, and I was trying very hard to get it down." He pounced on it, like a hidden truth. "He wanted to go natural—we all agreed. So he took folic acid and vitamin D, some magnesium and potassium. A little garlic. We had long talks about all those treatments."

I held my tongue. Which wasn't easy, because those methods were pathetic, and I could see the vital signs from where I sat. The blood pressure looked terrible. Brian found the time and space to document about supplements and other minerals but not about salt? And in the meantime, why not use plain old normal medications, like a diuretic?

Brian railed on. "The last time I saw him, he had this knee pain. Probably arthritis. It didn't get better with glucosamine and ginger, so I gave him prednisone. He left me a message the day before the stroke, telling me he was thrilled because his knee felt so much better."

Apparently Mulch never heard of ibuprofen. Without thinking, I shifted into problem-solving mode, something doctors do all the time whether they should or not.

"Makes you wonder," I mused, "if those steroids raised his blood pressure even more. Increased his risk."

He stared at me, staggered, and I realized what I'd done, essentially accusing him. So I blundered on, saying meaningless things like maybe the patient would improve. He kept staring, shaken. So I threw caution away and shared Clara's penicillin reaction. I even patted his arm, which made me feel like his mother, quite peculiar.

The penicillin story seemed to help. He calmed a bit, sat back and breathed. I guess there's nothing like discovering you're not the only idiot in the room who has done something dangerous and foolish.

"So what happened?" he asked, almost eager. "Did she sue you?"

I almost wanted to say she did, just for his peace of mind. You know things are messed up when someone hopes you were sued for malpractice. I felt too conflicted and didn't want to be there.

"You'll get through this. Please come talk to me whenever you need." I patted his arm again, an empty gesture and still weird. I stood to leave. I had patients waiting.

"Thanks, Norah. I think you're right—there's no case here." He actually rolled his eyes. "Those steroids, right? No free lunch, right? I don't think his wife even knows about that complication. Whew. Guess I should be more careful, huh?" He acted lighter now. "Did you have something you needed? Before all that?"

I thought about Janet Hancock and her feeble heart, en route to the hospital now. I thought about his stroke patient, ruined for life. Once the lawyers saw the chart, once they discovered the jolt of prednisone right before the stroke, along with the lack of standard medications, they would pursue that. They weren't stupid.

I also remembered how helpful Brian had been when Wanda took time off, how he pitched in and teased and made my life easier.

No one is completely flawed or completely good. Most of us are a mixed bundle of strengths and weaknesses, a ragged assortment of assets and failings. Practicing medicine is controlled chaos and you have to struggle to keep your head on straight. It's hard to do it well, but you also can't veer off down a side street at full speed. It felt like Mulch was flying down a dead-end alley at two hundred miles an hour.

And right now, what was the point? I had already faulted him and he already confessed. Sort of. Brian Mulch was beyond my control, and he would face his consequences. In front of the lawyers, in front of everyone. It might get ugly.

"No," I said, being generous, feeling complicated. "We can talk about it later."

42

Owen Parker changed his plans and decided to leave sooner.

He announced this unexpectedly on Saturday afternoon when I went to walk Blink. Owen grabbed a black dachshund named Stretch and joined me. The waiting room looked too busy, a crowded assortment of downy cats and nervous dogs, eyeing each other suspiciously. Stretch's whippy tail whirred like a happy propeller and his stubby legs blurred as he churned to keep up with Blink. He made me smile.

"Aren't you making all those people wait too long?" I asked, looking back over my shoulder to where Ralph stood scowling in the back doorway, shading his eyes with one hand and watching us go.

"They can handle a few more minutes. I'll be extra nice." He hadn't shaved, and I admit I'd grown used to that look. The shadow fit him. But he ignored me when I laughed at the idea of him being nice, and he went on. "The new doc wants to start right away. She just graduated from vet school and really needs the money. Huge debts like most, overwhelming. I don't especially care. It gives me more time to get settled in Durango."

I didn't know what to say. I'd expected another month to untangle my feelings and prepare a farewell.

"I'll miss you," I finally remarked. "I hope it works out. I hope you escape from. . .whatever you're escaping from."

"No." He stared into the park, where an old man sat crookedly on a bench and watched a small boy dig in the sand. "Not escape. More like persevering, but in a colder place. I'm tired of the heat."

We should all move away. Sometimes it felt ridiculous to live in this desert. But not right then, not with the chill nights and warm days of autumn, the world bathed in soft light under vivid skies. Perfect weather for eight months each year. Durango would be caked with ice and snow, searing wind, stinging frost. Maybe we should all just forego seasons and move to Hawaii, a steady climate where you didn't need three sets of clothing for the seasons. Where you could hardly travel twenty miles without bumping into a very large ocean. Unlike the Southwest, where you drove and drove for hours and still weren't where you wanted to be, still hadn't left the state.

"Hot or cold, pick your poison," I said. Blink cut me a wounded look because we only made one loop around the park and I steered us back. I felt bad for those people in the waiting room.

"Wait." Owen stopped under the old pine tree, where the sign bore scrapes from my pinecone barrage. He put his hands on my shoulders and peered into my eyes. "I need to know what you want to do."

I didn't know what he meant. It sounded as if he might desire a relationship after all, that maybe he wanted me to visit him in Colorado. I should never have kept returning to the shelter, a mixed signal. But there was Blink.

"What do you mean?" I asked, frantically trying to sort myself.

"I mean what will you do about Blink, of course. Are you going to take him home or not?" He squinted at me. "What did you think I meant?"

"Nothing," I stammered. What a dunce I was. "I mean, I need to get him together with Emcee first, make sure they get along. . ." My words trailed off, because why hadn't I done that already? I looked away at the old man on the bench, then back to Owen. I knew why I hadn't. "I guess I haven't done it yet because I like coming by."

"Good. I sort of figured. Me too." A crooked smile.

Behind him I saw Ralph far away down the street, advancing toward us on the sidewalk, his face a thundercloud. His heavy thighs gave him a rolling, swaying gait, like he rode a ship bearing down on us.

"Ralph's coming," I warned. "You're in trouble."

Owen turned and waved to him, then shook his head and made a firm go-away gesture. Ralph stopped and stood, crossed his arms and waited. He could muster quite an intimidating expression for a young person.

"Maybe do it today," Owen said quickly. "I'm trying to help simplify the place before I leave."

"All right, I will." I exhaled heavily, casting about for excuses. "I've just been distracted. There's been too much happening, new disasters. Sometimes I just hate people. And I'm being attacked online by that horrible med student. I may have to hire a lawyer."

"Great. Blink will be so happy. Ralph will do the paperwork

and—" He stopped, registering my remarks. His eyes narrow, his face dark. "What do you mean, attacked online?"

Ralph started toward us again, slower but steady. I explained rapidly about the nasty reviews, about George's unsuccessful attempts to take them down. How Jeremy kept posting new ones, and my average score had fallen to two-point-eight.

"That fucking little prick," Owen snapped, his eyes hot and furious. A savage expression that made me take a step back. His mouth snarled. "Give me a few days, okay?"

He saw me glance behind him again and he turned to find Ralph fuming up, getting close. He tossed me Stretch's leash and pitched me a grin, then took off sprinting up the sidewalk toward Ralph. I heard him laugh as he nimbly sidestepped, passing Ralph at a run, his white lab coat flapping as he dashed back to the clinic.

Ralph came up. He stood and regarded me, wordless, then he reached over and took Stretch. We walked back together.

"Are you going to miss him?" I asked Ralph.

"No, he's a pain." He shot me a sidelong glance. "But yes, probably."

I had to ask. "Why is he really leaving?"

We walked in silence, and I wasn't sure if Ralph would reply. Then he suddenly did.

"This is private, okay?" He glared at me, as if somehow I forced him to do this against his will.

I nodded and slowed my steps because we were nearly back.

"One of his partners, Dr. Sandusky. A quiet guy, super nice. Except last year he killed himself." Ralph stared at the sidewalk. "So I think that's why Parker's leaving. Leaving that behind, joining his friend in Colorado. Veterinarians have a really high suicide rate, you know."

"Oh. I'm sorry," I said quietly. I felt nauseated.

"Yeah." Ralph held open the door for me.

I wanted to find Owen, say something. But I'd promised Ralph discretion, and I suspected none of my words would be welcome anyway.

43

When Blink came home with me, Emcee seemed to grasp the gravity of the moment. Her reaction would make or break Blink's future. If she growled or snapped or cowered, anything negative, I would have to rethink it. She circled him cautiously, sniffing, then touched her nose to his missing eye, the skin sewn shut. Blink stood motionless and let her explore him, his tail barely swaying. Finally Emcee stopped and sat down, solemn. Then her mouth broke open in a smile.

Maybe it can work, she said, glancing at me. *He smells funny, like that dog doctor. But he seems nice enough.*

"You'll probably need an adjustment period," I suggested. There could be territory disputes, resentment, altered routines. Emcee didn't deserve much stress. If problems developed, I hoped maybe Emily or Wanda might want a dog.

Blink gazed about the large kitchen, a little dazed. He'd been living in a big cage, but nevertheless a cage, for months.

Is this where I'll be staying? he asked, peering into the family room.

Sweet, huh? Emcee turned and trotted outside, ducking through the dog door, and Blink followed eagerly. When I looked out, she appeared to be giving him a thorough tour of the yard. I could imagine her saying, *Here's the best place to pee.* Then by the yucca plant, *I once caught a lizard right here.* And that concluded the adjustment period. They got along great.

Maybe I should learn something about adapting from my flexible, unfaltering dogs.

The communications from Peter increased. More and more, I looked forward to his emails, his texts, eager when they appeared, disappointed when they did not.

HIM: *Anything new in the world of good and bad medical students?*

ME: *Good students keep getting better and bad students keep getting worse.*

HIM: *Perhaps you should take a break from students next year.*

ME: *And only interact with my patients and partners? Please picture my horrified face.*

HIM: *Well. You can interact with me.*

ME: *At least you listen to me. Or pretend to. No one else does.*

HIM: *I suspect you devalue yourself. Just a guess.*

ME: *Is that a criticism or a compliment?*

HIM: *What do you want it to be? I aim to please. . .*

It seemed impossible only a week had passed since the last committee meeting, that I had to wait another whole week until our next dinner. I almost called him, suggesting something sooner. Almost. The old Norah would have done it in a heartbeat. The current tentative Norah, swimming in uncertainty, kept her fingers off the phone and regretted it three or four times a day.

George Clark's smoking group grew larger, now up to fourteen people. Two of them were new to my practice, people whose friends from the first session encouraged them to sign up.

"I almost didn't make an appointment with you," confessed fifty-year-old Maura Whittle. She had long mahogany hair tinted with bright gold stripes, bold like a circus tent, and she smelled of tobacco and an eye-watering floral perfume she drenched herself with to mask the tobacco. She laughed, her mouth screwed to one side. "You've got some pretty nasty reviews online, in case you didn't know."

I wondered how many more potential patients never connected with me, too alarmed by Jeremy's comments. I would never know.

I found it draining to worry about two mental assaults at once, both Jeremy and the car-card whacko. After a long pause, the messages had resumed. Sometimes we got three all at once, then other times on different days.

FOR ZANE: *Screw You, Old Geezer.*

FOR BETSY: *Worthless.*

FOR ME: *Useless existence.*

The analysis of handwriting is called graphology. Some experts think it's valid, some think it's bogus. Occasionally, legal cases revolve on it. But effective or not, I couldn't help myself. I searched for cursive letters online, then I ordered a book and plunged in. All sources universally agreed that the double-looped Os meant something sketchy, that the writer was highly secretive. Often a liar.

Beware a person writing those Os.

I delved deeper. I tried to stop, chastising myself that graphology was not science, might be severely inaccurate. But I found it too intriguing. That slight backhand slant: a withdrawn person. That low position of the cross on the t meant unambitious. Could any of this possibly be true, or did people just make this stuff up? When I looked up parts of my own handwriting, though, it seemed pretty accurate. I forbid myself from analyzing Peter's. My graphology skills felt too amateurish, anyway.

I forced myself to quit thinking about it, to pay attention to George and his tobacco group.

Someone asked about CBD. Someone always did, sooner or later, because CBD was touted to remedy everything, from curing acne to preventing cancer. A very tiny study said it helped with nicotine withdrawal and everyone pounced on that with vigor.

I get it. We all crave a magical substance that fixes everything. But it doesn't exist, and it never will. At some level it's flimflam, and there's always been a convincing version of that, forever.

CBD, cannabidiol, is a chemical substance from the marijuana plant, only it doesn't make you high. Except for treating an uncommon seizure disorder, few studies have proved CBD does much else. But you can buy it on every corner for pretty much everything. I'm not saying it never works, I'm saying we have no idea. No convincing research has been done.

George was ready.

"I wish I could promise it will help." He sounded sad about it, which made him appealing. I'd say it even made him adorable if that wasn't disrespectful. "CBD won't likely hurt you. But I looked carefully at that study, and the conclusions seem flawed. Try the CBD if you want—it might help—but it won't be a magic bullet. You still have to put in all the hard work, I'm afraid."

With those few sentences, George displayed both empathy and support while imparting education about recent medical research.

I barely recognized him. When George first started, he seemed so young and immature, almost adolescent. Now I thought of him like a colleague, an engaging adult man. I had significantly miscalculated his potential, for in the last six months he grew up ten years.

After everyone left, we sat in my office to review the session, fortified with juice and graham crackers, a pleasant if rather pediatric snack. But I felt good, good about George, good about the meeting. Not a sensation I'd entertained much lately.

"Well, George," I began. "I'd say your project is a success so far. What do you think?"

"I'm actually loving it." As if surprised that could be possible.

"When you started last summer, you had no idea what specialty to pursue. Has anything changed?" I might have crossed my fingers.

He turned so serious that I felt bad, like maybe I shouldn't have pushed him yet. But I misjudged him, again.

"Believe it or not, I've narrowed it down to two fields. Don't laugh, but I've been thinking about psychiatry. That, or family medicine."

I couldn't help myself and I grinned. "From what I've seen lately, I think either might fit you really well. But explain your thinking."

"Well, I haven't worked with a psychiatrist yet, so that jury is still out. I mean, the jury hasn't even been picked, much less sat down to hear my case."

Now he made clever metaphors. Clearly, I underestimated George Clark from the beginning, which made me feel both foolish and relieved. Introverts can be tricky like that, so much simmering beneath the surface. Sometimes the potential is deeply sunken, so deep it never fully rises. Other times it waits shallowly, ready to emerge in the right conditions. I nodded for him to continue.

"The mix in family medicine is fascinating. Acute and chronic problems. Sometimes you make a quick fix, sometimes you uncover an old wound. A person's mood affects everything. Back pain for one person may be a nine out of ten, and the same back pain for the next person is a three." His eyes huge after such a long speech. "What do you think, Dr. Waters? What is the best part for you?"

That caught me out, asked to defend the profession I'd been fighting with so hard. But I knew the answer because it kept me going.

"The best thing? It's how I learn something new every single day.

Usually more than one thing." I thought a moment. "And the surprises. I don't mean the bad surprises. I mean the people who you never expected to make a change, and then they do. I love that."

George looked serious. "I know you're stressed. I see how much time you spend on your charts, how long it takes to do it right. Now that I'm charting, too, I understand. It's exhausting. But—" He gnawed his lip and the full squirrel resurfaced. George had crawled out on a limb, analyzing his attending physician to her face. I saw the whites of his eyes.

"But. . . ?" I wished he hadn't noticed my discontent, which I tried to throttle around students.

"Have you ever thought about using a scribe?" he blurted. "It might really help."

I felt grateful that he tried, so sweet of him, but I did not want a scribe. Not at all. A scribe is a person you hire to sit in the room with you and the patient; they perch there like a shadow, typing the note while you take the history and perform the exam. A specter in the corner, watching and listening, recapping.

"I can't function with a scribe," I said, testy. "My practice is too personal. It would upset the dynamic between me and my patients. I wouldn't risk that."

"You would think so, right?" George wasn't the least put off by my sourness. "But you sort of do that all the time, when a medical student follows and observes you."

I frowned. He was correct, of course. My patients were quite used to another person in the room.

"Here's my idea," he carried on, determined. "Next time I'm here, let me be your scribe and see how it goes. A trial run."

I bestowed a tolerant smile on my gentle student, so earnest. He wanted to please me.

"Sure, George. Let's give it a try."

I knew I wouldn't like it. It would probably add to my work instead of subtract, and it would alter my connection with my patients, no matter what he thought. But I would be nice about it.

44

Zane scheduled a meeting for physicians and staff on Wednesday at noon. He acted enigmatic, almost secretive, and not in an upbeat way. Like he would be announcing something adverse. . . . I worried it might involve his health, or maybe his retirement.

I found out accidentally the evening before. No one realized I still sat in my office with the door nearly shut, finishing charts. I heard murmurs up and down the hall, a normal thing, nothing that caught my attention. Then I overheard Nellie and Betsy by the staff restroom.

Being the newest physician in the place, I commanded a diminutive office in the very back, next to that bathroom. Although previously a large linen closet, my office represented quite an upgrade from my old job, where no one had an office at all, and we simply shared a scratched-up wooden counter. I considered my little private office space one of the best perks of my job. I also reaped the bonus of overhearing conversations between staff outside the restroom. It worried me a little that I enjoyed listening to those chats, trivial rumors about everything from Nellie's struggling marriage to Martina's wild sex life to Jo's rare sighting of Betsy's husband. One night when Betsy's car had stalled out again, Dickie picked her up in a gleaming blue SUV, so new that it still bore a temporary license plate. Which of course generated new rumors about her frugality since they obviously weren't dirt poor.

"What did he look like?" I asked Jo later, trying to suppress my curiosity, trying to act natural but dying to know why Dickie remained so elusive.

"I couldn't really see him," Jo replied. "It was already dark."

Served me right for being nosy. And absorbing those gossipy tidbits felt like a moral failing, something I should avoid. I promised myself to save this personal shortcoming for my psychoanalyst, whenever I decided to seek professional help.

Anyway, back to that evening as I worked away in my office. I heard Betsy accost Nellie outside the restroom door.

"I don't see why I need to stay for this," Betsy complained. Her voice strained. "I have. . .another obligation."

"It won't take long. Come on." Nellie's words clipped.

They moved up the hall. Then Zane's heavy tread plodded by. He now saw patients a few afternoons every week and seemed content with that schedule, although lately his mood had deteriorated. About to have his colostomy taken down and his bowels put back together, I guessed he might worry about mortality again. When you have a surgeon's fingers inside your guts and you're anesthetized to the point of not breathing, bad things can happen, even though they usually do not. I still felt haunted by his description of that duck, sliding across a glassy pond. Maybe haunted is the wrong word, because it wasn't spooky, but it occupied a brooding place in my head.

I discovered I'd left some papers I needed on the copy machine and headed up to retrieve them. The large copier squats behind the front desk, shielded by a partial wall. When I heard the wispy voice of Dale Cunningham join Zane's, I began feeling odd about the proceedings, so I took the back passage and ducked into the alcove for my papers, planning a quick retreat.

"Is she here?" Dale asked softly.

"Yes, she's gone to the bathroom—again." Nellie sounded grim.

"Let me do the talking," Zane said. His words low and depressed, but also an edge. "Do you think she knows?"

"She suspects," Nellie replied. "She's been as nervous as a cat on a string."

I'd never heard that expression and had no idea what it meant. I assumed Nellie mixed up her similes, though somehow it sort of worked. But I felt too much like a spy and poked my head around the wall to make my presence known.

"What's up?" I asked innocently. Instinctively, though, I knew what was up.

"Oh. Norah. I didn't know you were here." Zane looked briefly distracted, then nodded toward a chair. "Actually, this is okay. This is good. Do you mind just sitting here for a few minutes?"

"Um . . ."

"Please. It might be helpful. Later." His eyes and mouth drooped.

Like I could say no to Zane, especially as morose as he appeared. I nodded and sat, understanding my role as witness and covertly pleased to be there. As I've mentioned, I'm not always admirable. In case there were any doubts.

Betsy stormed back up to the reception area and paused at seeing me perched there. Confusion crossed her face, then I felt a brief malevolent blast from her glare. She switched to the others where they stood: Nellie, Zane, and Dale. Her usual pasty face had turned red and damp, a smudge of foundation near her jaw as if she'd just refreshed her makeup.

"I really must get home," she insisted, reaching for her purse. She wore scrubs I'd never seen before, a pattern of purple snakeskin. Or maybe alligator. "Can't we talk about this tomorrow?"

"Betsy. We know what you've been doing." Zane's words rumbled deep in his chest, as if reluctant to rise. A painful twist to his mouth, like the syllables hurt coming out. "We're going to have to let you go."

Her shocked porcelain face, that expression I'd seen so many times, like we were all insane. Her eyes darted between them and even over at me, a desperate animal seeking somewhere to flee.

"That's a lie. That's defamation. You can't prove anything!" she exclaimed, suddenly shrill, stamping her little foot.

Zane tilted his head. "What's a lie?"

Her haughty chin rose. "Whatever you just said. Whatever you just accused me of. Someone here is lying." Her glance flew to me, dreadful, then cut away and skewered Dale with loathing. "You're making this up just to earn your keep."

Apparently she didn't comprehend that we weren't paying Dale for his work.

"I don't think we accused you of anything. Yet." Zane handed her a typed page filled with names and numbers. She scanned it quickly and her face wadded up. Her chin trembled and her eyes filled and unexpectedly I felt bad for her.

"You can't...I never...I didn't mean...*I had to*," she floundered. A tiny sob, barely heard, as she stared at Zane, then switched her wretched eyes to me. "Please."

"Betsy," I spoke suddenly. My job had been to sit silently, but my brain cracked open and shook every cell in my head. "This wasn't your idea, was it? It was your husband, wasn't it?"

She whispered something so low I couldn't hear, her eyes locked, before her gaze slowly wandered back to Zane.

Then I remembered those thousands of dollars. Many thousands, tens of thousands. More. My heart closed.

Dale spoke briefly, that breathy sound. I don't remember what he said, some technical things about posting and billing. Something about deletions. Betsy stood unmoving, rigid as a post, except for her eyes flying up and down the paper that shivered in her hand. Then Nellie made comments, snipped and rote, instructions about severance and privacy. I watched Betsy, waited for her to move again, to react. She couldn't just stand there frozen forever.

"I don't...I couldn't..." she curled, nearly crouched toward Zane, imploring. "If you knew what he said. How he talked to me. If you—"

"I'm very sorry," interrupted Zane. I'd never seen him go stony like this, his face marble. It felt awful. "But so should you be sorry. I'd like to hear you say that."

Her face shut, a door slammed tight. Just her eyes alive, darting about, her trapped look banging into each one of us in quick succession. Searching for someone. Anyone. But she saw nothing and retreated a step. Then her face broke, wracked with fear, and she shouted at us all.

"You haven't heard the last of me. You'll hear from our lawyer. Every last one of you," she screeched in a strained, rusty voice. It sounded wooden, though, rehearsed. Almost as if she'd memorized it. Prepared for it.

For some reason she focused on me with the last ounce of her rage before she left, her eyes burning blue flames. Which seemed particularly unfair to me, but also felt terrible. Then she was gone, the paper from her hand floating to the floor.

Everyone remained silent, let her absence digest. I winced and finally stood up, headed for my office. Zane sighed and followed me, sat down wearily in the other chair, as if his own body was too much to bear. A soft murmur wafted from the front, Nellie and Dale talking.

"I started this practice over forty years ago, you know." Glum, he stared at the floor. "Just me, all by myself, because that's what doctors did back then. I hired a few staff, took on everything. I delivered babies, assisted with surgeries, took care of hospital patients. The whole shebang." He picked up a paperclip on my desk, fiddled with it, unbent it. At first I thought he reminisced for those good old days of autonomy and esteem, but I was wrong. "I almost ruined my family, Norah, because they couldn't count on me. The patients always came first. I never was there for all the important things my kids did. School. Sports. For some reason I thought my patients' problems were more important than my own children's disappointment."

"Different times," I pointed out. "Some docs still do that, start their own practices from the ground up. But most don't. It's gotten too complicated."

"Tara almost left me, and she probably should have. My kids were grown before I made peace with them. Now we get along fairly well, I guess." He gazed out my small window, dark now, blank. "I suppose it's normal to look back and wish you could do it over. Remake yourself."

"I'm sure it is. I wish it all the time." I smiled, rueful.

His heavy gaze sharpened and pinned me. "You're so uncertain these days. Why is that?"

"Tough year." I scowled at him for turning the tables. "What did Betsy do? How did she take the money?"

"She was pretty clever. When a patient paid in cash—sometimes even when they paid by check—she kept the money and destroyed the bill. You know how some people leave the line blank, where you write who the check is for. And by destroying the bill, I mean she destroyed all evidence of the bill, like it never existed. Sometimes she even eliminated the visit entirely, erased it like it never existed. She deleted the bills electronically so they never showed up as paid or unpaid. Poof. I mean, she left some of them, so there would be a little cash to make it look normal. So Nellie didn't notice."

"Dale discovered this?" All his careful hours, dredging through screen after screen, matching up visits with bills. No wonder Betsy freaked out when he poked into her schedules. It also explained my lower income, since I saw more uninsured patients who paid with cash.

"Yeah, he got suspicious pretty quickly. Then last week we created a decoy. I had a friend come in, pretending to be a patient, and he paid in cash. Cloak and dagger stuff, ridiculous. I hated doing that, but it proved the point." The corners of his mouth dragged down. "And those stupid notes on our cars. Her husband was doing that, you know."

"What?" I felt completely blindsided.

"I started wondering a few weeks ago. That's why I wasn't more worried." He saw my face and grimaced. "I'm sorry, Norah, really sorry. I wanted to tell you, but I wasn't certain enough until yesterday."

I should have been more upset, even angry, but Zane looked too despondent. "But why? What was the point?"

"A decoy. They knew we were getting close, so they tried to distract us, make us worry about something else. That's why Betsy started getting the cards too. So that she seemed like a victim as well."

My irritation at his secrecy flared, but my sense of relief soared. I considered Zane's miserable face and let relief win. My feelings of betrayal paled beside his; he'd practically been a father figure to Betsy.

"Should we prosecute?" I asked. "It must come to thousands of dollars over the last few years."

"Many thousands. It added up fast. I made Dale quit looking because I didn't want to know. Let me tell you, getting that man to abandon an unfinished task is quite a chore." His eyes looked watery, but then his eyes seemed watery much of the time. "And no. . .no prosecution. I mean, you can go for it if you wish, but it's hard to prove, even though we know. It would take forever and cost a fortune in attorney fees. That's why I just told her to leave." Zane stared out the empty window, his spirit drained.

We faintly heard Dale and Nellie, discussing qualifications for a new receptionist. Zane and I sat with our silence and pondered. I thought of Betsy's distress every time we got the windshield notes, just not the distress from what I'd been imagining. I thought of that message on her desk—*Don't You Forget*—obviously from her husband, obviously the same loops as the index cards. Graphology got it right. Secretive. A liar. The way Betsy methodically and tightly wadded up that paper and dropped in it the trash. Her peculiar smile, almost triumph. Or maybe her retaliation.

I reached into my bottom drawer and pulled out a slightly dusty bottle of red wine that a patient gave me for Christmas last year, over ten months ago. Fortunately it had a screw cap instead of a cork.

"Why don't you open that," I said, wiping off the bottle with a tissue and handing it to Zane while I went to the nursing station for coffee mugs. I returned with the cleanest ones I could find and poured us each a few ounces.

"Don't be too dejected," I said. I let myself sink into this new sense of reprieve. Now I only had the online reviews. Hey, one source of torture was better than two. I offered a faint smile. "I think things are looking up."

I suspected that sentiment might or might not be true, but he was about to go back under the knife, for heaven's sake. I guess it helped, for Zane smiled back at me and nodded. I tapped his mug with mine and gingerly took a sip of the old wine. It still tasted quite good.

45

HIM: *How come you never married?*

ME: *I could ask you the same thing.*

HIM: *I asked first.*

ME: *I was raised by a woman who thought men were only good for one thing, and that one thing didn't require vows. Just availability.*

HIM: *Do you agree with her premise?*

ME: *Yes and no. Some men are only good for one thing. Others have additional attributes.*

HIM: *Zinger. But I could say the same thing about women.*

ME: *Copycat. So how come you never married?*

HIM: *I was raised by an angry man and a browbeaten woman. I had no role models for marriage. It seemed like a dangerous voyage, so I never boarded that ship.*

ME: *You left your parents' orbit forty years ago. Are you telling me you haven't seen an admirable married couple in all that time?*

HIM: . . .

HIM: *I'm still thinking.*

ME: *Oh, come on. Besides, haven't you wanted children?*

HIM: *I could ask you the same thing.*

ME: *I asked first.*

HIM: *Some days it seemed like a good idea. Most days not. Too late now, anyway.*

ME: *Are you channeling my thoughts?*

HIM: *I hope so.*

ME: *Or are you a psychic? I bet your home has one of those neon hands in the window, one of those palm-reading signs.*

HIM: *How did you know? You want me to predict your future?*

ME: *Maybe. What does that involve?*

HIM: *Touching. That is, touching your hand, to read your palm. At least, starting with your hand.*

ME: *I'm thinking about it. A lot.*

46

Brian Mulch turned needy. Usually he held himself apart, looking down on the rest of us and our mundane approach to medicine. Our unenlightened views of alternatives. Now he hung around, wanting to talk, seeking reassurance. I understood his distress and did my best to be kind, but a little of him went a long way, and soon he became downright annoying. No thank you, Brian, I did not want to inhale essential oils for my stress, especially not lavender, a fragrance which I find irritating. An aversion of mine which for no good reason seems to appall some people.

The malpractice lawyers didn't take long to review his charts and recognize that the hefty dose of steroids he prescribed right before his patient's stroke might be a problem. I'm not saying the steroids caused the stroke, because maybe they didn't. Arteries clogged with fat from burgers and fries causes strokes. Smoking certainly causes strokes, but Brian's patient hadn't smoked in ten years.

And of course hypertension causes strokes. But Mulch hadn't even recommended the DASH diet for blood pressure, which surprised me, because that's completely natural and it's proven to help. Low salt, grains, fruits, and veggies. You can't get much simpler, and it often actually makes a difference.

If Mulch got lucky, the case would settle out of court. No blame assigned, just a chunk of money for the patient.

The next week, George Clark showed up ready to scribe.

"Don't introduce me as a med student," he suggested. "Just say you're trying out a scribe, and invite feedback from the patient at the end. I'll leave the room so you can get an honest answer. Okay?"

"Yes sir," I quipped, saluting him, amused at George taking charge.

"Dr. Waters. I'm serious."

"I know. I'm sorry. It just feels a little strange."

"Give it a chance." He looked disappointed in me, so I behaved. "And when you're doing your exam, be sure to say out loud what you're finding—normal or not normal—so I can put that in the chart as you go."

It *was* strange. My hands felt empty, lost, without a laptop to peck on and search. I'd been using electronic records for years, so now my fingers fidgeted and my arms didn't know where to be. I tucked them up and leaned back and talked with my patient. Direct eye contact almost the whole time, which felt oddly more intimate than usual. George slipped into a corner chair with a laptop and didn't interact, rarely raised his head unless I asked him about the patient's latest lab test or tetanus shot, data which he quickly produced.

At first, his quiet tapping on the keyboard distracted me, the soft patter of letters and words falling into place. But soon I no longer noticed. One time a patient showed me a crusty growth on his back, probably a keratoacanthoma, and I signaled George to take a look, but he shook his head. He wasn't supposed to be a medical student right then.

Old dog, new tricks. I got better at the game.

Two things happened by the end of the afternoon.

Number one: most patients didn't mind. After a few minutes, they forgot about George. Many enjoyed the visit, probably because of that eye contact thing, as I tell students all the time. The patients liked getting most of my attention instead of the computer in my lap. My own teaching stared me in the face.

Almost done, George typed a few more words, hit *Save*, and presented me with the laptop.

Number two: I found myself gazing at thirteen well-written notes. I still needed to review them, make a few tweaks, add a few items in my own words, but each encounter was ninety percent complete. I cannot emphasize this enough—ninety percent done. Normally at this point in the day, I'd be happy to have finished half my work.

"Pretty impressive," I conceded. Something strange churned inside me, roiled between my heart and my guts. I couldn't quite identify it, but it felt like *potential*. I quickly squashed that sensation, unwilling to believe.

A smile stretched across George's face. He pointed out how he also submitted the billing, including an additional code for counseling that I would have forgotten. Not only did he make my day easier, he earned me more income.

What the heck.

"Dr. Clark?" Carmen Borgata, the new receptionist, came tentatively up beside us.

Nellie could hardly have hired a person more opposite from Betsy. Carmen's glossy black hair waved off her shoulders and dark eyes danced in her friendly face. She wore relaxed, comfortable scrubs, and her low voice had a soothing quality on the phone. She also spoke fluent Spanish, a brilliant move on Nellie's part.

Carmen came with a few drawbacks. Young at only twenty years old, she had little experience. She seemed too awed by the doctors and occasionally got tongue-tied. Subject to terrible allergies, a personal civil war raged inside her body: eczema, sinus congestion, asthma. Naturally, I have a soft spot for asthmatics because of Ben, so I didn't care. Leave it to Brian Mulch, though, to express concern about her potential sick days.

I didn't have to retort when Brian said that, because Nellie bristled up to him and barked, "That's what I'm here for, Dr. Mulch. Now that no one's embezzling our money, I don't have to keep running back and forth to the bank. I don't have to drive myself crazy double-checking everything. I'll have plenty of time to pitch in."

No medical office runs effortlessly. I've checked in with physicians I know, to see if their staff and docs all got along, a happy productive family. I usually got tight faces or hysterical laughter.

"Dr. Clark?" Carmen asked again, pointing at a clipboard. Shy, self-conscious. "I can't find this code you used."

He shook his head. "Just call me George. I won't be a doctor for three more years."

"Really? But you seem so—" She left it hanging, pausing to sniffle and search her pockets.

I handed her a box of tissues. "George is a great guy, isn't he?"

George flushed and my phone buzzed again, the third time in the last few hours. At least I would get home early tonight with plenty of time to talk to Mom.

47

Arriving home to Emcee and Blink felt like coming before a committee. After the usual wriggling and jumping and celebrations, Emcee and Blink sat solemnly before me with big eyes, anticipating. If I took too long, they glanced back and forth at each other.

Food? asked Blink.

Any minute now, Emcee assured him.

Do you think we'll get a walk? he wondered.

Absolutely. Otherwise we would be so sad. Emcee inched closer to me, imploring.

"Quit ganging up on me. Who's in charge here, anyway?" I complained, as I obediently fetched their food and changed into my dog-walking clothes.

My phone rang as we returned.

"Hi, Mom," I said, moving through the house to the back yard. The mid-November weather had frosty corners, cold at night, and rain recently swept through Phoenix when the first winter storm struck the Rockies. Rain brings a unique joy after months without it; cloudy days become special, counterintuitively delightful. The desert drank and drank, soaking it up, cactus turning plump. Now the evening sparkled, clear and glittering, and the creamy curl of a quarter moon coasted down through the sky.

I lowered myself onto a sturdy wooden lounge because the dogs had a combined weight of one hundred twenty pounds. They jockeyed for position, stepping over and around me, finally settling with Emcee on my belly and Blink across my legs.

"There's empty cushions all over this porch," I pointed out to them.

You're warmer, Emcee said, her elbow in my spleen. Blink peered down his long nose and laid it on my thigh, quietly content. They did feel cozy in the nippy evening air.

"What's that?" asked Mom.

"Just talking to the dogs. How are things in Fun City?"

"Fun City?" she hooted. "More like Gun City. I just found out Johnny Quart packs heat all the time. Even when he patrols his little rock yard. Probably in case someone like me touches one of his cheap pebbles. Guess it's a good thing I didn't rile him up too much."

"How's your noodle barricade holding up, what with the rain?"

"Not great. It's all wonky now. The Mailman said he'd replace it for me with something more substantial. The last time The Mailman was here, Johnny stood in his front window, glaring through the blinds. He doesn't know I can see him there. He didn't even have his stupid toupee on his head so his scalp shone like an egg. I think he's envious."

"That's great, Mom. Your Italian neighbor, who probably has mob connections, is jealous and carries a gun. You may not need to worry about living old enough to get senile." It actually sounded disturbing. A paranoid old man with a gun can show up in headlines.

"He's hopeless. I've got more important things to tell you."

"I'm all ears."

I put my head back and watched the scrap of moon dip behind the hills. My mind shifted back two nights ago, dinner with Peter Calloway. For once we didn't talk about admissions or dismal online reviews or difficult people who never listen. We talked about travel, places we wanted to explore. We created pretend journeys, imagined disasters we might have to escape, like earthquakes in San Francisco and volcanic eruptions in Iceland. We predicted what travel together might look like.

"You probably get up at five and hike four miles before breakfast," he said sadly, shaking his head.

"You probably sleep in till lunch and then lie out in the sun all afternoon," I shot back.

He laughed, ran his fingers through his hair. "Right. Because my complexion really thrives on sunlight."

A swatch of hair stood up on his head, so I reached over and smoothed it down. I took my time, stroking the hairs into place. Then I rearranged it, tucked a few strays behind his ear, and withdrew my hand slowly. We stared at each other and his lips compressed, the freckles disappearing then returning.

"Maybe we should plan a trip together. Soon." His eyes gleamed in the unsteady light, the candle flame wavering. Green then blue, then green again.

At the car, he kissed me for the first time. Slow and delicious. I must have imagined it, or maybe it was the jalapeños we just ate, but those freckles on his lips tasted spicy and—

"You're going to be shocked," Mom warned, jolting me back to the present. "Really shocked."

"Probably not." I doubted she could surprise me much.

"Yeah? Well, The Mailman and I just got engaged. Can you believe it?"

"Very funny."

"No, Norah, I'm not joking. For real."

"What?" I stiffened, straightening abruptly. Both dogs startled, looked about for a threat. Seeing nothing, they relaxed and sent me reproachful gazes.

"I know, I know. I admit it's embarrassing. Completely out of character." She sounded defensive.

There's a reason for my reaction. During my entire childhood, Mom kept a framed quote in the kitchen, above the trash bin. Which meant I read it every day, multiple times.

Never marry at all, Dorian.
Men marry because they are tired,
women, because they are curious:
both are disappointed.

—O. WILDE, *The Picture of Dorian Gray*

Needless to say, I grappled to find the best words. "Well, you're right. This is surprising."

"I didn't expect it either." She hurtled ahead, as if to get it over with. "He just proposed, out of the blue. Down on his knee and everything. Said he'd never met anyone like me and probably never would."

"Can't argue that," I commented, still fishing for a better reaction, coming up blank. I felt like I'd fallen into a parallel universe. "Isn't he younger than you? By quite a bit?"

"Yeah, yeah. Big deal. That just evens things out, since men die younger than women. They don't have much staying power. In lots of ways." A short laugh. "So. . .what do you think?"

Get a grip, I told myself. Be kind.

"Are you happy about it?" I finally asked.

It may have been the longest silence from her I'd ever witnessed.

"Yes. I am. I'm happy."

I thought of all the times she tried to fix me, all the times she took it back. Don't quit your job—no, ditch your job. Toughen up—no, be nicer. Be kinder to Austin—no, get rid of Austin. Knuckle down and do your work—no, sell your house and live off the land. I had so many things I could say to her.

"Well then, Mom. That's good. That's what matters, right? That you're happy."

"Yes, honey. You're very wise." She seemed relieved. And it may be one of the nicest things she'd said to me in a long time.

Suddenly Emcee and Blink stood up, tested the air with their noses high, wet and twitching. What must that be like, the ability to sift scents like visible colors, using your nose to see a steak cooking or a chipmunk in a tree.

It's the neighbor's cat. I hate that cat! Emcee exclaimed, hackles up. They leapt off the lounge and dashed to the cement block fence, a thunder of barking.

"Gotta go, Mom," I yelled into the phone. "Congratulations!"

I highly doubted this engagement would last longer than a week or two. I gave it a month, tops.

48

Everyone left town over Thanksgiving. All right, not everyone; it just felt like it.

Peter Calloway flew off to see his mother and sister in Denver.

Mom and The Mailman ran up to Las Vegas to throw money away in the casinos. She has always been fond of the MGM Grand because of that huge bronze lion, which she saw being carved from Styrofoam on a Phoenix lot in the eighties. I almost suggested we get together for dinner so I could meet The Mailman, but she announced her plans first, which spared me the rejection. To be fair, she wouldn't see it as a rebuff, and maybe it wasn't. Maybe I was oversensitive. Introducing her daughter to her fiancé wasn't high on her list, and I should get over that. It still felt like avoidance, though, and made me wonder if something might be amiss there.

Since I no longer went to the shelter for Blink, Owen Parker faded from my radar. I thought about getting in touch, saying goodbye. Doing nothing felt wrong, but seeking him out felt wrong, too. And it's not like he came looking for me. Already I sensed him sliding away mentally, making his plans, leaving Phoenix. My heart ached for him, those shrouded sorrows, but I couldn't betray Ralph's confidence. I felt stuck.

I didn't mind that I would be alone for Thanksgiving. Emcee and Blink made decent companions for a holiday weekend, and I enjoyed solitude. Then something unexpected switched inside me and I did mind. I suddenly yearned for company, very un-Norah-like. What was wrong with me?

I battled myself for a few days, then gave in and invited all my partners over for Thanksgiving dinner. I'm not a great cook and I'm practical, so I offered it as a potluck. I figured one person might come, maybe two. Or maybe no one, since it was only three days away.

They all came, everyone except the new receptionist Carmen, who begged off because she had three siblings to manage at home. Zane and Tara, Zane still walking cautiously after his second surgery, his hand pressed to his wound. Emily and her two teenage daughters, who went berserk on a baking rampage and brought five desserts.

Wanda and Dale, the hummingbird and the ostrich, with their tribe of three boys and one reluctant adolescent girl, marginally brooding. Even Brian Mulch came, accompanied by a new girlfriend who clutched his arm, a skinny yoga instructor named Pacify with curly russet hair. She smelled fusty like incense, and she brought her dog—which no one should ever do without asking—a tiny hairless creature called Particle that spent the day in her lap, including when we sat at the table eating dinner. Emcee and Blink stared at it like it came from the moon, then backed away and went outside.

I don't think that's really a dog, Emcee said as they departed.

That woman holding it smells awful, Blink said. *She should go roll in the dirt.*

"Be nice," I told them, wishing I could join them for a while.

Unpredictably, we all had a blast.

Zane couldn't eat much, his guts still too raw from surgery, but by the end of the day he laughed with glee as Wanda's boys tried to teach him video games. The older boy, quick and clever, taught Zane shortcuts. The middle boy, timid and patient, showed him the bigger concepts. The smallest boy sat at Zane's feet and giggled every time Zane uttered outrages like *Wait, I can cut down a tree with a sword?* or *I can't put a pumpkin on my head!* Before they left, Zane made them promise to keep up his tutorial. Those boys were a riot, so earnestly instructing old Dr. Zane.

Within minutes, Emily's girls swept Wanda's somber daughter into their circle, asking her to help arrange their dessert table. They applauded crazily when she created a tower of brownies that looked like a Jenga game, making everyone stop what they were doing to admire and applaud it, and soon all three strategized the next display.

Even Brian Mulch and Pacify ended up in the back yard, unsuccessfully teaching Particle to chase a ball while Emcee and Blink tiptoed around the tiny dog as if they might accidentally break it. Blink playfully barked once, sending it to cringe and tremble behind Pacify.

Blink looked up at me, innocent. *I didn't mean to scare it. Really.*

Emily and I spent a fair amount of time in the kitchen enjoying a bottle of champagne.

"You're better," Emily announced, studying me as she refilled our glasses.

"Better than what?" I acted insulted.

She ignored my ire. "I like this Norah. I'm calling you Norah two-point-oh."

I laughed. "Emily, you forget how old I am. This is more like Norah twelve-point-nine. And besides, my life isn't exactly all rainbows and ponies. I'm still pretty upset about the online reviews. What a disaster. I'm fairly certain I've lost patients over that."

Her face furrowed. "And there's nothing you can do?"

I shrugged, felt defeated and a little queasy. . .not a good thing on a full stomach and five desserts. "Let's not talk about it, okay? It's too much of a downer for today, and I'm sorry I brought it up."

Emily immediately changed the subject and soon we were laughing again.

The rest of the weekend stayed quiet, and I enjoyed my seclusion. Peter and I texted a great deal. On Saturday, we were still at it after midnight. A few times I laughed out loud, drawing drowsy glances from the dogs.

Is she ever going to go to sleep? Blink asked Emcee, raising his head.

Hard to say. She doesn't usually act like this. But humans don't understand sleep very well. Emcee regarded me briefly, then put her head back down and dozed off immediately.

Then Sunday evening my phone rang. Jeremy, the bad medical student. That call must have been an accident, I figured, a butt dial. Completely taken aback, I didn't answer, even when it happened again an hour later. He didn't leave a message either time.

49

Our appointments always exploded on Monday after a holiday. People had put up with their burning urine and screaming hangover headaches and stabbing backyard-football muscle sprains for several days, and they could not wait another hour longer. Too much good food made blood pressures soar and blood sugars boil, and stomachs rumbled and rolled with indigestion and heartburn. I can't explain why at least some didn't go to urgent care before Monday, even though I disagree with half the medical decisions those places make and worry that a patient will get azithromycin for their migraine.

We all saw patients through lunch, grabbing bites in between. Zane came in to help, knowing how frantic things would be. I made him sit at his desk and handle phone calls and messages since his surgical belly pain still prevented him from standing up straight.

"And I don't want to come back in here and find you playing video games," I scolded, shaking a finger at him.

Zane beamed. "I'm really starting to get the hang of Minecraft."

"Good lord." I rolled my eyes and went back to work.

Though my patients were gone at five-thirty, I still had almost two hours of charting left. I missed my scribe, and I would finish at home later that night.

"Dr. Waters." The new receptionist Carmen Borgata appeared at my door, her face stern. "There's a physician here to see you. Dr. Null. He seems like he's kind of upset. I told him I wasn't sure if you were still here."

I liked her protective instinct, giving me an out if I wanted it. But my mind went blank—did I know a Dr. Null? Then it struck me like a sledgehammer, took my air. Not a doctor, but medical student Jeremy Newell. Which meant the calls the night before were not accidental and something was up. What an ass, calling himself a doctor to get past Carmen.

"All right," I said slowly, feeling seasick and wanting to run, knowing I couldn't. I cannot imagine my expression as I steeled myself. "I'll come see him."

"I can bring him back here to—"

"No. I'll go out there." I didn't want him in my little office, too small, too close. My stomach churned, bracing to be attacked again. Maybe he got in trouble after all, maybe some disciplinary action against him, although that seemed unlikely from what I'd written. I would meet him in the large empty waiting room, plenty of distance between us. A few people around if things went south, Carmen and maybe still Emily in her office. . .I wasn't certain.

"Are you leaving now?" I asked.

"I can stay." Carmen's eyes narrowed. She understood immediately, astute beyond her years. I wanted to give her a raise already. "I'll just be there working at the front desk."

"Thank you." I nodded appreciatively and found my feet.

Jeremy paced the waiting room. If he cut his tight blond curls any shorter he'd be bald. As I entered, his back was to me and I saw him pick up a magazine, give it a snarl, and slap it back down on the table. He strode to the front door like a caged animal, wheeled and then pulled up short at seeing me.

I said nothing. He started this parade, and I had no idea where it was headed.

"Dr. Waters." He hurried over, extended his hand out of habit.

"Jeremy."

His hand felt damp and cold. I watched his face morph from anger to caution and everything in between, his pliable upper lip that could sneer and frown at the same time, those icy eyes. Then a shudder passed over him and he began to plead. I didn't buy it, of course not. I just watched him, deadpan.

"Dr. Waters. I'm sorry. I am really, truly sorry. I never should have done those negative reviews. I was just angry, and I acted out. It was very immature of me, and I promise I will never ever do anything like that again." He clasped my hand like a supplicant, and for a moment I feared he would drop to his knees.

"Okay. . ." I said slowly, unsure where to go with this. This confession came unexpected and felt devious, the opposite of what I'd feared. Could I be wrong? Could I believe his regret? Carmen shifted in the corner of my eye, staring at us from behind the counter, then she quickly looked down. But I caught her hard expression, unforgiving. She had been there before.

"Just please stop doing this. I've learned my lesson," Jeremy implored. He realized he'd held my hand too long and suddenly let go, sort of threw it away. His mouth a painful rip in his face, distorted.

"What on earth do you mean?"

A bitter gleam. "Come on, don't play dumb. It has to be you. I'm not stupid."

"Jeremy. Believe me, I have absolutely no idea what you're talking about." I now felt completely lost. "You need to explain yourself."

His anger crashed back. "I don't know how you've done it. Especially those posts on social media that I never wrote. And those comments on the med student site, where we evaluate the professors. You shouldn't have access to that. I filed a complaint."

"A complaint?" I actually laughed. "I'm an old woman—I could be your grandmother. I'm sure you pointed that out when you criticized me to Candore. I can barely manage electronic medical records, and I screw up my email all the time. I don't even have any social media accounts."

A dim light in my brain appeared and began to brighten. I remembered Owen Parker on my front porch that night, while the mockingbird screamed overhead. *I actually am a computer sort of guy.* Then last week... *Give me a few days.* My thoughts flew to the veterinary clinic.

"Jeremy," I asserted. "It's not me. I am not remotely capable of tampering with any sort of computer stuff, anything online. Tell me what's happened." He looked so distressed that I actually added "Please."

He speared me with a feverish glare, his plea for a truce clearly a scheme. His lips so taut they barely moved. "I don't believe you. If not you, it's someone you got to do it. The school might put me on probation, which would go on my permanent record." His eyelids squeezed shut then sprang open, and he took a step toward me. He sounded like he was strangling. "My *permanent record*, Dr. Waters. Can you imagine what my brother would say? My family? Because of you?"

I moved one pace back to maintain distance. Carmen's voice came from behind the counter, tense and low. "Dr. Waters. I'm calling someone."

"Whatever has happened is not because of me. It's because of you. Your choices," I said coldly to Jeremy. My heart galloped, but he couldn't see that. "You should leave. Now. Please go."

His mouth worked back and forth but no words came, his face wild. Then he spun and left, slamming the front door and rattling the frames on the walls. I hurried over and turned the latch.

"Oh, Dr. Waters! Who was that?" Carmen came around the counter, her eyes huge, gasping a little. I heard her wheeze.

"Where's your inhaler?" I asked quickly. I knew that look, that hollow hunger for oxygen.

She fumbled in her pockets and eventually produced the little device, took two deep puffs and held her breath.

"Better?" I questioned, about to go get my stethoscope.

She nodded, exhaling. "Better."

I caught myself smiling. "Who were you calling for help?"

Now she laughed, a throaty chuckle. Maybe it was the asthma. "I have no idea. I mean, no one. I just pretended, just said that to distract him. Maybe scare him. He was so creepy."

"I think it worked." I regarded her with fresh appreciation.

Carmen sat down and fanned herself with a flyer, her skin glowing. "Whew. Sometimes that albuterol makes me all flushed." She put her head back against the wall and seemed suddenly very young, about twelve years old. But her eyes opened and simmered, tough like a veteran. She put the paper down and went on. "I grew up with a drug-addicted mom. She's in prison now, but since I'm the oldest, I had to protect my little sisters. I learned all kinds of tricks. So I guess I've had lots of practice."

I gave her a hug. You don't always need to talk.

We walked out together, watchful, but Jeremy had gone. Low gray clouds clogged the sky, more rain likely. Although my charts weren't close to finished, they would have to wait. I remained by my car until Carmen pulled away, then I headed for the Amigo Veterinary Hospital.

50

The smothered sky had gone nearly dark when I arrived, the rain drizzling and dripping as I parked and ducked inside. My lucky night, hardly anyone waiting in the lobby. But I stared, amazed to see the old woman with the furry orange tiger cat, that same woman from months ago with a skin cancer on her face. The cancer had kept busy, as cancers will, the hard bumpy crater just below her left eye now larger than before.

Cancer cells are diligent. They grow fast, sidling up to normal cells and shoving them out—sometimes quickly, sometimes at a slow and steady pace, but relentless. The cancer won't quit. Sometimes healthy cells fight back; they rally the immune system to slap the cancer away. Other times the cancer hits back harder.

I remember a spell when my mom called cancer cells "little Hitlers," encouraged by her eccentric friends. She created complex maps showing how the cells metastasized, traveling the lymphatic rivers of the body in platoons and making blitzkrieg invasions into other organs, with many references to World War II and actual aggressions. That is, until a dean at the university caught wind of it and made her stop.

When my second chance appeared at the vet clinic, I knew I should take it.

"Ma'am?" I pulled a chair over. Startled, her red-rimmed eyes bobbed up at me and she clutched the cat to her chest, making it hiss. It seemed resigned, though, and never struggled or tried to escape. The woman stroked it frantically, contrite, mumbling rapidly into its neck and sneaking furtive glances in my direction.

I pushed ahead. "I'm so sorry to disturb you. You don't know me, but I'm a physician. And I realize it's not my place, but I'm worried that you might have a skin cancer." I pointed to my own cheek to indicate where her tumor was.

Her hand flew to her face, covered the growth. That answered that. She knew, at least sort of.

"I'm sorry," I repeated. "I only want to help. You should show your doctor, in case it's serious. All right?"

She turned away from me, still furiously stroking the cat, which hunched in her lap with its eyes closed.

I tried. Sometimes that's all you can do.

The door opened and Owen motioned me inside. The old woman never looked up.

"What a great surprise," he said, a big hug, a cautious smile because he knew why I was there. No beard, his usual untidy hair, a clean white coat. He smelled like acetone. "I wasn't sure if I should contact you before I left."

I still felt upended from Jeremy and pulled back. I didn't want hugs just then. "Owen. What have you done?"

"Me? Whatever are you referring to?" His black eyebrows up, innocent. A dog started barking furiously behind a door and he turned, opened it a crack. His lips to the gap. "Quiet."

Silence. Whatever else he might be, the man was undeniably a dog whisperer.

"You know exactly what I mean. I just had a visit from Jeremy Newell. He begged me to stop."

"Oh, that." His nose wrinkled, as if smelling something dead.

"Yeah, that. You have to show me what you've done. I mean it. I have to know what he's accusing me of."

Owen looked amused. "I guess you do."

He drew me down the inner hall to a cluttered office with a metal desk. Two old plastic chairs. An impressive array of computers and monitors, jumbled wires. He leaned against me and opened a screen, entered a very long password. "Wait here while I take care of Mrs. Pickler and Petunia. Look up your reviews."

"Hey, maybe she'll listen to you," I implored. "I tried to tell her about that basal cell cancer on her face. That she should see her doctor."

"Ha. I tell her that every week."

"She's here every week? What's wrong with her cat?"

"Nothing." He disappeared.

I looked at my watch, impatient. Of course he should see the woman and her cat first, but I fretted about all the work I'd suspended and thought about my waiting dogs. That's the good and bad thing about electronic charts—I could finish my work at home. I could stay up all damn night long getting it done right.

I gazed around. I read flyers on the wall about heartworm and ehrlichiosis and valley fever in dogs. Feline leukemia. Groomers and pet products. Educational courses for veterinarians. Boxes stood open on the floor, half filled, Parker packing up. A litter of greeting cards on the desk caught my eye and I admit I snooped: thank you notes from clients, appreciative and sweet. That surprised me a little, which made me feel bad.

Finally I quit procrastinating and turned to the computer, brought up my review page. Before Jeremy's assault began, I had maybe six reviews at this particular site, all scored at fours and fives. Then came the negative hits, fifteen or so, all ranking me with ones and twos. I hadn't looked in almost a week, but I assumed my average dropped even more.

No. I sat stunned. The bad reviews had all vanished.

Twelve new glowing recommendations replaced them. Not all dated recently, either—some seemed to have come from months ago. I felt a giddy little surge in my chest, something that might be called happiness by those who are more used to it. Just to keep it real, a single score of three complained about the waiting room, dated from over a year ago.

Owen reappeared. He stood in the doorway and leaned against the frame, his signature stance. I jumped up and embraced him, because I couldn't help myself. His hand around my shoulders, then off.

"What? How?" I sputtered. I looked back at the screen to make sure it hadn't changed, as if the negative reviews might resurface.

He shrugged, self-deprecating. "Piece of cake. Not that hard."

I started to grin but stopped. Something was off, a piece missing, and my eyes narrowed. It made no sense that Jeremy would be so upset by this.

"There's more, isn't there? Jeremy said something about social media. And the med school website."

Owen pointed me back in the chair and sat beside me, took the keyboard. "Don't watch."

I averted my eyes as he typed. As if I would understand what he did. But my emotions careened all over the place. Humor, admiration. Chagrin, dismay.

"Okay." He nodded at the screen.

Jeremy's face stared at me, a proud photo, suit and tie. Owen scrolled down to a recent post, a photo of Jeremy shaking hands with Dr. Candore. Except thick white lines had been drawn into the photo, a dunce hat on Candore's head and large eyeglasses with googly eyes. The caption read: *Can you believe Dean Anthony Candore? What a spineless buffoon. Here's betting I'll replace him someday.*

My hand clapped itself over my mouth.

"Hold on, there's more." He changed windows and displayed an official-looking student page.

Many colleges have sites where students can comment on professors and teachers. They admire those who deliver the best lectures, which ones to seek. Which ones seem weaker. Disrespectful language is not tolerated and will be removed, but the monitoring sometimes lags behind the postings. Owen pointed out two messages, supposedly from Jeremy.

Dr. Murray never knows what he's talking about. Don't bother with his lame lectures.

Professor Acharya told us the wrong dose of dopamine. And she pronounces it wrong. Not sure where they find these teachers.

I felt horrified. Murray may be one of the kindest men I knew, and Acharya was brilliant. Both were widely admired, painstakingly careful, and would never make casual mistakes. No wonder Jeremy was in trouble.

"You did this? How?" I stared at him like a stranger. Which he essentially was, I reminded myself. I knew very little about him.

"I assume that's a rhetorical question," he said dryly. "Jeremy, or maybe some official at the college, keeps deleting these posts, and I keep putting them back. Maybe the same day, maybe a few days later. I hope it's driving him nuts."

"But you make it look like he's doing it? How can—"

"Norah. It's called hacking. And he deserves it, the jerk." Owen leaned back, his jaw hard.

I grabbed him. "You have to stop. I really appreciate the positive reviews, more than I can ever say. It's the best I've felt in weeks. But you can't—"

"Yeah, I can." His eyes shadowed. "I'm defending you. But I knew you'd probably react like this. You're too nice."

That annoyed me. "You're wrong. I am not very nice."

"It's not an insult," he laughed, then put his hand on top of mine, which still clutched his sleeve. "Like I said, I suspected you'd feel this way. That you wouldn't want to ruin him, even though he tried to ruin you."

He was right, of course. I did not want to ruin Jeremy, although I should.

"That's true," I admitted. "Even though it might be the best thing for future patients. There's something wrong with him. But. . ." My words faded.

"But what? Do you really think you can save him, Norah?" His face both tolerant and unforgiving.

"Not me, not personally. But perhaps someone could work with him, teach him to act more appropriately. Maybe I could speak with his advisor, recommend counseling. Maybe he could still grow." Even as I said it, I knew better. But don't we all deserve that chance? Was I only talking about Jeremy?

"No, he's too defective." Owen's face like stone. "He should go down in flames."

Owen was right and Owen was wrong. I couldn't decide which side of this fence would make me strong, which side weak.

"If he goes down, I want it based on the truth. Not deception. He has three more years to improve or fail." Even as I said that, I knew it was quite difficult to be thrown out of medical school. At my core, I also knew Jeremy likely could not change.

"Don't you dare forgive him."

I made an ugly sound, a noise somewhere between fury and disgust. "Don't worry. I don't have that kind of strength."

I looked at Owen and tried to weigh what he'd done, how I felt about it. About him. Fair enough, he had warned me. He told me that I did not want a relationship with him. Now he gazed back, defiant.

He finally spoke, almost reluctant. "I can fix it if you want. I prefer revenge myself."

"Fix it how? Hasn't it gone too far?"

"No. I already set it up." He shook his head, gentler now, as if fondly disappointed in me. "Just promise you'll think about it for a day before I do it."

"No promises until you tell me."

Owen appealed to the ceiling, then lowered his eyes to me. "I can quit doing the posts, just leave it at that. It will all fade away the next time they're deleted. Or if you prefer, I'll quit doing the posts *and* he'll get notices from those sites that I hacked, saying his accounts were compromised. Saying that materials were posted in his name, originating from somewhere in the Caribbean. Or Russia. Take your pick. It'll look very official. He can show it to the deans, and that will absolve him."

My emotional carnival ride climbed and dipped, made me dizzy with relief and worry and a thousand other feelings. I took a breath to steady myself.

"Owen. It—"

"Please. I'd rather not talk about it anymore, okay? Just let me know tomorrow if you want his absolution." He took one of his business cards, scratched through the phone number and wrote another number on the back, then an email address. He slipped the card in my purse then stood. His face now moody, melancholic—it wrenched me open.

"Wait," I insisted. I hoped Ralph would forgive me, because surely Owen would figure it out. "I want to know. . .I need to know. . .are you okay? I heard about your partner."

His eyes flashed. "Goddamn Ralph."

I winced. "You can't tell him I said anything." Owen silent, unreadable. I felt him retreat. "I just want to say that I feel bad, that's all. For him, and for you. And that I care about you."

I thought of the medical student Grace and my last words stuck in my throat, a kind of choke. His eyes flew up at me. A very long moment passed and he finally spoke, calmer.

"I'm all right. I mean it. You don't need to worry." He pulled me up. "Come on, I'll walk you out. How's Blink doing?"

The evening air hung cold and dense, a low slate overcast, a few raindrops. The raw odor of ozone. We talked about dogs until I climbed in my car and he shut the door.

"Just so you know," he said as I lowered the window. His eyes warm now. His fingers touched my arm. "There were a few times when I regretted making that rule."

I started to reply. I didn't even know what I would say, but he had already turned and headed back inside.

51

In medicine, change often occurs gradually. We slowly understand diseases better, find new ways to tackle them. Better research, improved outcomes. Who knew that post-traumatic stress disorder could be managed with eye movement exercises better than with sedatives? Or that treating everyone's pain with unlimited doses of opioids caused far more harm than good, actually worsening a patient's pain over time? It turns out that opioids aggravate nerve perception and make the tissues more sensitive, so the pain hurts more.

Occasionally, change occurs abruptly. A new virus emerges and shakes the world, sending us scrambling. Penicillin quits working. To navigate electronic records, scribes can become invaluable.

My practice shifted. Not the patient care, but the mechanics of the day, the players beside me, time itself. I began collaborating with Wanda Cunningham about both of us cutting back hours and sharing a scribe. I wanted someone exactly like George Clark, of course, but that would be a tall order.

Zane settled into his new routine, two days a week. He saw a handful of his old patients and could not have made much, but he said it suited him.

"Maybe you should retire altogether." I couldn't help myself and simply had to poke at him. "Leave all this stress behind. The personnel problems. The billing and insurance. It's endless. The unhappy patients. The ones who would rather believe someone ranting online about a whacky cure instead of their physician."

"Just because you want to quit doesn't mean I have to," he replied mildly, but his eyes sparkled. Since his second surgery, he had new energy. His white hair now longer and a little madcap. It didn't feel like sloppiness, but more like rebellion.

"I never said I wanted to quit," I protested.

"Norah. You've wanted to quit for at least a year."

"That's your interpretation." My best sour face, because he was right. "Besides, you have new hobbies now to keep you busy, like playing video games."

Zane roared with laughter. "You're right. I do, and I love it.

Wanda's boys come over on Saturdays now and coach me. I had to buy an extra monitor so we could play more games at once!"

"What does Tara think?"

"She thinks I've gone round the bend. But it keeps me out of her way, so she's pretty happy about it. That's another reason I can't retire—I'd drive her nuts if I was always home." He turned serious. "In some ways, with Wanda's boys, I feel like I'm making amends. For neglecting my own kids too much."

"It was a different time," I said gently. "Like a cult."

He nodded, still sad. "Medicine always came first. And frankly I liked it, being so valuable to my patients, proving myself. I loved making a diagnosis that someone else had missed. Such a triumph. But the imbalance with family life was messed up. . . . I can admit that now."

"Hey. Don't get me wrong," I asserted. "I don't want you to retire. Mostly because if you do, that will make me the senior doc here. I already feel old enough without that title."

He laughed again and I left. I had to get home and prepare for the evening, my first dinner with Peter Calloway that did not follow an admissions meeting. We were getting together on purpose. His invitation came via text.

HIM: *How do you feel about dinner on Friday?*

ME: *You mean there's a committee meeting on Friday this week? I didn't know that.*

HIM: *No, there's not. I want to divorce us from that paradigm.*

ME: *Divorce is a loaded word.*

HIM: *It's only loaded if you're already committed.*

ME: *Committed? As in, committed to an asylum?*

HIM: *Quit being so perverse. It only makes you more appealing.*

ME: *Heaven forbid. Shall we meet somewhere?*

HIM: *Am I allowed to pick you up?*

ME: *Only if you're willing to meet my dogs. Word of caution: they're large, hairy, and sarcastic.*

HIM: *I expect nothing less.*

I felt adrift, out of my element. For so long, my element consisted of bitterness and depression. And those pieces still swam around inside me, but now better flotsam floated in there too. Excluding my short fiery collision with Owen Parker, I'd been with only Austin for three years. Who, by the way, sent me a card in the mail. Humorous and hopeful, with a photo of a wistful dog on the front. *Thinking of you,* it said. Really? Austin is a writer and that's the best he could say? I ignored it and checked with my mom, to see if she still entertained him.

"No, I had to let Austin go," she pronounced. "Too bad. He had promise a few years ago. Then he went nowhere. What a bore. I'm not sure how you put up with him for so long."

"You liked him longer than I did." Maybe it's her age, that she doesn't remember that. But mostly she only recalls what she wants. I changed the subject. "What's up with your neighbor Johnny Quart?"

"Didn't I tell you? He might have died. I saw an ambulance in his drive last week, but no flashing red lights and no siren. Of course, they hate to make much commotion around here because they might trigger more heart attacks in all the old biddies who are peeking out from behind their curtains. If they get excited and you raise their blood pressure, they start dropping like flies. Anyway, I haven't seen him since."

"Well. That's too bad. No one has been by?"

"Not a soul. Of course, I've been out more than usual. The Mailman likes flaunting me on his arm."

"The engagement's still on?"

"Yeah, so far so good. I mean, we shouldn't wait too long because of our age. We don't want some lover's tragedy where one of us dies before we tie the knot. We're trying to agree on a venue. I want outdoor, but he wants indoor. He worries about sunlight and wrinkles. Guess he never heard of sunscreen, but he's kind of vain. I told him it's flu season, so indoors is a bad idea because that's how you catch it. People our age can die of influenza, you know."

"Outdoor sounds good to me," I agreed. "When do I get to meet him?"

"Huh. You really want to meet him before the wedding?"

"Mom. Of course I do. Although I imagined you two would run off to someplace exotic to get married, like the South Pacific. Thailand. Even the Caribbean. That feels more like you. Dancing on the beach in a grass skirt."

"I just told you. He's avoiding the sun."

"Maybe you should mention that he lives in the wrong state for that."

Having reached my fill, I made up an excuse and ended the call. Then I realized she dodged me about meeting the man, again, and I wondered again if she was hiding something.

Technically, he would be my stepfather. What the hell.

52

Peter arrived five minutes early, in black jeans and a white shirt. I hadn't seen him since before Thanksgiving and I'll admit I felt pretty eager. His hair looked soft and thick, those silver gleams. I had missed him, and went out on a limb and told him so. His eyes lit up and his freckles deepened.

Emcee and Blink greeted him cautiously. Judicious, they circled and snuffled him from toes to crotch.

"They're worse than airport TSA," he said, holding out his arms as if afraid to move. "What if I don't pass their screening?"

"Then I guess you and I are done." I shook my head, as if it couldn't be helped. "I don't make the rules."

As usual, Emcee took the lead. She came back and sat on my foot. *He seems patient. And he respects dogs. I like that.*

Blink stayed beside him, accepting a few strokes on his head, then glanced over at me. *It's kind of nice having another guy around.*

Emcee cast her eyes up, met mine. *Boys.*

"I think you made it," I whispered loudly to Peter. "I think you've been cleared."

He blew out a long breath, wiped imaginary sweat from his brow. "Whew. And not that it matters. . .just curious, you know, for future reference. Do they sleep in your bed with you?"

I gave him my best enigmatic look and said nothing.

We had much to catch up on during dinner. I laughed at his family stories, his mom and sister both in Denver, upholding a tradition of disastrous holiday dinners with everything from burnt-black turkeys to runny pumpkin pie. His temperamental old father now lived in Ireland and rarely communicated.

I updated him on Jeremy. When I described our confrontation at my practice, Peter flushed red.

"I wish I'd been there," he said roughly.

"You're doing that thing." I pointed at his hands, his right thumb mashing his left palm.

"Damn right I am." Heated, his lips tense, the freckles gone. "Don't ever stay there alone at night. All right?"

"Calm down—it's okay now. A friend took care of it." I quickly summarized Owen's work and my ultimate decision to rectify. Every day I felt bad about it; every day I felt good. Back to gray again, where no answer could be right. I tried to embrace that uncertainty.

"Jeremy deserved that hack," Peter agreed, somewhat mollified. "And I guess I'm glad you reversed it all in the end. But how do you have friends who can even do such things, that hacking? That's not a normal skill, and I'm pretty sure it's illegal."

Explaining Owen felt impossible. "He's kind of an unorthodox. . . friend. I don't know him very well."

"I think I'm a little afraid of you now," Peter admitted.

I waved my hand, dismissive. "Listen. I've got better things to tell you. Do you remember that timid med student, the one who couldn't talk to patients about sex? George Clark?"

"Yeah. You said he should go into radiology with the rest of us socially awkward people."

"I never said that!" I protested. "I said he should go into pathology."

"I know a pathologist who would—"

"Stop it. I'm serious." I told him how George scribed for me, how well it went. "I actually see a ray of hope. That maybe I won't spend the last dim years of my career fighting with computers every night."

"Good, because I've got a proposition." Peter shifted and dug in his pocket for a folded piece of paper and placed it on the table. "These are my top three vacation picks. You should make your own list, and let's see if they intersect."

"Right now?"

"Sure, why not. Just go wild."

I thought a while, then started writing. He sat back and finished his plate, sipped his drink. Watched me with those blue or green eyes.

One place intersected. The South Pacific, Bora Bora. Apparently it was me who wanted to go to there, not my mom. It seemed incredibly dreamlike, a hut on stilts over turquoise waters, tropical fish gliding below. Peter gave me the biggest grin I'd ever seen and promised to start making plans. Then he pulled out his wallet and extracted a small, laminated card, three inches square.

"I got you a Christmas present," he announced, suddenly sheepish.

"Only now I'm having second thoughts. I think I'm jumping the gun, that we're not ready for this. And it might be too corny. Too sappy."

"Oh, no." I felt embarrassed because this hadn't occurred to me so far, gifts and Christmas. I've never been accused of being overly sentimental. "Things have been so crazy. I haven't even thought about Christmas yet."

"No problem. But it seems like a dumb idea now." His lips skewed and he tucked the card back into his wallet. I think he blushed, but the light was too dim to be sure. "I think I should save it for later. Just forget it."

"Hey, that's not fair. Now I want it." I put out my hand. "Come on."

He studied the card again, made a doubtful face, then reluctantly passed it over. Mostly black, it displayed a radiologic image, a wedge of white and gray lines, a maze of striations and segments. Unfocused and grainy.

"An ultrasound?" Puzzled, I turned it over, as if an explanation might be on the back. "Is this an echocardiogram? I'm pretty bad at deciphering these cardiac images. Is there something wrong with the valves?"

"No, it's a normal echo. But it's mine." He tapped his chest. "My heart."

It took me a few seconds.

"Peter Calloway," I eventually managed. I may have flushed myself then and appreciated the soft lighting. "I did not imagine you to be quite this romantic. You continue to surprise me."

"Is an echocardiogram romantic? Radiologists are awkward, remember? It's a bunch of black and white fuzz." He frowned, uncomfortable.

"Hey." I seized his hands. "How would you feel about going with me to a wedding in Sun City? To see an eighty-six-year-old woman marry a seventy-five-year-old man?"

He looked perplexed.

"There's something you should know," I said. "Let me tell you about my mom."

Acknowledgements

Tremendous thanks to the women physicians who offered their insights on how they keep practicing family medicine and who somehow found the time to tell me about it: Lindsay Alaishuski MD, Natasha Bhuyan MD, Stephanie Briney DO, Uzma Jafri MD, Kelly Luba DO, and Andrea Patton MD.

To Melissa Miller DVM for her priceless advice and guidance, keeping the veterinarian stories accurate and authentic, and who works at the *real* Amigo Animal Clinic.

To the dauntless readers who helped pull it all together: Ted Cavallo, Cindy Alt RN, Cheryl Pagel MD, Therese Zink MD, Patricia Cox, Jackson Lassiter, and Patricia Camalliere.

Enormous thanks to Margaret Dalrymple, editor, for her keen critical sense of character and plot and her uncanny ability to guide me without telling me what to say. I'm in awe.

To the amazing and supportive people at University of Nevada Press who have given me this rare opportunity: JoAnne Banducci, Caddie Dufurrena, and Jinni Fontana. And to copyeditor Jennifer Manley Rogers for her careful touch and insight.

To radiologist Katherine Cavallo Hom MD, for helping me try to capture that specialty's unusual essence.

To Rebecca Nicole Kennelly, Esq., for her valuable advice on the legal aspects of harassment and graphology, and her enthusiastic brainstorming.

To Gregory Rutecki MD, for sharing his deep and thoughtful reflections on medicine and family.

To Deb Schoeny for sharing a few slices of administrative challenges.

To Pamela Wible MD for her dedicated and courageous work with physician burnout and suicide. To any discouraged and depressed physicians or veterinarians reading this, or to their colleagues and friends, please contact her now at www.idealmedicalcare.org.

Resources

ON PHYSICIAN BURNOUT AND MORAL INJURY

https://www.kevinmd.com/blog/2019/05/burnout-vs-moral-injury-does-it
-matter-what-we-call-it.html

STUDIES ON BURNOUT

http://www.annfammed.org/content/current

https://www.whitecoatinvestor.com/should-your-child-become-a-doctor/

https://www.medpagetoday.com/blogs/suicide-watch/84905?xid=nl
_mpt_blog2020-02-17&eun=g1007166d0r&utm_source=Sailthru&utm
_medium=email&utm_campaign=ItsAcademic_021720&utm_term=NL
_Gen_Int_Its_Academic_Active

ON VETERINARIAN SUICIDE AND BURNOUT

Not One More Vet: https://www.nomv.org/

https://time.com/5670965/veterinarian-suicide-help/

PHYSICIAN HOURS SPENT PRACTICING PREVENTION

https://www.ncbi.nlm.nih.gov/pmc/articles/PMC1447803/

About the Author

SANDRA CAVALLO MILLER is an author, poet, and retired academic family physician in Arizona who has helped launch hundreds of medical students and residents into their careers. She is the author of four novels, including the Dr. Abby Wilmore series at the Grand Canyon Clinic—*The Color of Rock, Where Light Comes and Goes, What the River Said*—and a novel about a public health physician in Phoenix, *Where No One Should Live*. Her unlikely path to medicine includes degrees in anthropology and creative writing at the University of Illinois before attending Rush Medical College, and her essays and poetry have been published in *JAMA, PULSE-Voices from the Heart of Medicine, Under the Sun,* and *Embark,* among others. She lives in Phoenix, Arizona. For more information, visit her author website at skepticalword.com.